NO ONE NEAR

A DCI EVAN WARLOW THRILLER

RHYS DYLAN

WYRMWOOD
BOOKS

COPYRIGHT

eBook ISBN - 978-1-915185-18-1
Print ISBN - 978-1-915185-19-8

Published by Wyrmwood Books.
An imprint of Wyrmwood Media.

EXCLUSIVE OFFER

OTHER DCI WARLOW NOVELS

THE ENGINE HOUSE
CAUTION DEATH AT WORK
ICE COLD MALICE
SUFFER THE DEAD
GRAVELY CONCERNED
A MARK OF IMPERFECTION
BURNT ECHO
A BODY OF WATER
LINES OF INQUIRY

CHAPTER ONE

'Oh. My. God. It's like something from a film.' Georgia stood under the tallest arch of the remains of the Abbey, chosen because of the backdrop, with the Parish Church of St Michael and All Angels on her right and the hill of Talley Woods behind. She'd made Cam take loads of photos in the freezing, clear air. And even though it was now a ruin, the fact that the Abbey had its origins in the twelfth century, instigated by The Lord Rhys, one of the true old kings of Wales, and that the hamlet of Talley was right there, just yards away, made it somehow so much more real.

Georgia turned to beam at Cameron Sadler. She looked happy, her face pale from the cold air, even under the hat with earflaps and pleated yarn ties. But the walk from the Abbey, around the lake – well, to one side of it – and back, though only half a mile or so, had been bracing and brought colour to her dimpled cheeks. They'd lingered in the churchyard to read half a dozen of its ancient gravestones. Cam had even joked and said if they looked around and saw a woman in black shuffling up the street, there was no way he was following her.

She'd laughed at that. They'd been completely alone at the Abbey, and Cam knew she was a huge Harry Potter fan. Him referencing Godric's Hollow had made her day.

'Told you it'd be worth it.' Cameron held out his hand. Georgia took it and stepped out from under the arch. 'Saw the photo online and knew you'd love it here. And, like I said, it doesn't rain all the time in Wales, despite what people say.'

Above them, the sky was a cool pale-blue, except where the low December sun was arcing towards the horizon and a bank of clouds. Georgia let go of cam, clenched her fists and waved them back and forth in a show of child-like excitement before grabbing Cam's arm again and leaning in. 'If it stays this cold, we'll be able to see the stars,' she said with a touch of awe.

'Hmm.' He glanced up. 'But the forecast says freezing rain and maybe snow. A storm anyway.'

Georgia pouted. She looked pretty, even doing that. 'Which forecast said that?'

'The BBC.'

'Well, find one that doesn't say that, and we'll have that one.'

Cam laughed.

'Besides, if it does rain, we'll stay in and play games.'

'What sort of games? Did you bring Pictionary? Or that one where you have to make whatever sound is on the card?'

Georgia hugged Cam's arm a little tighter. 'I meant the sort of games people on their honeymoon play.'

'Honeymoon? I almost forgot.'

Georgia punched him playfully on the arm. 'Come on, I'm getting cold now.' Georgia pulled him towards the path back to where they'd parked. They walked on together, kitted out in gloves, hats, thermal jackets, and walking boots.

'Did you know honeymoon is *mis mêl* in Welsh? Honey month.'

'Miss male? Who told you that?'

'Ed. You know he speak-a da language.'

'I did not know. Is he from around here?'

'A bit further west. But he told me about this place. Loves coming up here when he's home.'

'Let's hope he's not waiting in ambush in the woods with a six-pack of lager, then,' Georgia said with a prim smile and a batting of her eyelashes.

'Ed's alright,' Cam objected.

'He's a borderline alcoholic, even if he was your best man.'

'He's gone skiing for Christmas. No chance he's here.'

'I hear wistfulness in your voice, Cameron Sadler.'

Cam stopped and turned to Georgia. 'If it was a toss-up between honeymoon games with you and a black run with Ed, you'd win hands down.'

'Perhaps with hands tied behind your back, if you're lucky.'

Cam stared at her in astonishment. 'If the cold weather has this effect on you, we're moving to Lapland.'

Georgia kept a straight face for all of ten seconds and then ran off with Cam in pursuit.

'Oy, Mrs Sadler, wait for me,' Cam yelled.

That brought Georgia up short, and she turned with both hands on her cheeks, the grin back with a vengeance. 'Mrs friggin' Sadler. Can you believe it?'

Cam caught up. 'Right, come on, no more messing about. Bits of me are threatening to fall off after taking all those snaps of you in the ruins.'

'I don't want any of your bits if they're cold,' Georgia said, her face tilting in coy suggestion.

'Come on. The car might still be warm. We're not that far from the cottage, but the roads might be tricky, and I'd rather find the place in daylight.'

They'd tied the knot on December 17th.

A Saturday.

In December.

A decision forced upon them, as with so many young couples, driven largely by delays and deferments caused by the damned pandemic. They'd planned for 2020.

Yeah, right.

By the time the summer of 2022 came around, Georgia Stephens and Cameron Sadler waited no more. They sent out some save-the-date cards, choosing a time when everyone at the school they taught at would be free to come, and crossed their fingers. They had twenty at the ceremony, thirty more at the party in the pub afterwards. And yes, it had been a Saturday in December and the people who were there were those they'd wanted to be there.

Initially, they'd toyed with a big family affair, church service, a marquee for over a hundred in a field, but they didn't have that kind of money to toss down the drain. Their priority was to get a place of their own and deposits weren't cheap these days. Same went for the honeymoon. But a Christmas away staying at a secluded NON cottage – No Owner Nearby – in Wales ticked all the boxes. Especially when it came to not offending their families. Instead of bending over backwards to keep the Sadlers and the Stephens happy, they'd do the family thing after New Year and before term started.

It was a plan both newlyweds were relieved about. In Georgia's case because it avoided the chaos of two older sisters and their kids running rampant, and in Cam's case, he could hide from the austere, prim and proper regimented Christmas his mum and dad had always opted for. They'd have to do without him and his bride for this year.

They'd both talked about it, shared, and shelved the angst that had been a factor in their choice of wedding date, finally deciding to put themselves first. This year, they'd have their first quiet, magical Christmas in a cottage away from it all. As Mr and Mrs Sadler. They'd stayed in London on Sunday and travelled down west first thing on Monday as a married couple.

They reached the Abbey entrance and Georgia looked east, out over the hills and fields once more, beneath a looming sunset burnishing the low clouds orange and pink. She caught her breath. So far, the trip was turning out to be everything she'd hoped it would be. And, if the bed turned out to be a nice, soft one, it was going to be a Christmas to remember.

She'd made Cam look up the proper pronunciation of the cottage they'd booked: *Cân-y-barcud*.

'Khan uh bar-kid,' was what Cam had finally worked it out as. The song of the kite. As in the red kite. A bird brought back from the brink of extinction by establishing feeding centres across the vast spaces of central Wales.

'Do kites sing, then?' Georgia'd asked.

'Mewling whistle, Google says. We'll find out, I expect,' Cam had replied.

The NON website had the cottage listed as 4.9 out of 5 in their reviews section.

"Remote CROG loft cottage nestled in the hills in a peaceful valley close to great walking, with mountain biking and horse riding nearby. Ideal for those keen on exploring the hills, beaches, towns, and villages of West Wales. Or for those wanting to get completely away from it all. Open-plan ground floor. Kitchen with gas cooker and hob. CROG loft double bed as mezzanine. Centrally heated with an additional wood burner. Wi-fi is provided but limited and not for streaming."

A real getaway.

It sounded amazing. The pictures were even better. Now all they had to do was find it.

From the Abbey ruins at Talley, Cam drove north past the titular lakes before looping west and then south along single-track lanes that rose and fell over four miles. But always with a view of the woods they'd walked up receding in the distance. They passed a few farms and the odd cottage until Cam came to a stop at a 'T' junction.

'What does it say after we pass this farm?' He peered at the faded sign on a post at the lane leading to the farm entrance. 'Tal Farm.'

Georgia read the email. 'Take the left turn for half a mile. N.B. this road is not on Google maps. Key is in the combination lockbox.'

She grinned. 'Not even on the map. I didn't know places like this existed.'

They got there at four fifteen, five minutes after sunset, with the clouds drifting south over the sky, providing a natural light show of reflected cinnamon that bathed the whitewashed walls of the rectangular dwelling. It looked so simple and charming. A box with a chimney on either end, one door at the front with two sash windows on either side.

Idyllic. Exactly as described.

The only thing detracting from perfection was the Land Rover Discovery parked in front. Cam pulled in behind it and sent Georgia a puzzled look.

'The owner?' she asked.

Cam shrugged. 'I thought the point was we wouldn't be seeing anyone.'

'Maybe he's come with champagne and caviar?' She grinned and opened the door. 'Come on. I'll grab the small suitcase and you bring in the big one.'

They took out the luggage. Cam groaning as he lifted out the big one. 'I'll come back for the supplies in a minute. Let's get inside.'

The light was fading fast and the temperature falling with it. As they came around to the front of the car with its headlights on, Georgia's breath plumed out of her mouth in a yard-long stream.

'Is there a light on in there?'

'Something is. Or is it the fire, you think?'

Georgia was closest to the door. 'Where's the key box thing? I don't—' She stopped.

'Find it?' Cam asked.

'No. But weirdsville. The door isn't shut.'

'Not locked, you mean?'

'No, it's open. By about three inches. Shall I knock?'

'Why not?'

Georgia did the needful. And with each contact of her knuckles, the door opened a few more inches until, with rap number four, it swung fully inwards.

'Hello?' Georgia called out.

No one replied.

'Perhaps he's outside chopping logs. What was the owner's name again?'

'Royston Moyles.'

This time, Georgia used the name. 'Mr Moyles? Are you here?'

Nothing. Not a peep. In fact, the last time Georgia had heard such silence was… never. There was always some sound in the flat they shared on the school grounds. And traffic. And the clatter of trains on the main London line, the odd siren. Nothing like this complete absence of sound.

'Is the fire on?' Cam asked from behind her.

Georgia stepped in and her eyes flicked to the wood burner, and the logs that had burned down but were still red embers in the grate. 'It is. Oh, look. There's a little Christmas tree and some tinsel on the stairs.'

'Right, let's get in and shut the door before the place gets too cold.'

They dumped the luggage on the open-plan ground floor next to the one settee while Georgia looked around, the smile once more on her face. 'It's so cute,' she said. But then she frowned and sniffed. 'Can you smell something?'

'What, like a candle?'

'No, something that might need a candle. Something a bit poo-ey?'

'We're in the countryside, Georgy. Farmers spread muck.'

'Lucky I brought a candle, then.'

The walls were thick. Rendered white back to the original. The windows had shutters on the inside. The kitchen block was a peninsula with all mod cons and red door panels to add a touch of pizzazz to the place, which, Georgia thought, it didn't need. Behind that, at the other end of the room, was a table and chairs. Rustic, as per the vernacular, if you excluded the red cabinet doors. And in the corner next to the table were the white-painted open stairs leading to the mezzanine.

'Right, I'll get the supplies while you throw a log on the fire and inspect the bed.'

'You're keen,' Georgia said.

'Your fault,' was Cam's rejoinder.

Georgia found the logs in a large basket next to the burner. She used a poker to open the glass door and threw on three. Then she stood and glanced up. The mezzanine stopped halfway across the room supported on ancient beams and with a waist-high matchboard wall behind which must be the bed.

She went to the stairs, glancing out of the window at Cam, bending over to fetch the boxes of supplies they'd stocked up on. In the headlight beams, stair rods of rain were now visible. She gave a little disappointed shrug and put her foot on the stairs. She'd taken six steps up when she let out a scream loud enough to shatter the peace for miles around and bring Cameron running back in.

He found her slumped in the corner next to the stairs, white with fear, trembling uncontrollably. As he reached out a hand, she vomited on his shoes.

'Jesus… Georgy, what is it?'

'Up… upstairs… oh my God, Cam. Oh, my God.'

Cameron turned and took the stairs. When his head cleared the mezzanine floor level, the reason for Georgia's scream became all too clear. His breath seized as a bolt of shock and nausea threatened to overwhelm him, too. A metal bedstead stood beneath the wooden A-frame that made up the roof. Through two roof windows, the evening sky, with the ochre clouds now a thin ribbon in the west, looked down. And what it saw, like Cameron, was the body of a naked man strung from the crossbeams of the A-frame, ropes binding his limbs and wound around his throat.

But not a man anymore. This was a purple-faced corpse hanging face down. Strangled, it looked like, by his own weight.

Cameron Sadler knew three things instantly.

First, judging from the stuff that had run down over the man's body, over the small of his back and around the flabby flanks to pool on the bed, they'd found the source of Georgia's funny smell.

Second, he'd never seen a dead body before, but he knew enough from films and books that this was a very unnatural death.

And third, that his honeymoon was over before it had begun.

CHAPTER TWO

IT WAS a different kind of cold in London, Warlow decided. He hadn't thought about it much before. But today, at minus three, under cloudless skies and with a north easterly adding another two degrees of chill, it concentrated the mind. And perhaps there was a grain of truth in that appreciation. At home, in West Wales, it was wetter and milder. The wind, whistling down the east coast from the north, a wind that he met on every corner in the Capital, never made it further than Swindon. If it did, as was promised over the next couple of days, it spelled trouble. He had a vague memory of this dry, biting cold from his time in the Met. But he'd been younger, fitter, in more of a headless chicken rush all the time. Not that today was exactly leisurely. There was just over two hours left before his afternoon train home and he was yet to secure the purchase he'd been searching for.

He stood staring at the surrounding people. The many surrounding people. You forgot just how busy this city was, even on a Monday morning when the majority of people should have been at work. Okay, it was the week before Christmas and Coaldrops Yard was within throwing distance of King's Cross and St Pancras stations. Jodie, his soon to be daughter-in-law, had suggested he come up here for a last look around. But since he had no idea of what he was looking for, all he did was amble from one place to the other, listening to banal Christmas songs oozing out of the shops as he passed.

It should have been straightforward. He knew who he was buying for. Jess Allanby, a Detective Inspector and colleague in the Dyfed Powys Force, and her eighteen-year-old daughter, Molly. He'd never been any good at presents. But he wanted to do something special for them and so toyed with the idea of taking them out for a turkey and tinsel lunch on Christmas Day. But Jess had put the kibosh on that from the outset.

'Not the same,' she'd said when he'd tentatively broached the subject. 'And Molly would throw a blue fit. It's her way or the highway, with all the trimmings.'

It was then that Jess asked what he'd be doing, whether he'd be in London with his son Tom and his partner Jodie or not. But Tom was rostered to be on call as an ENT surgeon and Jodie, a nurse, had thus decided to work the day shift, too. Not much point Warlow being in London while they were at work. He knew his mistake as soon as he'd mentioned that to Jess. Her eyes grew wide, and she'd said, 'Right, then you can come to us.'

That was when he'd suggested Christmas lunch at a hotel.

That was when he'd been shot down.

That was when he accepted the invitation and realised, he needed to get them something nice as a thank you.

Christ, he hated shopping.

Jodie became his saviour and not for the first time. She came up trumps for Molly for her eighteenth when she'd suggested a Fjällräven laptop bag that went down a storm. And for Christmas, Jodie's suggestion of some Bluetooth trackers Molly could attach to her belongings, to avoid having to buy yet another phone or set of keys, would fit the bill. Molly liked practical things. She was like her mother in that sense.

It was Jess that was proving difficult to sort out. He simply did not know what to buy a forty-something-year-old woman without coming across as one of the three of the lesser known of Snow White's companions: clueless, trite, or sleazy. And he hated the thought of a gift for a gift's sake.

Jess was someone who already had everything she needed. So, what could he get her she didn't have but would appreciate? Not jewellery, not perfume, not clothing, not a candle, God forbid. He'd been in and out of the trendy shops, most he'd never heard of before, like Fox and Badger, Hatty, American Village. He became a serial loiterer, window shopping, but rarely venturing inside.

Ironically, when he finally took a step over the threshold to get out of the bone-chilling cold into a lovely smelling place called Earl of Eden, he found his inspiration. Not on the shelves, though all the stuff looked very nice in a shiny new thing way, but in a small black object on a shelf behind the desk. The music coming out of them was jazzier, hinting at the season, but not as in your face as the inane pop songs dug up for December and played incessantly. He traced the noise to a Bluetooth speaker. Small, but with an excellent sound. And then he remembered Jess telling him that Molly was always complaining about the music Jess played through their old wired system. But with a Bluetooth wireless speaker, Jess could take it into whichever room she liked, couldn't she?

His grin of relief made the girl behind the desk ask if he was okay.

'Just enjoying the music,' he said, knowing he sounded inane.

She smiled back, hoping, no doubt, that Warlow would not be one of the flaky ones. But he was already heading for the door. He could get one of those speakers in John Lewis on Oxford Street.

Warlow glanced at his watch. There were a couple of hours to kill and he could walk it in half an hour, buy the thing, and get the Elizabeth Line to Paddington from Bond Street. He only had a backpack for his clothes, having travelled light to spend the weekend with Tom and Jodie for an early mock Christmas. And he'd insisted on taking them out for a meal as his treat last night on the only evening they both had free to be with him.

They'd spent most of it ironing out the trip to Perth – the Western Australian one – in January to visit Warlow's other son and his newborn little girl. And, in Warlow's case, to also meet his grandson Leo, who was all of eighteen months. It made for an animated and excited little meeting.

Now that there was a plan, Warlow headed back along streets he knew well from a long time ago. When the snazzy regeneration of St Pancras hadn't even begun. When going to King's Cross on a job meant taking a dive into the city's underbelly.

He took York Way and joined the throng, across Euston Road to Gray's Inn Road. As always in London, there were half a dozen ways to get to where you wanted to go and there may have been a more direct route, but this was the one Warlow took. A familiar route. One that he'd walked many times when he'd investigated the killing of two young prostitutes as a DC working out of Holborn.

The city had changed, but these streets were the same. They'd begun the investigation in January in a bitterly cold winter. Traced the girls' movements from their flat in Judd Street to their patch at King's Cross where the young women stood out in the cold: smoking, shiveringly underdressed, touting for business. He'd done house to house on Doughty Street and Millman Street. Even called in to the Great Ormond Street Hospital for a tea when it got too cold.

Strange how much of an effect that case had on him. Probably because the girls had been so young. No older than Molly Allanby at seventeen and eighteen. He'd walked up and down the area so many times that he knew every step. It drew him back like some dark magnet. He'd even taken Jodie and Tom to a restaurant on Lamb's Conduit Street that did amazing Middle Eastern cuisine, which, coincidentally, they both adored.

There'd been none of the cool shops that Jodie mentioned to him on that street back then. But now, as he walked along towards Theobald's Road and Bloomsbury, it all came back to him. How they'd set up a sting operation with one of the female officers who'd stood in the January cold. Looking for a punter one of the girls wrote about in her diary. A Mr Posh. They'd followed several likely suspects, but eventually found James Ridgeway with several pairs of underwear in his garage in Cambridge. One of those pairs belonged to a victim. Ridgeway commuted to the British Museum twice a week as part of his doctorate research from a Cambridge college. He'd bring his murderous desire with him and leave to go home to his prim and proper existence in the university town after indulging in his nefarious tastes.

Mr Posh was still in prison. Would be for a long time yet.

Warlow bought the speaker in John Lewis. A Wonder-boom 2 which, according to the sales assistant, gave you a lot more bang for your buck than some of the better-known names. By the time he sat in his airline-style seat on an afternoon Paddington to Swansea train, memories of Mr Posh were fading. But only after he'd gone through it all in his head, as the hypnotic movement and the sounds of the train lulled him into almost a fugue state. He recalled the near misses they'd had, the sloppy reports that almost… almost let Ridgeway slip through. He'd learned a lot during his time on that case. That details mattered. That luck sometimes played a part. He'd interviewed a train guard who'd been off sick for two weeks with flu and who'd remembered Mr Posh because he'd left an umbrella on a seat and came back to fetch it. In doing so, he'd dropped some papers, and the guard saw an envelope with a British Museum logo. If that guard had taken another few days off work, Warlow would not have interviewed him. If Mr Posh hadn't left his umbrella, the envelope would not have been seen. These were breadcrumbs that could have been so easy to brush off the table. Random moments in the universe that on their own had no power or meaning, but when aligned had the capability of trapping a monster.

If there was one thing that case taught Warlow, it was never to disregard the smallest detail until it was looked at thoroughly, catalogued, and designated insignificant. Until then, everything had meaning.

As the train pulled out of Bridgend, Warlow took a call from Superintendent Sion Buchannan.

'Cold enough for you, Evan?'

'The brass monkeys have run for the hills.'

'How was London?'

'Lovely to visit, but I'm glad I'm on the way home.'

'Yeah, has that effect on me, too. Where are you?'

'Approaching Port Talbot.'

The slight hesitation in Buchannan's reply prompted Warlow to interject before he could speak. 'Why is it I get the feeling you're not ringing to sing Jingle Bells to me, Sion?'

Buchannan sighed. 'We've had a shout. I'm ringing

because I think you'll need to make a detour. And yes, it's late, and the weather is turning to crap. In fact, there's been a weather alert for everything south of Mid-Wales, and that means that the gritters haven't been out on the smaller roads. But you could cut across country rather than head down the M4.'

'Implying I'll be on those smaller roads?'

'Oh, yes. The body was found in a rental cottage up near Talley. Well, I say near Talley, between Talley and Abergorlech.'

'Nice pubs up there.'

'I knew you'd see the bright side. I'll text you the address. Jess is on the way. I haven't rung DS Richards or DC Harries. But Gil Jones is in the loop. Jess thought we'd give him a heads up since he's the closest at Llandeilo. He's dealing with the couple who found the body.'

'I'll contact Catrin and Rhys. I've got another fifteen minutes before I get out at Neath.'

'Jingle all the way,' Buchannan sang.

'Oh, what fun,' muttered Warlow under his breath and ended the call.

CHAPTER THREE

DETECTIVE SERGEANT GIL JONES sat at a snug alcove table in the lounge of the Cawdor Hotel, Llandeilo, feeling the glow of the open fire just feet away. Red ribbons and holly had been draped over the mantlepiece. Soft Christmas tunes were playing over the PA. Opposite him huddled Georgia and Cameron Sadler, looking a damned sight better than they did when they'd walked in fifteen minutes before. He'd sat them down and ordered them both a G and T and a cup of tea for himself. Being a Monday, and since the weather was rapidly turning from cold to atrocious, the lounge was half empty. Still, it was early. Gil suspected the place would fill up. Roads were becoming treacherous, and he'd already seen one couple ask at reception if there were any rooms at the Inn.

He'd spotted no donkey, though, and the woman, though of childbearing age, looked more like someone who'd enjoyed a few too many custard slices than pregnant.

Not that he was judging. Not in this day and age. And especially not while he was on his own journey towards fitness. Or at least something less than a forty-inch waist.

He knew from personal experience that said journey was not a smooth ride.

He'd spoken to DC Craig Peters, his team member DS Catrin Richards' traffic officer partner. There'd been several accidents already, mostly on the smaller roads. Ironically, the main A roads had been treated, and that was giving drivers a false sense of security. But when you couldn't drive up even the slightest gradient unless you had a 4x4, you might as well have been in a force-ten blizzard.

It had rained just after five. Not for long. A typical squall. But it had been heavy. The water had hit pavements and metalled roads that had been at subzero temperatures for days, turning the rain instantly into sheet black ice. Conditions that made you wish you'd opted for that slightly more expensive four-wheel-drive version of your snazzy SUV after all.

He said all this to the Sadlers.

'We only just made it to the town,' Georgia said. 'No way we'd even try to get home in this.'

Gil felt sorry for them. He hoped the G and T helped. But, in the meantime, he needed to ask the Sadlers some questions.

'Mind if we go over the circumstances of earlier?'

Georgia and Cameron exchanged resigned looks. 'Fine,' Cam said.

He took the lead, running through the wedding and their decision to get away from it all via the NON website. He itemised the walk in Talley Woods. The sunset, and the open door to *Cân-y-barcud*.

'Was there a key in the lock?'

'No,' Georgia answered. 'They were on the countertop in the kitchen. Only the kitchen was also the living room. Open plan.'

'So, you pushed the door open and walked in?'

'We thought there was someone there because of the

Land Rover,' she explained. 'I knocked, and that pushed the door open. The fire had been lit. But I noticed the smell right away, didn't I?'

She glanced at Cam, who squeezed her arm with a tender little smile.

'Smell?' Gil asked.

'A bad smell,' Cameron explained, wincing. He took a sip of the icy drink and shivered slightly as it trickled down his throat. 'I thought it was muck spreading. That's what I said, anyway. But the man... the dead man... he'd lost control of his bowels and it was all over the bed.'

'That can happen. At the end, I mean,' Gil said.

'Do you know who it is?' Georgia asked suddenly. Her untouched gin and tonic clicked and fizzed gently as the ice cracked and settled. Unlike Cameron, Georgia had kept her hands in her lap. Gil suspected it was to stop them from shaking.

He pondered her question, knowing he didn't need to answer it. But these were not stupid people. Besides, they'd seen the Land Rover. Logic dictated that it must have had something to do with what they'd found. Even so, he didn't answer directly.

'How did you book the property?'

'All done online.'

'You never spoke to the owner?'

'No. Knew his name, obviously. But the deal with NON properties—'

'NON?'

'No Owner Nearby. So many of these places are annexes to bigger properties or outbuildings with the owners next door. Can be intrusive. Once we had kids knocking on the door at seven am. That was on a farm. By half past, they were jumping all over the bed.' Cam smiled with the rueful fondness that only came with distance.

Georgia recalled the incident with a glance in Cam's direction, but her smile was uncertain and a shadow of his.

'So, you communicated with the owner only online?' Gil persisted.

'Royston Moyles? Yes. Wouldn't know him from Ada—'

'It's him, isn't it?' Georgia threw out the words as a challenge.

'We're awaiting formal identification, but the car is Moyles's, and his clothes were found at the side of the bed. He's the right age and build. His features aren't exactly matching the driver's licence, but…'

'Oh, God,' Georgia whispered and turned her head away.

'I don't need to tell you that this information is highly confidential. We haven't yet contacted Moyles's next of kin.'

'We won't say anything.' Cam reached over and clasped Georgia's hand. The knuckles were white when they crawled up from between her thighs.

'Was this some kind of sex thing?' she asked, her face as white as the knuckles. 'You read about people trying to hang themselves while they…'

'Autoerotic asphyxiation,' Gil said. 'I doubt it. From what the Detective Inspector on the scene thinks, it's not self-induced.'

Georgia looked like she'd swallowed an oyster for the first time.

Gil reached over and lifted her drink. 'Why don't you take a sip? Steady your nerves.'

She let go of Cam's hand and clutched at the glass. The sip became a healthy mouthful. Then a second.

'And when you drove to the place, do you remember seeing anyone, or any vehicles?' Gil asked.

Both Sadlers shook their heads. 'It's a quiet road. I

mean, dead quiet. There's a good couple of miles that Google hasn't even mapped.'

'*Arglwydd* yes. You wouldn't want to go out there unless you were after a bit of quiet, that's for sure. What you were after, wasn't it?' Gil addressed Georgia, hoping the drink had taken her mind off the image of Moyles.

'That's exactly what we wanted. It's been a hectic term. Last few weeks before Christmas always are,' she said.

'Ah yes, you teach. One of my daughters does, too. She's been to five nativity plays. Three she was playing the piano for. I was at two of them. I'm now fluent in *Little Donkey*, both in Welsh and English.'

That brought half a smile to Georgia's lips. She looked around at the cosy lounge as if seeing it for the first time, before settling in on Cam's face. 'I've just realised we have nowhere to stay.'

Gil's phone started playing the theme tune from *Rocky*. He made no apology as he took the call and spoke a few words in Welsh into the phone before smiling at the Sadlers.

'Weather is getting worse. More rain is due, but the temperature is falling, too. Could be a bit of snow in it and the roads are bad. We're getting the gritters out to pave the way for us lot to go back out to *Cân-y-barcud*. But I've had a word with the manager here. He's had a couple of cancellations thanks to the weather warnings. He has room here for you.'

'Really?' Georgia's delighted relief was genuine.

'Plus, I've negotiated a special honeymooners' rate. They have deals on, only available online. But I've swung that. Bed and breakfast plus an evening meal for £60.'

'That's ridiculous,' Cam said. 'You can't get fish and chips for that much in Berkshire.'

'It's a special rate, as I say. Shall I say yes?'

'Please,' Georgia said, and dabbed her eyes. 'You're so kind.'

'All part of the service, ma'am,' Gil said. 'We will need a formal statement from you. But we can do that in the morning. Doesn't look like you'll be rushing off. There's enough here in town to keep you occupied for a few hours. Galleries and a few shops. Obviously, *Cân-y-barcud* is a nonstarter.' He paused, realising what he'd said. 'That was not meant to be a pun. The NON bit. What I am trying to say is that you won't be able to go back there.'

Georgia shivered. 'I wouldn't want to. I threw up, by the way. Full disclosure for DNA and stuff.'

Gil nodded. 'Good to know. Now, there is parking for residents around the back. If Cam does that while you see the manager, we can get you sorted out.'

The Sadlers shook his hand and walked towards the reception desk.

Without even thinking, Gil started whistling the tune to *Little Donkey*.

He'd got two bars in when his phone rang again. The name Evan Warlow appeared on the phone's screen.

'Evan, survive the big smoke then, did you?'

'I did. But a brief respite, by the sound of it.'

'I've just spoken to the witnesses. Honeymoon couple. They got the scare of their life.'

'Anything useful?'

'Not much. The place is meant to be a NON property. That was the deal. NON as in No owner near. There's a market for it, apparently.'

'NON. Never heard of it. But this one turned into ODOS, obviously.'

Gil pondered that one. 'No, new one on me.'

'Owner dead on site,' Warlow said.

Gil sighed. 'Clearly, you've had too much time alone on that train with a six-pack.'

Warlow sang out a low note of derision. 'I'll be with you in half an hour. Just coming through Pontardawe. We can go up together.'

'What about the kids?' Gil didn't have to explain that reference. Both he and Warlow were twice the age of DS Catrin Richards and DC Rhys Harries. But the label was applied with more than a hint of affection from both men.

'I'll get on to them,' Warlow said. 'No point in them risking life and limb. I'll get them into HQ. They can set up in readiness for the morning.'

'Tomorrow.' Gil voiced the word in a low rumble. 'Only six days to Christmas, Evan.'

'I know. These bloody criminals have no respect for peace and goodwill.'

'Tom and Jodie, okay?'

'Fine. Big plans for Australia. West Coast wine country and all that.'

Gil glanced out of the window at someone slipping and sliding on the narrow pavement. 'It'll be what, thirty-something degrees out there when you go?'

'It will.'

'Can't see a reindeer on a beach, somehow. I've always struggled with that.'

'But there's no snow in Palestine at Christmas, either. If we're going to be pedantic about it. Where it all began, I mean.'

'True. But there might be in Bethlehem. I mean the one between here and Llangadog. We've had a couple of people call in to the hotel looking for it whilst I've been sitting here.'

For years, people would come to the village in the Towy Valley on the opposite side of the river to the A40, named after the nonconformist chapel of Bethlehem that had been built there, simply to get their letters and cards stamped at the village post office. That had long since closed, but some people still came to take a snap outside the chapel and add a tag to the image along the lines of "Here we are at Bethlehem for Christmas. LOL."

'Right, well, have you eaten? Can I get the Lady Anwen to make you a sarnie?' Gil asked.

'No, I'm fine. I loaded up on M&S at Paddington. Besides, from what little I know, best I see it on an empty stomach. We'll go up in the Jeep. Let's hope we don't need to go off-road, but if we do, at least we'll be prepared.'

'Looking forward to it already,' Gil said, not meaning a word of it.

CHAPTER FOUR

DC RHYS HARRIES was tying baubles to the higher branches on the Christmas tree. He didn't need a stool. Whereas Gina Mellings, the woman he shared the house with, most definitely did.

'If it's going to cause problems, why don't I cook and have them come here?' Gina asked in a voice that suggested this discussion was not in its early stages.

'But it isn't just my parents,' Rhys replied. 'There's my aunty and uncle and at least four cousins. I mean, it's a proper circus, clowns included.'

'All the more reason for us not going, then. It'll be the same at mine. My sister and brother and a four-year-old and ten-month-old...' She paused to look up. 'Move that gold one over six inches and put this silver one in its place. You're out of sync now.'

Rhys took a silver orb from Gina. 'I've even thought to ask my mum if she could make hers just after midday. We have a bite there and then go to your mother's for seconds, at say two?'

'What? Eat two Christmas dinners?'

'Yeah. Well, by the time you load up your plate with second helpings, it's like having two dinners, isn't it?'

'Not on my plate it isn't,' Gina said.

'It's just, I don't want to upset anyone,' Rhys said, his words heavy with angst. 'I'm willing to sacrifice seconds at mine for the sake of keeping everyone's cap straight.'

'We could go to my mother's for dessert instead.'

An avalanche of horror spread over Rhys's face. 'And miss my mother's Christmas cake?'

Gina shook her head. 'How the hell is this going to work, then? You don't expect us to go back to your mother's for dessert after having had a second Christmas dinner at my mother's, do you?'

Rhys, looking very sheepish now, could only offer a feeble shrug. 'Could do.'

'God. It'd be simpler if we buggered off to Tenerife for five days.'

Rhys pondered this. 'Don't think I can. I don't have that much leave left.'

'I wasn't being serious. I was being hopelessly optimistic.'

Rhys grinned. 'I like it when you're being hopelessly optimistic. Though I think they cancel each other out. Didn't someone sing a song about that once?'

'Olivia Newton-John, one of my dad's favourites. Ever since he saw her in those black trousers in Grease. And it wasn't optimistic, it was *Hopelessly Devoted*.'

'That'll be me too, then.'

'What, fancying Olivia neutron bomb, as he called her?'

'No, being hopelessly devoted,' Rhys said, reaching up to fix the silver bauble.

He had to stretch, but when the silence from Gina got too much, he turned with an anxious face. 'Did I say something wrong?'

'No. Exactly the opposite.' Gina's voice dropped low. 'Hopelessly devoted. To your mother and to me.' The mock serious look on her face dissolved into a smile. 'Don't worry about Christmas dinner. We'll sort something out.'

Rhys smiled. His default state whenever food was mentioned.

'The good news is your mother plated up a Sunday lunch from yesterday for us for tonight. All that needs is a few minutes in the microwave.'

'Great,' Rhys said, resisting the urge to dab at the corners of his mouth where saliva was threatening to leak out at the mention of his mother's Sunday roast. Luckily, his phone saved him. He looked at the caller ID and frowned.

'Hello, sir?'

'Rhys. *Shwmae*? I haven't seen you since Friday. Play Saturday?' Warlow asked.

'We did, sir. And won against Crymych.'

'Bloody hell. And you're still in one piece?'

'Gave as good as we got, sir.'

'Have you eaten?'

'Not yet.'

'Right, well, get some food down you. We've had a shout. DS Jones and I are going to the scene to meet DI Allanby but given that the roads are turning into an Olympic ice rink, I'd like you and Catrin to get to HQ and establish a beachhead ready for us to get cracking first thing tomorrow. It'll mean a couple of hours to get things set up. You okay with that?'

'No problem, sir. Nothing on the telly anyway.'

'That's what I like to hear, unbridled enthusiasm. You are going to go far, DC Harries.'

'Thank you, sir.'

'Gina, okay?'

'Fine, sir.'

'Give her my regards. Now, chow down, and I'll let Catrin know you'll be there in half an hour.'

'Will do, sir. And, sir, where is it, the shout?'

'Somewhere between Abergorlech and Talley. On the dark side of the bloody moon.'

Warlow rang off.

Gina stuck her head around the living room door. 'Who was that?'

'The Wolf. There's been a—' He stopped there. The last time he affected a bad Scottish accent and tried to say the word "Murder" she'd thrown a cushion at him. 'An incident. The Wolf wants me in for a couple of hours to set up an Incident Room. He sends his regards, by the way, and his apologies for dragging me away from you.'

'He didn't say that.'

'The regards he did, apologies no. That was all me.'

Gina, herself an officer in the Dyfed Powys Force, shrugged. 'Obviously needs his key personnel in.'

Rhys grinned. 'Exactly. Key personnel. But he said to make sure I'd eaten first.'

'Right, get changed out of those joggers and I'll get a plate into the popty ping.' Though not actually the Welsh word for microwave – more an onomatopoeic Wenglish bastardisation – it was a colloquialism both Gina and Rhys used with frequent delight.

'I love it when you talk… food.'

'Five minutes,' Gina said. 'And don't put your white shirt on until you've eaten. I don't know what your mother puts in her gravy, but we ought to paint it on bomb shelters because it would easily survive an atomic blast. It's a sod to get out of any clothing.'

———

HALF AN HOUR LATER, as Warlow approached the outskirts of Llandeilo, DS Catrin Richards looked up to see Rhys Harries pull open the Incident Room door.

'Hiya, sarge. Got in alright, I see.'

'Craig sent a mate to fetch me. They've clocked half a dozen accidents since half five, he says. People sliding all over the place.'

'It's not funny out there. I don't envy the Wolf and Gil going up country.'

'Abergorlech?'

'No, thanks, I've had one already.'

Catrin, who was posting up images on the Gallery, turned towards Rhys with a pained expression. 'I swear, sometimes I hear Gil's actual voice coming out of your mouth.'

'Could be worse.' Rhys grinned.

'How?'

'Could be something else coming out of... a different orifice,' Rhys said, obviously floundering for a better punch line.

'I rest my case.'

Rhys walked over to the Gallery to stare at a formal photograph of a man in a suit and tie. 'So, who is it, then?'

'Royston Moyles, aged sixty-two. Was a county council-lor, which explains this snap.' She tapped a painted nail against the board. 'No longer a county councillor, he was still a chair of the local community council and on a few committees, was a school governor, and owned property and bits of land all over.'

'Your actual pillar of the community, then?'

'Yes.'

Rhys leaned forward to peer closer, a head and some taller than the DS. What he saw was a jowly man with saggy brown eyes, thinning hair that he was compensating for by sporting a pair of impressive sideburns.

'Gil would be very suspicious of the whiskers.'

'Yes, I mean, why? Was he born in 1880?'

'They call those something, don't they? Lamb chops?'

'Mutton chops,' Catrin corrected him.

Rhys raised an eyebrow. Moyles's facial hair extended down to the edge of his jaw on either side of an otherwise clean-shaven face, fluffing out a good inch towards the bottom. Catrin walked over to her desk and picked up a printed-off map on which she'd ringed the property.

'Blimey, it is out of the way,' Rhys said as she pinned it up.

'That's the attraction, apparently. People who want to get away from it all book it.'

'Not much to do out there. Good mountain bike trails and a bit of walking but bugger all else.'

'They were on their honeymoon,' Catrin explained. 'The people who found him. I daresay they'd find something to do.'

'Honeymoon,' Rhys repeated.

Catrin waited. When Rhys spoke a word out loud, it triggered a train of thought that ended up in a question of some sort. She was not disappointed, therefore, when he said, 'You and Craig planning on tying the knot, sarge?'

'Maybe,' was her enigmatic reply. She could have said a lot more. She could have said that it cost money to get married and that their priority at that moment was to get through the IVF programme they were in the middle of. She could have said that if it didn't work, they'd go the private route. That took cash and their savings would not stretch to both a wedding and expensive medical treatment. For now, the NHS was coming up trumps. But if that failed, private medicine was the next step. Catrin deflected the question with one of her own.

'How about you and Gina?'

Rhys laughed. 'Oh, no. We've got a way to go before

anything like that. We want to travel a bit. Enjoy it while we can. Us moving in together is a kind of test.'

'How's it going so far?'

Rhys turned his gaze on Catrin. 'Pretty good. I have no complaints.'

'What about Gina?'

'She has a few, but I am a work in progress, apparently.'

'I know how she feels. Why don't you start by doing a background check on Moyles? We haven't contacted the relatives yet. There is an address and I think Warlow will want to do that once he's happy the corpse is who we think it is. That's if the roads allow. See if there's anything on the PNC, run a DVLA check on the Land Rover. Oh, and there's the Sadlers. They're the people who found the body. Gil talked to them, but best we do a background check on them, too. You know the drill.'

'I do. Cup of tea before we start?'

Catrin didn't hesitate. 'Don't mind if I do.'

CHAPTER FIVE

To BE fair to the gritters, they'd done their job. The road up as far as Tal Farm was pretty good. A little crunchy under the tyres and all that salt and grit would do the undercarriage no favours, but needs must. There was no point Jess hanging on. She'd volunteered to visit Moyles's widow on the outskirts of Llansawel, to the north of Edwinsford. Warlow arranged to meet her back at Llandeilo once she'd finished and he had done what he needed to do.

Once they took the left turn along the unmarked and unmapped roads, things became, for lack of a better description and, in Gil's words, "Bloody dodgy as." Other vehicles had been on the route, so a path of sorts had been made across the icy road which, now that the temperature was way below freezing, had become a treacherous, semi-slushy, black run. Luckily, the way was fairly flat with no real gradients until they came to within a quarter of a mile, where they were met at the bottom of a small hill by a uniformed officer who exited his response vehicle parked in a field gate entrance. He flagged Warlow down and spoke through the wound-down window, his words visible as feathery vapour in the cold air.

'Might be best if you leave the car here, sir. Not everyone has got up the hill.' He motioned towards the dark ribbon of road silhouetted against the "aurora policiaris"—another of Gil's sayings—of light beyond at *Cân-y-barcud*. 'I can let you into the field, behind me, sir. Ground's as hard as concrete, anyway.'

Warlow complied. As he and Gil crunched over the frozen grass to the roadway, the Uniform sang out another warning, 'I'd stay on the verges too, sir. A couple of people have gone AOT on the climb up. Funny, the first two times. Pitiful when it happens again.'

Arse over tit was not something Warlow wanted to emulate. And the thought of having to pick Gil up, should he stumble, was a nonstarter.

'I know what you're thinking, Evan,' Gil muttered. 'I am looking where I step.'

They took it slow and easy up the narrow lane, their torch beams picking out the footsteps of those who had gone before. Gil led, Warlow following. Not the usual two-abreast way of approach, but the last thing either wanted was a broken limb on this dark and freezing night.

When Gil crested the rise and stood on flatter ground, breathing hard as Warlow joined him, both men stood to survey the sight in front of them a couple of hundred yards away. Glaring white arc lights picked out the little building, and the vehicles parked all around it. The sight was more akin to a landing site on the moon than a getaway cottage.

'No Apache village today, I see.'

Gil's reference to the usual array of Tyvek tents at a crime scene was well put, even if, as Warlow suspected, it would no doubt trigger someone if they ever heard him say it. For once, the investigators were inside and under cover.

A good plan since Warlow could feel the cold seeping into his toes already.

'This is the only road in, then, I see,' he muttered.

'Looks like it.'

Warlow studied his surroundings. Away from the light show at the property, the world was dark. Not even the lights of the response vehicle in the field behind were visible now. Under other conditions – the type not involving dead bodies – this really was a place to study the stars with light pollution at a minimum. They walked on along a gradual descent, still careful to find some traction on the grassy verge.

'You all set for Christmas, Gil?'

'The little ones are excited. School winds them up, of course. But it's their time, isn't it?'

'You're not a fan?'

Gil let out a negative growl. 'Not really. Too much to eat, too much to drink, and the weather too shite to burn it off outside.'

Warlow recalled the awful Christmas jumper complete with floppy antlers that, for reasons of expediency, Gil had worn out of season not so long ago. 'You don't know anyone by the name of Bob Cratchit, do you?'

'Don't you start. The kids all call me Scrooge. The Lady Anwen thought it would be funny to give me a stuffed sheep wearing a jumper in the style of a stripy humbug last year. Baa-humbug it's called. It sits in my chair when I am not using it. The children – mine and the grandchildren – think it's hilarious. But if I hear Noddy Holder screaming out the name of the season never again, I would not be disappointed.'

'I'm with you on that one.'

'But the Lady Anwen makes a mean mince pie, I have to admit. What about you? Is Tom coming to yours?'

'No. We had our Christmas lunch on Sunday. He'll be

digging out turkey bones from some poor bugger's throat, I expect. No, I'm home alone with Cadi. Unless this damned thing drags me in. Though Jess and Molly are hosting me for lunch on the day.'

'Tidy,' Gil commented. 'Of course, you would have been welcome at our place, but to be honest, it's like a creche on acid most years.' They'd reached the gate leading to *Cân-y-barcud*. A Uniform, wrapped in so many layers it was impossible to tell her actual body shape, proffered a clipboard to sign. The arc lights were glaringly bright behind her.

'Who needs a bloody Christmas tree?' Gil grunted and made his way across to the front door.

Alison Povey, whether because of some sixth sense or a covert messaging system setup with the Uniform at the field a quarter of a mile back to alert her when the boss was on site, stepped out of the door just as Gil and the DCI approached.

'Ho, ho, ho,' she said by way of greeting.

'No party hat?' Gil observed.

Povey, like all the other techs, wore a Tyvek suit with the hood on and a mask, which she pulled down over her chin now to continue the conversation. 'Not yet. That all comes later.'

'Please don't tell me the killer entered down the chimney,' Warlow said. 'Or things really will kick off.'

Povey beamed at them and made a show to look over their shoulders. 'Just the two of you, is there?'

'Who else were you expecting?' Gil asked.

'A third wise man. Who else? And since the chimney is a stovepipe with a six-inch diameter, Father Christmas would have to be a shape changer. No sign of a break-in. My guess would be that the killer was known to the victim who let him, or her, in.'

'Talking of victim… unless we go in soon, my lips are going to freeze,' Warlow said, or rather stuttered.

Povey turned to the door. 'Follow me, gentlemen. Welcome to Santa's grotto. Please put on your charming snow suits which are just inside the door.'

Gil and Warlow exchanged glances. 'See why I bloody hate Christmas?' Gil muttered once more.

Povey kept talking as they followed her in on the marked-off areas it was safe to walk on.

'As you will see, it isn't an enormous space to work in.'

'Bijou,' Gil said, glancing around. 'Any signs of footmarks? It was dry and dusty up until the rain.'

'Lots. We're eliminating the visitors, obviously. But otherwise, I think whoever did this cleaned up after themselves. But we'll keep looking.'

'The Sadlers could only have been in here for a few minutes, according to them,' Gil explained.

'Yes. They hardly touched anything by the looks of it. Except for a nice little splodge of vom.'

'Mrs Sadler mentioned that,' Gil said.

'Any signs of a struggle?' Warlow glanced around at the neat open-plan room.

'No. So, either what happened to Moyles was done under coercion or he did it voluntarily.'

Both Warlow and Gil sent her quizzical looks.

'I meant possibly as part of a sexual… indulgence.'

'Nicely put, Alison. Perhaps we'd better see.'

Povey called to the techs who were up on the mezzanine to come down. 'Not enough room to even pet a moggy, let alone swing one.'

Warlow and Gil waited at the bottom.

'Evan, if you'd go up and move left to the bottom of the bed. Gil, you'd better stay on the top of the stairs.'

The body had not been moved. Neither had what had been deposited on the bed. But the cottage's open door had got rid of the smell downstairs. Up on the mezzanine, however, it remained ripe. Warlow was wise enough to realise that those brilliant little TV scenes, where the vital clue is found by prising open the fingers in a clenched fist or a shut mouth to find a deposited trophy, were good for viewing figures, but complete nonsense in reality. Povey's team would probe and photograph every inch of the corpse and the room. Not having the Home Office Pathologist there yet was a pain, but it meant Warlow had all the time in the world to look over the remains of Royston Moyles.

More's the pity.

The "rope" the Sadlers had described had been wrapped around the corpse, starting at the legs, and winding up over the midriff to the chest. It went up and back with a double loop at chest level, and then over the crossbeam of the open A-frame above. At ankle level, the same double loop effectively suspended the body. Both hands had been tied with the same material behind Moyles's back. The rope had frayed ends and loose threads along its length and was clearly nylon.

'Looks like this has been used before.'

'Agreed,' Povey said. 'It's the sort of stuff you find lying around on farms all over the place.'

In its head and face down position, lividity was staining the corpse's abdomen. It would also have stained the face, because it was the lowest point on the body, were it not for the dark purple it had already become because of asphyxiation from the separate loop of blue rope around the neck – a noose which also ran up over the crossbeam and back towards the body.

'If this is something sexual – what does Rhys call it now, a paraphilia – then I'm obviously reading the wrong books,' Gil muttered.

'This isn't anything sexual,' Warlow said. 'Look at the

ropes. Someone knew what they were doing. The more he'd struggle, the tighter it would become.'

'Not quick, then,' Povey said.

'Not quick at all. By arching his back, he'd relieve some of the tension, but the knot would shorten the rope. How long can you do that suspended from the ceiling?'

'So, there is no way he could have done this to himself?' Gil asked.

Warlow swung his head in a no. 'I've seen the odd accident from people trying to indulge themselves. There was a bloke who liked to use a mannequin outside in the rain. No problem at all with that. But not in the middle of the cricket pitch in Whitland, as the schools let out.'

'Did he have an accident, then?' Gil asked.

'Yes. Two first-team players caught him red-handed. Or something handed. He was lucky to get away with just the three broken ribs and a headless mannequin. But this is nothing like that.'

Gil's pained expression ran the length of the corpse and back again. 'Now I feel even more sorry for the Sadlers.'

'They won't forget their honeymoon in a hurry, that's for sure,' Povey said from the bottom of the stairs.

'Okay, I've seen enough.' Warlow began backing towards where Gil was. 'No point hanging about here.'

'Oh, please.' Gil winced at the pun.

Warlow frowned. 'Unintended, I promise.' He turned to Povey as he got to the bottom. 'Let me know when Sengupta gets here, and the body is moved. I'll probably want a gander by daylight.'

Povey walked them out. 'I suppose you two are off now for a slap-up meal and a brandy?'

Gil ran with it. 'Elementary, my good woman. Mrs Hudson will bring it in on a tray. And I'll smoke a pipe while DCI Warlow plays the violin and ingests some narcotics.'

Povey giggled. 'If you are in Llandeilo later, I may catch up with you.'

'Maybe,' Warlow said. 'I doubt I'll be heading back to Nevern in this.'

As if orchestrated, a few flakes of snow began whistling in on a sudden breeze.

'Ding dong merrily on high it is, then,' Povey said.

Neither man replied as they trudged off into the darkness.

CHAPTER SIX

JESS DROVE OUT AS FAR as Talley Abbey and parked in what had once been a pub off the main road. There she'd arranged to meet an old friend from rural crime. Hana Prosser worked with her and the team on a couple of cases. One tragically involving her own father. Though she was well south of her base at Newtown, the type of vehicle she drove was well suited to off-road, so she'd been drafted in.

They met as old friends and Jess had no qualms about being driven to Llansawel to talk to Janet Moyles in Hana's "beast" of a Ford Ranger.

And so, while Warlow and Gil stood surveying the crime scene from the crest of the rise they'd carefully negotiated, Jess and Hana, who in a month's time would shed her PCSO status to become a fully-fledged constable, sat in the Moyles' kitchen watching the widow go through the ritual of making them a cup of tea.

She'd taken the news that her husband Royston had been found dead, remarkably stoically.

Remarkably stoically.

But Jess had been in situations like this before, and appearances could be very deceptive. What Mrs Moyles had not done was accept and assimilate that information fully yet. And though Jess had experienced grief in all its miserable forms, Janet was exemplifying denial par-excellence.

But Janet wasn't simply in denial. She, or a part of her brain that knew to accept was to give in to a cartload of horror and despair, was having none of it. She'd wittered on about the fact that there was a community council meeting in the new year and she needed to tell the clerk about that. That the vice chair was away for Christmas and she wouldn't be able to tell him. Some safety mechanism in her head was delivering all this tripe while she fiddled with cups and a kettle at the sink.

'Sugar and milk?' she asked, reaching into the fridge.

'Janet, why don't you come and sit down?' Jess said.

'Sugar or milk?' Janet repeated blithely.

Jess glanced at Hana but answered anyway, 'Milk only.'

'Me too,' Hana chimed.

'So, no sugar. Hardly anyone does these days, do they?' Janet muttered brightly. 'I remember when people took one or even two teaspoons of sugar in theirs. My Uncle Ifan, he used to take four, and heaped, too.' She paused without turning around to face the officers seated at the kitchen table. 'Four, would you believe it?' Janet chuckled.

Jess noticed for the first time that she was talking to her own reflection in the kitchen window. Everything was ready now. The kettle had boiled, bags were in the cups, a milk jug sat on the counter next to the sink.

The DI didn't see the change when it came, but she heard it.

At first, for a few seconds, it sounded like it might be the kettle again, though it only finished boiling a few minutes before. Yet this, a tiny noise from a constricted throat, came from Janet Moyles' throat as she stood with both hands on the edge of the sink rim, looking for all the world as if she was about to vault upwards and through the window.

But she didn't.

Instead, she trembled. At first, they were slight movements, but quickly sped up to an uncontrollable shake. Hana got up and crossed the space to where the woman stood, placing her arm around her shoulders, and guiding her back to the table where she flopped into a chair, causing it to scrape across the tiled floor with a tooth-twinging screech.

Jess didn't speak. There was no point. Janet wore a look on her face reminiscent of old images of concentration camps in Europe or Asia. Hopelessness writ large. All Janet could do was sit, the keening slowly diminishing, staring about her at the tidy kitchen and seeing nothing of it. Seeing instead, Jess was certain, a void where once had been a neat and ordered life.

Hana filled a glass with cool water and brought it back to the seated woman.

'Drink this, Janet.'

Janet's eyes flicked towards the uniformed officer and her neat blonde hair, flinching away from the voice as if her presence was something she'd not registered until that moment. But she took the glass in wavering hands, put it to her lips, and sipped.

It didn't matter that some of the liquid spilled down over her chin. All that mattered was that she did sip and the physicality of that reflex movement and the cool liquid in her throat ruptured her moment of madness.

She blinked. 'Is this… is this real?'

'I'm sorry, Janet. I'm really sorry,' Jess said.

Janet's face crumpled, and the glass clattered back to the table. A great sob erupted from her mouth, followed by a reflexive intake of breath, repeated over and over. She sounded like the slow-motion version of the little engine that could, lost in the goods yard, looking for a way out.

'Is there anyone we can ring, Janet?' Hana asked, her hand rubbing the woman's back.

Janet nodded. Small, vague movements. 'My sister. She lives in Llandovery.'

'What's her name?'

'Lois.'

'Do you have her number?'

Again, in response, Janet turned a bewildered look towards Hana.

'Lois's number, Janet?' Hana repeated the question gently.

'On the fridge. She has a new phone.' The answer came out more a whimper than a firm statement.

Hana went to the fridge and picked off a note held by a sheep-shaped magnet. She took out her phone and walked out of the kitchen to make the call.

Jess leaned forward over the table. 'Janet, I know this is hard. What I'm telling you is difficult to take in, but I need to ask you some tough questions.'

Janet sipped some more water. 'Did he slip? Was it a heart attack?'

'Royston's death wasn't an accident, Janet. And it wasn't a heart attack.' Jess recalled that suspended body. 'We think he was deliberately killed.'

Janet's eyes, wide already, now expanded to a point where it looked like another couple of millimetres might let them pop out of their sockets. 'What?'

Hana came back in. 'She's on her way.'

Jess kept her gaze trained on Janet's face. 'I wish I didn't have to say these things, Janet, I really do. But can you think of anyone who might want to do Royston any harm?'

'Harm?' The word floated out of Janet's mouth, warbling as it emerged.

'Did he tell you where he was going today?'

'Just out. He always goes out. We have stock in fields all over. We have properties.'

'Did he say he was going to a property?'

'No. But he goes to one or two. We rent them out.'

'Why does he go to these properties?'

'Just to check that the cleaners have done their jobs. We have some people from the village. Not locals. They're from Europe. They're hard working. But Royston likes to check. To make sure everything is right. We want to keep our stars.'

'Stars?' Jess asked.

'Star rating, ma'am. For the rentals,' Hana said.

Jess shrugged. It had been a long day. 'When was the last time you spoke to Royston?'

'Lunchtime. We had lunch here. Left over lamb from yesterday.'

'How did he seem to you? Was he anxious? Did he complain about anything bothering him?'

Janet thought, staring at the glass in front of her. 'No. Nothing. We talked about the fields in the lower acre. They get soaked and we have some stock still there. But nothing... unusual.'

'And no one strange has called at the house? Or telephoned?'

Another straightforward question, but one that didn't register with Janet. 'How?' she whispered.

'How?'

'How was he killed?'

Jess hesitated, wondering if telling Janet now would help or hinder matters. But in situations like this, her rule of thumb was to tell them if they asked. Some people did not ask. Janet had.

'Strangulation.'

Janet huffed out air, like the breathing they taught you to do when you were in pain. 'Have you told Charles?'

'Charles?'

'Charles is Roy's business manager. He needs to know.' This time, Janet found the number on her phone and showed it to Jess who had to put her own hand over Janet's to stop it shaking. 'It might help if you wrote down everything that happened today. Right from when Royston got up. Could you do that?'

Jess threw Hana a glance.

'Do you have any paper handy, Janet?' Hana asked.

'Over by the phone. The landline.'

It gave her something to focus on. Hana sat next to her, encouraging her to write. Jess sipped her strong tea, studying the kitchen as she did so. It was the absences that struck home.

No snaps of grandchildren on the fridge.

No framed photographs of children on the wall.

But there were images of Royston and Janet. Younger versions. On cruise ships. Sitting at a café on a beach somewhere. Not local.

Captured moments of happier times.

The officers waited until Lois arrived. By then, the single sheet that Janet had begun had grown to two, both covered in her small, neat writing. The words had expanded to include names and numbers of Royston's closest friends and his business interests. All valuable intel.

'There'll be a liaison officer coming very soon, Janet. She is going to stay with you and help you.'

'But Lois—'

'As well as Lois.'

Hana drove Jess back to Talley Abbey and her car.

'Thanks for the lift,' Jess said. 'And the moral support.'

Outside, frost twinkled on the surfaces of the parked cars.

'Any time, ma'am. So sad, though. She seemed so alone. And the way she reacted; I've seen nothing like that before.'

'Shock does all sorts to people, Hana. But you did brilliantly. Cajoling her into writing all that down. You're going to make a great officer. I bet Tomo isn't happy about you leaving.'

Tomo, the sergeant that had mentored Hana in rural crime, would undoubtedly miss her.

'I'm not looking forward to my last shift with him, that's for certain.'

'I bet he's delighted for you, though.'

'He is, ma'am. So he says.'

Jess got out of the car.

'Oh, and say hello to DCI Warlow for me, please?'

'I will.'

'Sorry I missed him.'

'I'll let him know. But you may yet bump into him. Early days in this case yet.'

CHAPTER SEVEN

GIL AND WARLOW arrived back at the hotel at around eight. To a busier place than they'd left.

At least a dozen stranded motorists rescued from cars that had spun off into ditches, or collided with another vehicle, or were simply left with spinning wheels on traction-less gradients, had been brought in by beleaguered officers. That, combined with the townsfolk realising that if they were going anywhere on a black-ice night such as this, it was via gritted pavements to their local watering holes and not to anywhere far afield, meant an almost full house. Word had spread and curiosity was dragging all the cool cats out to gawk.

It was almost Christmas after all, and the telly was rubbish.

Gil saw no hope of finding a table in the bar or the lounge with the comfy seats. Instead, he and Warlow settled at a table in the main restaurant while they awaited Jess's arrival. Even though they had no intention of eating anything, staff and management were being very accommodating.

Arrangements had already been made for Warlow and

Jess to stay at Gil's place this treacherous night. A house that, like everywhere in the market town, was within easy walking distance of the hotel.

Gil fetched some drinks from the bar. A pint of best for himself, half a lager for Warlow, and a still fizzing white wine spritzer for Jess in anticipation of her arrival.

'I've spoken to the Lady Anwen. She has a shepherd's pie in the bottom oven. Once Jess arrives, we can be off.'

'You checked with Jess? About her staying, too? I mean, I'm fine. Cadi's with the Dawes and happy as Larry.' Warlow spoke with total confidence there. His black lab had a co-conspirator in the shape of the Dawes' golden lab, Bouncer. She would have no complaints.

Gil took a swig of beer and stared over at the full tables in the restaurant with eyes focused somewhere else altogether. 'I knew a Larry once,' he said. 'Not happy, though. In fact, he was a miserable bugger. Probably something to do with the fact that he worked for a cesspit cleaning company. You know, those big tankers where they dip in a tube like a big straw and suck everything up out of your septic tank when it becomes too full.'

'Ah, God,' Warlow agreed. 'You can always tell where one of those is around. Especially if you're downwind.'

'Absolutely. Same applied when the driver of said tanker walked into the bar of an evening, no matter how much Imperial Leather he blasted himself with. As far as I'm aware, he's still working and goes by Crappy as Larry.'

'Thanks for sharing. But back to my point,' Warlow said. 'Jess has Molly.'

'She does. But she'd be mad to even attempt getting back to Cold Blow this evening. It'd be more like Frozen Blow. Besides, I've checked. Molly is with Bryn, her boyfriend.'

'Of course. He's home from university. How long do they get at Christmas? Four weeks, is it?'

'Something like that. Point is, she's safe, anyway.'

Warlow sipped his drink and looked at the glass before setting it down. 'I suppose it should be mulled wine, given the season. Warm the cockles and all that.'

'Ugh.' Gil growled. 'Never touch the stuff. Reminds me too much of Sangria.'

Warlow had a second to pull back and ease out of this little cul-de-sac of a conversation there and then. But a part of his self-flagellating psyche had to follow through to see exactly where this was leading.

'Okay, so what's wrong with Sangria?'

'Nothing. When it's going down. But all that fruit makes it vile coming back up.' Gil shook his head. 'Reminds me of holidays in Spain in my youth. I've had too many Costa del headaches after Jackson Pollocking the bathroom floor with Sangria. And mulled wine is only the warmed-up version.'

Warlow, momentarily speechless, stared at the sergeant. 'Once again, thank you for that imagery.'

'You're welcome.'

Warlow looked around. 'This place is buzzing.' A group of eight large-in-the-circumference department men entered the room and found seats at a table. Gil motioned to a waitress and asked who they were.

'Darts team from The Black Horse. Their minibus broke down in Carmel.'

A stranger might, flippantly, ask if she meant the town that Clint Eastwood had once been the mayor of in California. But Warlow knew the Carmel she was referencing was on the A476 halfway between where he sat and the A48. Notorious not for cowboys, but for speed cameras and getting snow before anywhere else in the county if there was any about.

'Waifs and strays,' Warlow muttered. But his eyes followed the server, who was being motioned to by a man in a waxed jacket under a matching flat cap. The jacket was unzipped revealing a yellow checked shirt and a green tie beneath a suit which might have been fashionable when steam trains ran up and down the valley.

The waitress pointed a finger in Warlow's direction.

The man approached. He must have been in his sixties, ruddy of complexion with unnaturally white teeth that seemed too big for his mouth.

'You gentlemen with the constabulary?'

'We are,' Gil said, regarding the speaker with interest.

A hand shot out. A soft hand with the nails cut short. 'John Napier, solicitor. I'm a friend—' He caught himself. 'I was a friend of Royston Moyles.'

Warlow sat up, his eyes narrowing. 'Was?'

'Mind if I sit down?'

Gil pulled out a chair. Napier removed his cap to reveal a bad comb-over of gingery hair and got to it. 'Janet Moyles rang me. One of your colleagues has called with her. Left her in a bit of a state, I'm afraid.'

'News of a death is never cause for celebration,' Gil said, his eyes never leaving the solicitor's.

'Agreed. But Janet insisted I speak with you. Is there anything else you can tell me?'

'Depends,' Warlow said.

'Look. We know he was killed. That the death was unnatural. But your officer would not give Janet more information than that.'

'That officer is a Detective Inspector, and she has given Mrs Moyles what information we can give at this moment in time.'

'But surely—'

Warlow cut across. 'Mr Napier, as a friend of the family, I'm sure you have Mrs Moyles's best interests at heart. But this is a police investigation and we cannot, at this stage, say any more than what we have already.'

Napier gave a terse nod and took in the bustling room. 'Never seen it like this. The weather has caught everyone by surprise.'

'True,' Gil said. 'Were you and Mr Moyles close?'

'I've known him for years. I've been the family's legal advisor, but I considered Roy a friend. We shot clay pigeons together when we were younger. Fished together. We worked on community action groups, park-renovations, that sort of thing.'

'You're local, Mr Napier?'

'I live a few miles out of town.'

'When was the last time you saw Mr Moyles?'

'We usually met for a drink on a Friday night, three or four of us.'

'Last Friday?' Gil asked.

'Yes. At The Farmer's. The Farmer's Arms. Three pints maximum, or three glasses of red in my case. Just enough to set the world to rights. We share a taxi home,' he added hastily.

'How many of you last Friday?'

Napier paused. 'How is that relevant?'

'Because we'll need to trace his movements.'

'But Friday was three days ago.' Napier smiled as if three days were a lifetime.

Warlow waited.

'There were three of us, as per usual,' Napier said, eventually.

'How did he seem to you?' Gil asked.

Napier sat back a little, as if he wanted to object further, but then seemed to relent. 'His normal self. Roy was always so full of life. Willing to help people. He'll be sorely missed, I can tell you that.'

'And you are unaware of anyone who might want to do him any harm?'

'Harm? There are dozens of people in this town who

owe… owed Roy Moyles a great deal. For work he did on the council, in the schools, helping farmers. I can't believe it, I really can't.'

Warlow took out a card. 'This is my name and number. I'd appreciate it if we could have yours. No doubt we will need to speak to you over the next few days while we piece together our understanding of Mr Moyles. But now is not the time. Not here.'

Napier reached into an inside pocket for a wallet and offered Warlow his card in exchange.

'We would also hope that, for now, you kept this information to yourself. We had to break the news to Mrs Moyles, but if you think it's chaotic here now, wait until the press finds out. The longer we can delay that, the better.'

'Completely understand,' Napier said. 'And if I can be of any help, please feel free to contact me.'

He stood up and wound his way through the crowd.

'Pillar of the community.' Warlow had one eyebrow raised when he said it.

'Napier or Moyles?'

'Both.'

'All that glitters, right?' Gil said.

'Hmm.'

'I hope that white wine spritzer's mine, is it?'

Both men turned to see Jess standing behind them. In following Napier's exit, they'd missed her entrance.

'Got your name written all over it, ma'am.'

Gil shifted seats and took the one Napier had previously sat in, letting Jess have his. She took off gloves and a faux fur earmuff, which, Warlow thought, gave her the look of a Russian princess, and sat, unbuttoning her coat as she did. She then took a swallow of her drink and sighed. 'God, I needed that. It's like a circus in here.'

'What are the roads like?' Warlow asked.

'Bad and getting worse. Hard to believe it's all meant to melt away by tomorrow.'

'The night is still young,' Gil said darkly.

'We've just had a visitor.' Warlow ran through Napier's visit and the spilled beans regarding Moyles's death.

'Janet Moyles was in a state when we left.'

'What was your impression?'

'Married couple. No kids, very… what's the word you like to use again, Gil? Parch-is?'

'*Parchus*. Very respectable.'

'That's the word.'

Warlow clamped his lips together before speaking again. 'It's what Napier was trying to tell us, too.'

'Doesn't tie in with what I saw at that cottage,' Jess said.

'No, it does not,' Gil agreed.

'We need to scratch the surface,' Warlow said. 'See what we can find under the veneer. Let's hope it isn't anything too unpleasant.'

Both Gil and Jess exchanged knowing looks that suggested Warlow was being optimistic. The good ship pleasant had already set sail and sunk somewhere beyond the horizon in this case.

'Molly, okay?' Warlow asked.

Jess took another gulp of wine before answering, 'She's fine. Nice and warm at Bryn's.'

Gil's mobile chirped a message notification. He glanced at it and looked up. 'Right, well, we've got ten minutes to finish our drinks before the Lady Anwen sends out a search party. Food is almost on the table. I suggest we get to mine, and then I'll ring Catrin for an update. Let her and Rhys get off home if they can.'

'Good idea,' Warlow said and downed his lager, while from somewhere in the hotel, a chorus of *Oh Come All Ye Faithful* rang out.

CHAPTER EIGHT

WARLOW INSISTED they talk to Catrin and Rhys the minute they got into Gil's. He'd apologised to Anwen and promised to keep everyone for only five more minutes. To which Anwen replied with no words, but a long-suffering look that said she'd heard all of that before with bells on. They sat in the Jones's nicely furnished living room, now decorated to the hilt with a lit-up Christmas tree, paper chains hanging from the ceiling and handmade Christmas cards on a mantlepiece. Gil caught Warlow's glance.

'Before you ask, I didn't make those. They are my grandchildren's work. The large, round, red blob with the black hat is me, apparently. Strangely, that figure appears, and in the same proportions, in all three of the girls' art. Obviously, they all have the same defective vision. I've booked them an optician's appointment for the new year.'

Jess and Warlow sat on the settee, Gil in an armchair he'd moved around so they could use the coffee table as a focal point for Warlow's phone.

Catrin and Rhys's faces, the DC's over the shoulder of the DS's, stared back at them from the brightly lit Incident Room at HQ. Behind them, the sparsely populated boards

Warlow liked to call the Gallery and the Job Centre had a few posted-up notes and images, but all too small to read on this video call.

'Catrin, what can you tell us?' Warlow asked.

'Royston Moyles has no record with us, sir. The PNC does not have him in the database. His DVLA record is clean. Rhys has found the property on a couple of online rental sites.'

Rhys leant forward a little, his customary grin tickled by something he was seeing.

'You three all look nice and cosy there.'

'We're at Gil's. We should be cosy,' Jess said.

'Are you having food there?' Rhys suddenly looked stricken.

'Shepherd's pie,' Gil said. 'A la Anwen. And there's a crumble of some sort to follow.'

Rhys's grin became a little forced. 'Sounds great.'

'We'll take a picture of it and send it over,' Warlow said.

Rhys's smile slipped.

'Haven't you eaten, Rhys?' Gil asked.

'Yes, sarge. But that was hours ago. Shepherd's pie sounds—'

Rhys slipped out of shot as the camera on the monitor they were using jerked away towards Catrin. 'If you don't stop food taunting him, we'll be here all night.'

The camera swung back towards a less smiley Rhys. '*Cân-y-barcud* is listed as a quiet place. A haven that is not cheap. It's on three or four websites, NON being one of them. No owner near is more like no one near in this case. Looks like it's fully booked up over Christmas and the New Year.'

'Last week?' Warlow asked.

'No, sir. Last week it was empty, but before that, three weeks were full.'

'Did it say that on the website?' Jess was intrigued.

'No,' Rhys explained. 'That bit I got from Moyles's business manager. More a PA really. Chap called Charles Brewer.'

Catrin came back into shot. 'I spoke to him. He's stuck six miles out of Llandeilo and did not want to travel this evening. But he says he'll meet you tomorrow at the hotel. He can be there early. I thought it would be better than dragging him into Carmarthen.'

'Good idea,' Jess said. 'Hopefully. Povey will have an update for us then, too. And the HOP will have been to the scene.' Jess got nods all around.

'Right.' Warlow glanced at his watch. 'You two get off. If the weather does what it says it's going to, we'll have a briefing tomorrow morning, time TBA. Agreed?'

'I'll text you what Brewer told me, sarge.' Rhys pretended to write something in the air with an imaginary pencil.

'How are you getting home?' Warlow asked.

'Craig is sorting out transport, sir,' Catrin said. 'We'll run Rhys home before we go to ours.'

'Text me when you're back safe. Both of you,' Warlow said. An order, not a request.

As he hung up, the door to the room opened and a girl of six or seven, clad in jeans, fluffy Olaf slippers, and a Frozen sweatshirt appeared. 'Anwen says if you don't come now, she's going to give your supper to the dog.' She delivered this warning confidently and with a complete lack of self-consciousness.

Gil stood up, raised his finger, and in a theatrical, comedy villain Dracula-esque voice said, 'Who are you and what are you doing in my house?'

The girl, clearly unfazed by Gil's overacting, rolled her eyes. 'And she said she knows you don't have a dog, but she'll borrow Archie from next door.'

'Curse that woman for the banshee that she is,' Gil announced.

The little girl half turned and called back over her shoulder, '*Mamgu*, Gil called you a banshee.'

Warlow laughed.

Gil kept a straight face. 'DI Allanby, meet my grand-daughter and master criminal ringleader, Eleri.'

Warlow, a more frequent visitor to Gil's had made Eleri's acquaintance, but this was a first time for Jess.

'I don't believe for one minute she's your granddaugh-ter,' Jess said. 'She's far too pretty.'

Eleri smiled and Warlow caught a glimpse, in that natural unforced grin, of the girl and the woman she would be. Gil better buy a big stick because he'd need it to ward off the suitors.

'Right, you heard the banshee, uh, Anwen. Dinner is served.' Gil moved his chair back.

But before either Warlow or Jess could stand, Eleri asked a question in her native tongue.

'*Wedodd mamgu bod y bobol hyn yn chaso dynon drwg, tadcu. Ydyn nhw?*'

Warlow smiled, but kept it restrained. He didn't want Eleri to feel she was being made fun of.

'Translation?' Jess asked.

Gil did the needful. 'She's asking if you're all here to chase bad men.'

Jess answered, knowing that this little girl was completely bilingual and slid into her native language as naturally as water ran down glass, 'We are, Eleri. Just like your granddad.' She got up and walked over to the little girl and got down on her haunches to be at her level. 'And he is very good at it.'

'Are you good at it?'

Jess threw Warlow a glance.

'We are the best,' he replied. 'After your *tadcu*, of course.'

Jess stood and held out her hand. 'I'm Jess, by the way. Can you show me the way to your grandma's kitchen?'

Eleri turned and led the way. 'But you must step over Mali, my cat. She's too lazy to get up.'

She waved a hand at a striped stuffed toy, legs akimbo on the floor.

Gil watched them leave with a shake of her head. 'Is it any wonder I'm worn to a bloody frazzle?'

'She's a treasure,' Warlow said.

'And there are two more like that. What bloody chance do I have?'

'Granddaughters,' Warlow said. It seemed to be all that was needed.

'Forgot,' Gil said gruffly. 'You're in the club, too, Evan. We are indeed lucky men. Now, glass of red with the shepherd's pie, or would you prefer a beer?'

The shepherd's pie was wonderful, the wine – just the one glass – a great accompaniment. Eleri sat with them while they ate and waited for her mother. Gil explained that his youngest daughter dropped Eleri off while she and her partner attended ballroom dancing lessons every Monday night. Something that would be ending soon as Eleri's brother or sister, currently incubating in her mother's womb, would make dancing nigh on impossible for a while.

'Is that why you don't dance, *tadcu*?' Eleri asked, pointing at his admittedly reducing, but still ample, abdomen.

'I hope that child in your mother's womb is a boy. He and I will form a blood pact against girls with stuffed cats,' Gil said with a snarl that made Eleri giggle. A knock on the door sent her scrambling to let her mother in. Anwen and

Gil followed leaving Jess and Warlow alone to respond to Eleri's sing-song goodbyes.

After she left, Warlow and Jess insisted on clearing up and then sat at the kitchen table with Gil, while Anwen watched TV. Gil went through the information that Rhys had obtained regarding Moyles's movements.

'Rhys has spoken to the cleaners. They visited the cottage on Saturday. Gave the place a going over. But because no one had stayed there for a few days, there had been little to do. Yesterday, he went to church. He was a regular.'

'Still comes across as a man of the people,' Jess said. 'Either he's been in the wrong place at the wrong time—'

Gil made a face. 'A random killing, ma'am? A lunatic on the loose in the hills?'

'I know it's not likely, but it is a scenario. The other being a planned and well executed killing. By someone who knew where he might find Moyles at that precise time.'

'Something to dwell on.' Warlow stifled a yawn. 'Right, I'm for bed. I was in London twelve hours ago. Hard to believe.'

'What, that there was an actual train running to bring you home?' Jess asked, before adding. 'Think the public would notice if we went on strike?'

'They might when the Barbarian hordes finally invade,' Gil said. 'But until then, probably not.'

———

WARLOW LAY in bed waiting for his brain to hit the brakes.

It wasn't the first time he'd lain in this bed enjoying Gil and Anwen's hospitality, and it likely would not be the last. Llandeilo, though only fifteen miles from Carmarthen, was a more central staging post for the mountainous hinterland of central Wales and ended up being a very convenient watering hole. Still, this wasn't his bed in his home. And he missed his dog.

A few yards away, Jess Allanby was no doubt having similar thoughts, though in her case she was missing her daughter instead of a dog. At least, he assumed she would be when she wasn't trying, like Warlow, to piece together the nuggets of information they already had.

And she would be doing that because she had an SIO's brain, complete with everything that came with it, such as an awareness that, though the hand they'd been dealt was devoid of any aces and complicated by the weather, it was still the upper hand for now, at least. As far as interference was concerned, anyway. And for interference, read the public. Yes, of course, once the press got wind, they'd be swarming like flies around horse manure, but these days there was also the TikTok brigade to consider. There was always a chance that the press might look upon yet another murder as not fulfilling the editorial feel-good pre-Christmas brief. No doubt once the big day was over, they'd pick up on Moyles's death and go to town. But what Warlow didn't want was a gaggle of amateur social media sleuths taking selfies outside *Cân-y-barcud* over the holidays, or inventing silly, spurious theories in order to gain followers or, nauseatingly, likes.

He was the first to admit that having to respond, even to peers who should have known better, to nonsensical ideas and criticism from people who had never seen a dead body in their lives, was a challenge,

And one he preferred not to have to face if he could help it.

So, that set the clock ticking.

Tick tock.

The season, and the weather, had given him a window in which to operate. Still, the ticking of that damned clock was loud in his ears. He wondered if it might lull him to sleep. But it didn't. Not for a long while. He forced his mind away from it and thought about other things. His boys, the dog, and inevitably, Jess Allanby lying in a bed a few yards away. But he trod on those thoughts smartly because they were becoming frequent flyers on his flights of fancy. And that wouldn't do.

No? Why not, Evan?

Time and a place was his usual answer.

Ironically, there probably would not be a better one.

Warlow turned over in the bed and listened to the wind rattle the windows like an animal in a cage.

CHAPTER NINE

TUESDAY

THE WEATHER BROKE at around 4am.

Nature, not that she needed to after the freezing rain, announced her presence with a clap of thunder and some lightning. Warlow awoke in a strange room and heard the rain pummelling the slate roof, convinced that he'd be unable to go back to sleep. But the weather's lullaby had other ideas. He drifted off and by the time he'd got downstairs a little after seven thirty, the table in Gil's dining room looked like something out of a Harry Potter feast scene, with three matching tureens taking centre stage.

Tureens.

They were striking pieces of pottery in a blue pattern with detailed grey scenes around the lid handle. He had a peek into each. Scrambled eggs in one, bacon in the other, thick half tomatoes in the third. Gil, apron on, stuck his head around the door.

'Tea or coffee?'

Bewildered, Warlow asked, 'Are we expecting a male voice choir?'

Gil glanced over his shoulder before whispering, 'I did try and hold her back. But she's gone into full master chef mode. And this is one of the few chances she has to use her mother's Llanelli pottery, so who am I to deny her that?'

Warlow reciprocated the whisper, 'You know I rarely eat break—'

He was cut off by a red-faced and beaming Anwen, her hair held up out of her face by a clip, clutching another, smaller tureen, in both hands. 'Beans,' she said and then caught herself. 'Morning.'

'Morning,' Warlow replied. 'This is some spread, Anwen.'

She made a dismissive noise like the bray of a small donkey.

'My.' Jess entered the room to stand and stare. 'Have we got company?'

'Yes,' Anwen said in a high-pitched voice. 'You two. Now tuck in. Toast?'

Politeness made Warlow take a spoonful of everything. But the taste of the bacon and the silkiness of the eggs made him have seconds.

When they arrived at the Cawdor Hotel at nine, Warlow knew what a Christmas turkey felt like.

Completely stuffed.

Alison Povey stood in reception and waved to the three senior officers as they walked in. She looked very different in her civvies, and not in a white Tyvek boiler suit with the hood cinched tight. Today she stood in black jeans, her upper body hidden under a puffer jacket. She kept her dark hair short and wore a constantly amused expression that belied her job as the lead crime scene investigator.

'Did you stay here last night, Alison?' Warlow asked.

'No. I have a friend in town. You at Gil's?'

'We were. Are you going back out to the site?'

'Sengupta's there now. Once she's examined, we'll get the body out and get on with having a proper go at the bedroom. It's been a frustrating few hours.'

Povey was amazing at her job, but delays like this didn't help anyone. She picked up on his silence. 'I know you hoped I'd have something for you, but things might be different by the end of the day. Will you be heading back to HQ?'

'At some point. But we're meeting Brewer, the victim's PA, here.'

Povey smiled and glanced around at their surroundings. The hotel was busy already. Those that had stayed overnight because of the circumstances found out quickly that taxi services were limited and tied up with school runs this early. And if they expected lifts from the police, they were mistaken.

'I think the local round table is organising volunteers to drive people to their vehicles.'

'Good. Sooner the better. We'll need a bit of peace and quiet,' Warlow said.

'I'll chat with the manager. See if she can find us a spot,' Gil said.

With that, Povey said her goodbyes and stepped out into the drizzle with a last wave of her hand. 'Have fun.' She grinned at Jess and Warlow, yanked up her hood, and trotted off.

———

BREAKFAST WAS in full swing at the hotel. Not that the stranded motorists had been allocated rooms. They'd been given blankets and allowed to sit in the comfy lounge all night. But to be fair to the hotel, this morning they'd also been given free coffee and tea and a local baker had brought in hot rolls.

By the dozen from the look of it, as a tray carried by a young bloke eased past Warlow.

But Gil found them a different alcove, more secluded even than the night before's, in the large dining room. Once they sat, Gil grinned at them both.

'What?' Jess asked.

'Don't you get an Agatha Christie vibe? Lots of guests in a hotel? Inclement weather locking them down in a cauldron?' He glanced across. 'Lend me a monocle. There must be an American heiress here somewhere.'

'Thank you, Poirot,' Jess said.

'More like *poeri*.'

Jess raised a questioning eyebrow.

Warlow answered, '"Spit" in the local dialect.'

Gil took no notice and pretended to twirl a non-existent moustache. He was still doing it when a younger, clean-cut man in corduroy trousers and a hacking jacket over a jumper, shirt, and tie introduced himself.

'Hello, I'm Charlie Brewer.'

Gil stood up and introduced himself, Jess, and Warlow. Clean and tidy were the words that sprang to Warlow's mind. Early thirties, with a quick smile that, under the circumstances, seemed inappropriate.

'Thanks for talking to us, Mr Brewer,' Gil said.

'Please, it's Charlie. Everyone calls me that. And when Sergeant Richards called last night, I wanted to help.'

Warlow threw Jess a quick glance.

'What exactly did she tell you, Charlie?' Jess asked.

'Only that there's been some kind of incident at a property I help Roy Moyles manage.'

That explained the smile. *He didn't know. And why should he?* They'd deliberately not broadcast Moyles's death. John Napier had known because Moyles's wife told him.

'Mr Brewer,' Warlow kept things formal, 'I'm sorry to have to tell you that Mr Moyles was found dead yesterday.'

Charlie Brewer's first reaction was to laugh. But it emerged a brief, stilted affair that froze on his lips when he realised that sitting around a table with three detectives and the chance that they'd turned up as a prank was non-existent. He went very pale, very quickly, and sat back.

Gil leaned in.

'Deep breaths, Charlie. It usually helps.'

It did. After a dozen tremulous and deep inhalations and exhalations, Charlie sat up, a little colour back in his cheeks.

'Sorry, I uh… wow, that's a shock.'

'I'll get you some tea,' Gil said. 'Sugar and milk?'

'One sugar,' Charlie replied.

'I'd make that two, then,' Warlow said to Gil's departing back.

'How?' Charlie asked. 'Did he die, I mean?'

'That's yet to be determined,' Jess explained. 'But as you will have gathered from us being here, we know that Mr Moyles's death was not natural.'

'Christ,' Charlie said.

'We can't go into any details yet,' Jess added. 'But we need to ask you some questions. Do you feel up to that?'

'Of course.'

And, to his credit, he was. Once Gil came back with the tea and the sugar kicked in, Charlie became an open book on speedread setting. They learnt how he'd gone to Hartpury College to study Agricultural Enterprise and to play some sport. But his cruciate ligament had put paid to that after only half a season. Once he got his qualification, he'd come home and got a job-share with an estate management company and filled out the rest of his time working with Royston Moyles, and his small portfolio of six properties. Three short-term, three long-term, as well as land owned and rented out to various farmers for grazing and silage.

'So, Mr Moyles didn't farm himself?'

'No, his heart wasn't in it. We got on because his background was much like mine. Unusual for this neck of the woods. I went to a private school, like Roy. But I had some land and property to inherit when my parents died. Roy was running that now.'

'But renting fields and properties isn't exactly a cutthroat business, right?' Jess asked.

'Just the odd irate tenant if the shower leaks or a toilet doesn't flush. That's about it.'

'Hardly need to call out the Cosa Nostra, then?' Gil said.

Charlie's ambiguous smile made Warlow appreciate that he might never have seen *The Godfather* but had enough instinct to guess that Cosa Nostra wasn't the Salvation Army.

'And no public or private enemies that you were aware of?' Jess asked.

Charlie looked shocked. 'Royston is… was a complex man. If I had to pick holes, then… my girlfriend says he's a letch. Nothing terrible. Just insisted on a hug and a kiss on the cheek whenever he could. And not just with her. Overfamiliar might be a better term. With women.'

'Did it ever become a problem?'

'No. I mean, my Sara, she's my partner, always tried to make sure she never sat next to him. Said he's always inching his chair to be as close as possible. But never anything… inappropriate.'

Jess stiffened in the chair next to Warlow. 'Except for the excessive hugs and the sloppy kisses.' Jess threw in one of her laser stares for good measure. Thin ice indeed in these days of hyper-awareness.

But Royston had been Charlie's boss, and that established an instant power gradient. Employment politics could mask all kinds of unacceptable behaviour. Charlie was not to blame here.

'Was he having an affair?' Gil asked.

'Royston? No.' Charlie looked horrified at the thought. 'He was a staunch churchgoer—'

'And we all know what a bastion of sexual propriety that is, don't we?' Gil muttered.

Charlie winced. 'No affairs. No way. He was hardly a catch, as my mother would say.'

Warlow smiled. Though young, Charlie had an old and disarming way about him.

'All the more reason to grope his employees' girlfriends, then, right?' Gil asked.

Charlie sighed. 'It wasn't like that. He made her feel… uncomfortable. Always a hand on her back, the hugs…' He paused, his brows furrowing, the discussion making him think about things Warlow suspected he'd prefer not to.

'Anything else?' Jess asked.

'There are the trees,' Charlie said.

'Trees?' Gil repeated the word as a question.

'We have land up near Llanfynydd. Close to twenty acres. There are a couple of old copses there, but he'd got a grant for reforestation and wanted to take out some of the older trees to allow access. Some protesters got to hear about this and have been camping out on the land.'

'So, there was contention?' Warlow asked.

'Words have been exchanged.'

'We'll need a location for that,' Gil said.

Charlie said he'd text the address. Gil gave him a number, and they watched as Charlie's fingers moved with the dexterity of the young over his phone's screen until Gil's phone pinged a receipt. But that was it in terms of any conflict Charlie could come up with. No pressing money matters, no financial issues. Moyles drank moderately, did not take drugs. His only vice, it seemed, was money. In that he liked it.

Twenty minutes after he'd sat down with them, Charlie stood to excuse himself.

'We've not released this information to the public yet, Charlie. For now, we'd be grateful if you kept it to yourself. Until we confirm a few things.'

'I said I'd give a couple of people lifts back to their cars.' He glanced out of the window. The rain had stopped and traffic ran normally outside. The black ice had defrosted almost everywhere. 'But this,' he glanced at Gil, 'this is a bit of a shock.'

'Are you in the round table?' Gil asked by way of distraction.

'Very much a junior member, I'm afraid.'

'Never mind.' Gil held Charlie's gaze. 'Get on with it. Keeping busy will help, you as well as the others.'

Across the room, a woman looked in his direction and gave a hopeful wave. 'That's Mrs Roach, deputy headmistress, at the primary school. Her car is in Manordeilo.' Charlie craned his neck to look at the crowd of people around the trestle table set up to serve coffee. 'But I can't see Roger.' He turned to the police. 'Do you know Roger Hunt? Wildlife photographer. Used to be on TV.'

'Name rings a bell,' Gil said.

'He's used some of our properties in the past for long weekends. Comes down to catch the dawn light. But he's in a property up near Gwynfe this time. Not ours. His car skidded off the A40 near the Plough, not far from Mrs Roach. I'm giving them both a lift.' He turned back to scan the room. 'He's here somewhere.'

As he stepped away, he let out, 'Oh, there's Dan Hughes. He and John Napier and Royston made up the three amigos on a Friday night. I can fetch him for you.'

As Charlie moved away, Gil muttered, 'Chatty sort, isn't he?'

'Verbose is the word you're looking for,' Jess said. 'When did he say he'd seen Moyles last?'

Gil consulted his notebook. 'Friday afternoon. They'd had a quick chat about bookings before Moyles hit The Farmer's Arms. Why? Think Charlie's a candidate?'

Jess thought it over before answering, 'Can't rule him out. Moyles sounds like a pest and that probably got on his nerves. His girlfriend didn't like Moyles, obviously. But I wouldn't put Charlie at the top of my list.'

CHAPTER TEN

THE ROOM FILLED UP, and the conversation grew louder. It looked like a lot more people were taking advantage of the free coffee and rolls, another tray of which had been brought in. An aroma of bacon and coffee percolated through the air.

Warlow, though, had never felt less hungry in his life after Anwen's feast of a breakfast. 'We had Uniforms take names and addresses of everyone here last night, yes?'

'We did, but will that help?' Gil asked.

'Who knows,' Warlow admitted. But in the back of his mind lingered the thought that some people had been stuck in their cars with nothing to do except observe the world around them. Who knew what those observations might throw up? Not a box Warlow wanted to leave unticked. 'We need to take a run out to where these protesters are, too.'

'Surely they won't be there in this weather,' Jess said.

'One way to find out.' Warlow reached for his coat.

'Right, well, I'll leave that to you and Gil. Think I'll wind my way back to Rhys and Catrin at HQ via this Hughes bloke if Charlie gets hold of him,' Jess said.

'Good idea. He might even give you a bacon ro—'
Gil's little joke was cut short by the sudden noise of something clattering to the floor, followed by a yell from near
the coffee table. All three officers looked up to see people
gathered around someone on the ground. They all moved
at once, pushing through the knots of people holding
coffee cups and rolls to find a patch of floor strewn with
bits of bacon and splayed baps next to a face-down
wooden tray. Next to the mess knelt the kid who'd carried
the tray in earlier. Next to him, Mrs Roach, also on her
knees and still masked, fussed.

'I am so sorry,' she said. 'I have no idea how that
happened. Someone jostled me and—'

'It's fine.' The young man righted the tray and started
piling the spilled bread on it. Then he frowned and considered Mrs Roach again as realisation dawned. 'Oh, it's you,
miss. I didn't recognise you under the mask. You've
changed your hair and stuff.' He'd used the word 'miss'
automatically and Warlow suspected that perhaps they
were rekindling a teacher-pupil relationship.

'Oh dear. Everyone okay?' A man, bearded with grey
streaked hair a tad too long for someone of his age,
appeared behind Mrs Roach. His face looked weathered
and familiar to Warlow. Though something told him that
this was a slightly worn and almost bedraggled version of
someone Warlow vaguely recognised. In his ear, Jess whispered, 'That's the photographer chap, Roger Hunt. *Wildscene* bloke.'

Charlie Brewer appeared with a big, overweight man in
tow who peered down at the mess. 'What happened here?'

'It's my fault, Dan,' Mrs Roach said, looking up. 'No
idea how it happened. I must have tripped or something.
But I bumped into poor Thomas here and—'

'Looks like we're going to need more rolls,' the man
called Dan said, smiling. 'Don't worry about it.'

A deputy manager holding an iPhone tutted. 'Just as I was about to take some snaps for the website. Can't take a picture of these dead bacon rolls, though. I'll get someone to fetch a mop and a bin bag.' She tutted loudly and shuffled off.

'Thomas,' Hughes said. 'You ask the kitchen for a mop. I'll text the bakery to get some more brought over.'

As quick a way of defusing a drama as Warlow had ever seen. Everyone went back to eating and drinking with the six-foot circle of spilled rolls a no-go area for now. Charlie saw Jess and Warlow and made the introduction.

'These are the police officers I was telling you about, Dan.'

The portly man offered his hand and leaned in to keep his voice low. 'Not the best of circumstances but happy to help.'

'So, you wouldn't mind answering some questions?' Jess asked. Warlow smiled. No flies on the DI.

'Not at all,' Hughes said.

'We can go back to the table we just left, if that's okay?'

Warlow watched Jess and Hughes walk back across the room. Charlie was still standing there. 'Mrs Roach, I'm ready when you are.' He held out a hand and helped the woman up off her knees.

'I don't know what I was trying to do down there anyway,' she said, recovering her composure.

'All we need now is Roger Hunt.' Charlie scanned the faces.

'He was here a minute ago,' Warlow said.

'You know him?' Charlie asked.

Warlow suspected young Charlie was a little star-struck at having a celebrity around. But all the DCI did was grunt and add, 'He was pointed out.'

'I saw him heading in the loo's direction. Great minds, or small bladders as my Uncle Lorrie used to say.' Gil grinned. 'If I see him there, I'll give him the nod.' He turned to Warlow. 'And I'll meet you outside in the Jeep, sir.'

Warlow eyed some paper cups next to the pump coffee dispensers. 'One for the road?'

'Does the pope?' Gil replied and sauntered off, whistling his standard going to the loo tune, The Police's *Don't Stand So Close to Me*.

———

DS CATRIN RICHARDS, unlike almost everyone she met who was looking forward to the holiday so much, wanted Christmas over and done with. Her and Craig's first IVF cycle had failed.

Nothing unusual in that because they both knew the statistics. In the United Kingdom, the success rate for the first attempt hovered around 50/50. The consultant she'd seen had made all that perfectly clear and had warned them not to be disappointed. But of course, they had been. More so than either of them had expected to be. As a result, they'd waited a little and taken stock. More a psychological respite than a physical one. But now, they were both ready to try again, and it had all been geared up for the new year. January the third, Catrin would begin her stimulation treatment. A week of injections with lots of scans until her eggs were ready to go. Then the trigger shot and the egg extraction.

She'd go under for that. Last time it had been quick and easy and she'd bounced back from the general anaesthetic within a day. It had all gone so smoothly. But none of the fertilised eggs had made it past day five. So, there'd been no transfer of embryos. All that treatment, all that anticipation, had been for nothing. Of course, there'd been more tests for both her and Craig, but the answer had been nothing more than sheer bad luck.

It happened. That was the way it sometimes went. The way the blastocyte cookie crumbled.

And so, this year she'd tuned in to everyone's Christmas grumbles with a fixed smile. Water-cooler chit-chat about what they hoped for, what they didn't want, what they were going to buy for others. All the while keeping her own powder dry but wanting to scream out that what she and Craig wanted could not be bought, not really. Admittedly, if the NHS treatment failed, they could pay for another chance either here or abroad. But that was all it was, a chance.

Christmas or no Christmas, you could not buy a baby.

Of course, she'd played it down to the others when the first cycle failed. But accepting failure had been psychologically difficult for a highly organised, high achiever like her. And so, she'd listened to the advice that followed from the professionals. Stay fit, eat well, get on with it. She'd done that. All three. Especially the getting on with it. Working for the Wolf in a team that she loved, keeping people safe, putting bad people away.

That old chestnut.

Perhaps.

But if she was going to bring new life into this world, and she'd do her damnedest on that score, too, she wanted that world to be as safe as it could be.

So, come on, Christmas. Bring it on. Carols and chocolates, crackers and cake. She'd do it all with one eye on the new year and what it might bring.

Because if there was one thing Catrin Richards was not, it was a moper. And she was looking forward to one day telling the team she'd caught. In her head, she heard Gil's voice.

'That would be worthy of a standing ovulation.'

At her desk, on her own, Catrin shut her eyes for a count of ten. My God, she was even beginning to think like him and Rhys.

Smiling, she called up a number for Royston Moyles's phone provider and punched it in.

'Morning,' she said to the voice that answered. 'This is Detective Sergeant Catrin Richards with Dyfed Powys Police. We'd like the call detail records of a person whose unnatural death we're investigating. We have a warrant for the following number. Can I send that through to you, please?'

CHAPTER ELEVEN

CHARLIE BREWER PULLED in behind Mrs Roach's Toyota, which had its rear end jutting out into the carriageway. Just as she'd left it the night before.

'I was so lucky to have made the lay-by,' she said.

'You were,' Charlie said. Even now, at 10.30am, they'd passed half a dozen cars sitting scattered over the A40 where the owners had left them the night before. And the Toyota's front wheels were turned at right angles to the body of the car.

'Please don't comment on the parking. I skidded it in as best I could.'

'Then it's a neat skidding if ever I saw one.' Charlie surprised himself at how even he was keeping his voice steady. But the big sergeant had been right. Ferrying Mrs Roach and Roger Hunt was proving to be a distraction. He'd go back into Llandeilo and see if he could help anyone else after this. Better that than thinking about Royston. 'Where are you, Roger?' Charlie asked.

Hunt pointed through the windscreen at a silver Skoda two cars ahead with its nose jutting out. 'That's me.' He blew out his cheeks. 'Difficult to believe I left it like that.

Luckily, nothing was moving last night. Still, best I get it shifted sooner rather than later.'

Charlie got out of the car and opened the back door for Mrs Roach. Patches of melting ice crunched underfoot, the edges crenellated against meltwater. Nearer the verge, though, it looked as firm and black as ever. Blotches of hoar frost nested between the tufts of grass, but where the watery sun had reached the road, everything was turning to water.

Charlie walked Mrs Roach to her car and stood back while she fired up the engine. He retrieved a scraper from his car and got the worst of the ice from her windscreen. It came away in slushy sheets. With the heat on and belted in, the teacher wound down the window to give him a heart-felt 'Thank you,' before pulling away and joining the thin stream of traffic on the A40 heading east.

'Nice lady,' Charlie said as Hunt passed him on his way to the Skoda. 'Any idea why she wears that mask?'

'Some people still do. If they're vulnerable. Plus, she works in a school, doesn't she?'

'Yeah, well, they're all Covid petri dishes, aren't they?' The car gave a couple of chirps and the blinkers flashed when Hunt pressed the key fob. 'Good. Battery isn't flat, then.' He turned when he got to the driver's side door. 'Thank you for the lift, Charlie. Much appreciated.' He had his own scraper and cleared the windscreen before clambering in. He closed the door but wound down the window to thank Charlie once more but hesitated before driving off. 'Are you okay? You look a bit peaky.'

'I'm fine,' Charlie said. 'Got a bit of bad news this morning, that's all.'

'Oh?'

For a second, Charlie wanted to do nothing more than blurt it all out to this man who had taken the time to ask if he was okay. But the big sergeant's words rang in his ears.

They'd asked him to be discreet. Soon everyone would know, but they'd used the words unnatural death and that could mean all sorts, couldn't it? The last thing he wanted to do was jeopardise their work.

'Don't worry about me,' Charlie said, and, wanting to deflect the concern now that he'd somehow let his anxiety show, added something banal. 'Will we be seeing you in the new year at one of our properties?'

'You never know,' Hunt said. But the smile that came with it, though polite, looked fake. Charlie let it go. This man was probably used to being accosted in supermarkets for his autograph. He'd probably developed that smile as a way of not wanting to offend, when the truth was he'd just spent a sleepless night in a hotel armchair, and all he wanted to do was get back to his cosy bolthole for a kip.

The Skoda's engine started first time.

It moved off in the same direction as Mrs Roach, though Hunt would probably turn right at the Llangadog roundabout and head east towards Gwynfe instead of continuing straight towards Llandovery. Charlie sat for a moment, wondering at the wisdom of taking a mountain road this morning, even though the thaw had come with a vengeance. Ah well, at least he'd done his bit. Now the rest of the morning beckoned, and he wasn't looking forward to it. There'd be paperwork to do, emails to answer, and he'd have to speak to Mrs Moyles.

He shuddered.

Should he cancel all bookings at *Cân-y-barcud* for the foreseeable? He'd need to warn the booking sites if so. And the police asked him to be sure to report anything odd if he found it.

That had been the female officer. The one he didn't know. Sergeant Jones was a familiar face around the town, often accompanied by one or more of his grand-daughters. And DCI Warlow had found fame on a

YouTube channel run by paranormal investigators when he'd physically rescued a blogger from the hands of a psycho killer. At least those were the words the blogger had used. But DI Allanby had been very interested in Charlie's comments about Royston's little foibles. He hadn't been sure about bringing them up, but there was no denying it. They'd have heard it from someone, if not from him, that Roy was a bit of a letch, as Sara would say.

He thought of her now. A fitness-obsessed physio. She would not be mourning Royston's demise, that was certain. Called a spade a spade did Sara.

Charlie hissed out a breath, put the car in gear, and pulled out. He did a U-turn at the Cwmifor turnoff and headed back towards Llandelio and the little office he shared with Royston Moyles above John Napier's solicitor's office. Better he start breaking the bad news about book-ings to people. What was the term Gil had suggested he use with the clients for now?

Ah yes. Due to unforeseen circumstances.

―――――

JESS ASKED Dan Hughes whether he minded her recording their conversation on her phone.

He did not.

'Thanks for talking to me. I can see that you're busy.'

'Least I can do under the circumstances.'

'Circumstances?'

For a second or two, Hughes looked horrified, but then recovered quickly. 'Okay, cards on the table. I realise I'm not supposed to know, but John Napier isn't the only one Janet Moyles rang after you left her yesterday. I was going to pretend I didn't know, but I'm hopeless at stuff like that. So, I know he's dead. And it's been bloody difficult coming here today knowing that and not letting on. Please don't blame Janet. It's only natural she turned to us.'

'Were you close?'

'John told you we used to have a few pints on a Friday night, no doubt. Close enough to do that week in, week out.'

'Was Moyles popular?'

Hughes smiled, showing teeth with a perceptible Mike Tyson-like gap between the front incisors. 'Not everyone thought he was the cream in their coffee.'

'Oh?' Jess already knew this, but she wanted to hear it from someone who really knew him. And not as an employee.

'A marmite sort of bloke was Roy. I mean, he could charm the sparrows off the bushes when he wanted to. Had that public school edge when it came to conversation. But he was a belligerent bugger, too. And I'd say opinion-ated. Of course, John and me, we took the piss out of him something terrible. But popularity wise…' Hughes paused, considering his next answer. 'Let's just say his enthusiasm got him into trouble sometimes.'

'Enthusiasm is an interesting word.'

Hughes paused, knowing he'd have to expand his answer. 'He used to own a pub in town. Did you know that?'

Jess jerked her head in a quick no.

'Yeah. The Lion,' Hughes continued. 'Popular in its heyday. I'm talking ten, or fifteen years ago. But he over-reached himself just at a time when the economy took a nosedive. Things went pear-shaped for him and he had to declare himself bankrupt owing lots of people money. Many of those were local tradespeople and business owners.'

'Hang on, I thought he owned property and land?'

A wry smile played over Hughes's lips. 'He may have

been a class A bullshitter, always talking the talk, but he wasn't thick. That stuff is all in his wife's name.' An eyebrow flicked up. 'She's put up with a lot over the years. But she stood by him. A bloody saint she is.'

Jess narrowed her eyes. 'Are you a saint, too? How come you stood by him?'

'I'm no saint,' muttered Hughes. 'But you do, don't you? I mean, time passes. And not all his schemes were rubbish. Plus, he could be good company. A laugh. But I didn't do any business with him. I made that a rule. That's how friendships end, isn't it?'

Jess angled her head. 'So, would you say he had enemies, then?'

'There are people in town who might not do a TikTok dance on hearing of his death, but they won't shed a tear, either. It has irked quite a few people to see him carrying on these last years as if bugger all had happened. But that's the nature of business. For every success, there are half a dozen failures. And the bloody pandemic put a lot of people to the sword.'

But Jess pressed the point. 'Did someone dislike him enough to murder him, you reckon?'

Hughes sat back, flinching from the bluntness of her questions. 'Whoa. That's a hell of a question to ask a simple baker. But I don't think I know anyone who hated him enough to do that. They might not piss on him if he was on fire, but I doubt they'd pour on the petrol and throw the match. He reinvented himself over the years. Bankruptcy forces you to do that. And Roy was a bit of a chameleon in that way. Irritating as hell, but not irritating enough to make someone do… this.'

From somewhere in the belly of the hotel, a brass band started up with *Good King Wenceslas*. Or at least a few instruments did.

Hughes smiled. 'Gwaun-Cae-Gurwen Band. The hotel

gets a few of them along this time of year to cheer people up. They usually make a bit of money.'

Jess smiled. 'This place is like something out of a black-and-white film. Not in a bad way. Good to see people rallying around.'

'Hard to believe a murder could happen in a town like this, isn't it?'

Jess snorted. 'Not for me, Mr Hughes. Scratch the surface of most communities and you'll find something unpleasant wriggling in the black earth underneath.'

Hughes frowned. 'Then I'm glad I'm not in your job. That's all I can say.'

CHAPTER TWELVE

CHARLIE WAS as good as his word regarding the contentious woodland and sent Gil a pinned map and instructions on how to get there.

'It's up towards Llanfynydd,' Gil said. 'On the other side of the Cothi River from Brechfa.'

'Ah, Brechfa,' Warlow mused.

Neither man needed reminding of Brechfa Forest and the first case they'd worked on together. The murder of a man by his childhood friend and cycling partner. A case that had led down a dark and harrowing alley involving child abduction and the consequences of a childish prank gone badly wrong. He hoped they weren't heading in that same murky direction now. One glance at Gil told Warlow he was having identical thoughts.

'Please do not start humming *Teddy Bear's Picnic*.'

'Wouldn't dream of it,' Gil said. 'According to the map, the land is next to an existing forest, but there are old burial grounds up there.'

'Oh, great.' Warlow gave a pained shake of his head. 'We'll have the dead to contend with as well.'

'Ah, right, the dead.'

Warlow sent Gil a wary glance. 'We're not going to hear dead dad jokes now, are we?'

'Wouldn't dream of it. Though I did hear they'd set up a bit of a gambling den near the burial grounds. Called it dicing with death.'

'Oh, for God's—'

'Word is they're making a killing.'

'Please—'

'And you do know that if you're ever being chased by a tribe of taxidermists, the worst thing you can do is play dead.'

'Put the bloody radio on, for God's sake.'

They took the A40 back towards Carmarthen and turned off at Dryslwyn, past yet another scene of crime where a young boy had been abducted at Cwrt Henry, and thankfully returned to his parents unscathed. They drove up past the holiday cottage time-share village on the Pant-glas Estate and took a right towards the village of Llanfynydd.

But, as with many of these rural addresses, its proximity to the actual centre of habitation it was linked to by postcode left a lot to be desired. Halfway to Llanfynydd, Gil ordered Warlow to turn left along a steep lane bordered by winter-bare hedges that wound upwards but soon flattened out into a long straight single-track road along a ridge bordered by fields.

'This must be Roman,' Warlow said as they bumped along.

'It is. Came on a drugs raid up here once in freezing weather. Ended up being a hail seizure.'

Warlow, open-mouthed in disbelief at the monstrosity of that pun, could only mutter, 'What the hell did they put in your coffee this morning?'

On their right, the fields rolled away with glimpses of the Black Mountains foothills. On their left, the ground stayed high until it, too, flattened out to reveal a vast expanse of sky. Unusual enough to be somewhere in this part of Wales, where none of the land was above you, for both men to be intrigued by the views. But eventually, the tarmacadam gave way to crushed stone and the Jeep's tyres rumbled and snapped over the lane until, at last, the fenced field gave way to moorland and the forest loomed ahead.

Warlow parked in a turnaround. The road ended here, marked by a single-bar gate leading into the forest. But a little way back, another gate, this one with the addition of a sprung walkers' gate next to it, led off to the right.

'We park here, I take it?'

Gil got out of the car after a cursory, 'Yup.'

They backtracked to the gate. Three hundred yards to the right was a copse of deciduous trees where a colourful homemade banner had been draped across some kind of wooden structure. No one challenged them as they approached, though a brown and white dog of no discernible breed that Warlow could make out barked enthusiastically at them, its tail wagging.

By the time they were within thirty yards of the first trees, the message of the banner had become legible.

NATURE: PERFECT NOT PROFIT.

Behind the banner, a fortress of wooden pallets had been erected with painted warnings and the inevitable "ban the bomb" logo. From somewhere in the middle of all of this, wood smoke rose in a spiral towards the sky.

The dog's barking elicited a yelled, 'Bruno!' in response. A woman's screech of rebuke.

'Think that could be one of the undead?' Gil asked.

'Unwashed, more like it,' Warlow said.

When Bruno ceased to desist, a shape emerged from behind the stockade. The woman could have been aged anywhere between seventeen and twenty-seven, and looked shapeless in layers of jumpers, the topmost in a bright

array of fair-isle colours. Her thick trousers also looked like
they were multi-layered. Her hair, in dry brown cornrows
tipped with pink, seemed to sprout from the top of her
head where it had been bunched together into a kind of
topknot. She was a walking charity shop clothes horse with
hands invisible under the extended sleeves of the jumpers.
The only bit of her skin on show – her face – was ruddy
from the cold, and on seeing them hardened into wary
inquisitiveness.

'Another eviction notice, is it?'

Warlow placed the accent as Cardiff or further east,
but still this side of the Severn.

Behind her, a rangy man, bearded, his head shaved to
show off a coiled snake tattoo winding around like a
hatband, emerged to stand at the woman's side, legs
splayed. He wore army boots, camouflage trousers, and an
army jacket over a T-shirt displaying some illegible graffiti
art. Warlow, after a quick assessment, counted at least a
dozen piercings in and around his face.

'I'll take the papers,' the man said, stepping forward.
'We need fuel for the fire, anyway.' His was not an accent
Warlow recognised. Perhaps there was a hint of the low
country there.

'We're not here about any eviction, sir,' Gil said. And,
as expected, his use of the word 'sir' brought the man up
short and his expression clouded with irritation.

'I am not a sir. Gender is a capitalist construct. You can
call me Lizard.'

'Good to meet you, Mr Lizard,' Gil said.

Lizard glowered.

'Are you the only two here?' Warlow asked.

'Who wants to know?' Lizard spat.

Gil made the introductions. Confirmation that they
were police officers gave Lizard a chance to plot silently.

'Just the two of you, is it?' Warlow asked again.

'No, there are six of us. Lawfully occupying an area designated as a historical monument,' the woman said, not hiding the challenge in her tone.

'We sleep with the dead,' Lizard added.

'Never works for me,' Gil said. 'My wife says my snoring would wake the buggers.'

Warlow stepped forward. 'Are the others here? It would be easier if I talked to all of you at the same time.'

'Two of the others are foraging. Emma and Gatch went into town for supplies.'

'And you can't contact the foragers?'

The woman looked confused.

'Okay.' Warlow smiled. 'Mind if I ask you some questions, then?'

Lizard bristled. 'We don't have to speak to authorities we don't recognise.'

'No, you do not,' Gil agreed. 'But I am not a hologram and it would be easier here than in an interview room, wouldn't it?'

'You can't arrest us for squatting here.'

'No,' Gil agreed. 'But this has nothing to do with that. Though, on second thoughts it might do?' He threw Warlow a glance.

Lizard sneered, but the woman was intrigued. 'What's it about?'

'The man whose land you're occupying,' Warlow explained.

'Moyles?'

'When did you see him last?'

'Why?' the woman asked.

'There's been a serious incident involving Mr Moyles. We're trying to establish his movements.'

'Not bloody dead, is he?' Lizard said, delighted at the thought.

'Calm it, Liz,' the woman said.

'Oh, come on, Fran. What if he is?' Lizard looked gleeful at the prospect.

Fran, her name now out in the open, turned back to Warlow with a little sigh that told the DCI living with Lizard had its own peculiar set of challenges.

'We saw him a week ago. He comes up here on a weekend with his dick-swinging mates. They all have double-barrel shotguns.' She grimaced. 'Not my favourite time of the week. Hunting rabbits, they say. But it's all intimidation. He thinks he can scare us off.'

'But he hasn't.' Lizard grinned.

Gil stared up at the tree they commandeered. 'And why don't you want him to cut the trees down? He wants to plant more, doesn't he?' Gil cast his gaze over the Oaks and Limes around him.

Fran let out a hollow laugh. 'Is that what they've told you? That he wants to plant trees?' She gritted her teeth. 'Mr Moyles is pally with a certain energy company called Gridfast. And they have a plan to link up two wind farms in the middle of Wales with the grid in Carmarthenshire. They could put the cables underground, but their preferred method is gigantic pylons marching across the landscape because it's a lot cheaper and Mr Moyles would be delighted if those pylons came across his land because he'd get a healthy wedge for letting it happen.'

She turned, breathless from her outburst, to regard her surroundings and wiped a sleeve over her eyes before sniffing loudly. 'These trees have a right to live. They've been here for longer than you and me. It's criminal.'

'Yeah, and any bulldozer is going to have to go through me first.' Lizard folded his arms across his chest.

'Fran… okay to call you Fran?' Warlow asked. The corded hair danced on her head as she gave him permission. 'Did you know Moyles at all?'

'No. We've exchanged words, but I don't know him. I

don't want to know him, the privileged Gammon that he is.'

'Plus, he's a perv. In the summer, when the girls are in shorts, he is up here twice a week,' Lizard said.

Okay, thought Warlow. Identity and gender name calling had become part and parcel of altercations with anyone having an agenda. And this was agenda central. But the girls-in-shorts thing fitted an emerging pattern.

'Is he? Dead?' Lizard asked.

'We're not at liberty to divulge information in an ongoing investigation,' Gil said.

'That means, yes,' Fran said. 'Otherwise, you'd say he'd been injured or was in hospital.'

Lizard did a little dance and started whooping until Fran turned on him. 'Liz, for Christ's sake.'

That took all the wind out of his sails and he stopped with a hangdog look.

'It's likely we'll need to talk to your friends at some stage,' Warlow said. 'For background. It might not be me. But someone will come, so be aware that it will not be about the eviction, okay?'

Fran, who'd also now crossed her hands over her chest, more to ward off the cold than in defiance, finally agreed, 'Fine. I'll speak to them. But they'll be saying the same as me.'

'How?' Lizard called out to Warlow and Gil's departing backs.

Gil half turned.

'Did he die?' Lizard shouted.

'Not well,' Gil said and turned away to hurry after Warlow.

CHAPTER THIRTEEN

Warlow got halfway back along the Roman road from the protesters' camp before his phone rang. It was not a number he recognised. He took the call through the car's speaker.

'DCI Warlow.'

'Mr Warlow, it's Charlie Brewer.'

'What can I do for you, Charlie?'

'It's…' the words trailed off into a huff of air. 'I've just got to the office. Royston's office, and it's… well, someone's been here. The place is a wreck.'

'Someone's broken in?'

'Looks like it. Everything's upside down. And I mean everything.'

Warlow felt Gil's eyes boring into the side of his head as he eased his foot down on the accelerator and the Renegade's springs squeaked in protest as they sank into the odd hole.

'Where are you now?'

'I'm here. I opened the door, took one look, and rang you.'

'Well done. Exactly the right thing to do. What's the address?'

'Corner of King Street and George Hill, Llandeilo. We're above Napier's Solicitors.'

'I know it,' Gil said.

'Right, stay where you are. No one goes in or out, including you.'

'Okay. Will do.'

When he'd ended the call, Warlow turned to Gil. 'Best give Povey a ring. She'll need to send someone over for this.'

Gil scowled. 'And there's me thinking we'd have a quiet run up to Christmas.'

Warlow snorted.

'What did you think of our eco-warriors, Lizard and Fran?' Gil asked, scrolling through his phone.

Warlow sent Gil a fleeting side-eyed look before turning his attention back to the road. 'Why is it that the social justice crowd always have a Lizard in their ranks?'

Gil grunted. 'If he wasn't flexing his muscles there under the guise of a cause, he'd probably be doing something stupid. So, they have their uses, the old radical activists. Especially in camps like that, which, admit it, are basically care facilities for the dangerously enthusiastic. This way Lizard can be an objectionable oik for a reason. I can see him being just the sort of clown who'd enjoy gluing his shaved head to a piece of art or playing dead ants in the middle of the M25 if he wasn't here.'

'Yes, well, activists need their shock troops, and good old Lizard looks like he might be the kid who always got into trouble at school.'

Gil settled back for a reminisce. 'When I was in school, we had things for the non-academics to do.'

'Is this the beginning of a Monty Python sketch?' Warlow asked.

Gil raised a finger. 'Hear me out. Practical stuff, like stripping down cars or woodworking or growing things in greenhouses. And I don't mean plants that give you the munchies. We're talking Maris Piper or green beans, even tomatoes. Now there's none of that because there's integration and you need to have a bloody diagnosis. Don't get me wrong, I'm all for avoiding stigmatising kids. But my mates who enjoyed fixing cars instead of French bloody verbs loved it. These days kids are divergent. At least that's what they said on Loose Women last week. Question is, are they naughty-divergent or neuro-divergent?'

'You don't waste your downtime, do you?'

Gil dredged up a faux smile. 'This was all via the Lady Anwen. Even she was almost sucked in. Tantrums, or throwing your food on the floor, or wanting to watch TikTok rather than read a book is now executive dysfunction, or anxiety, or information processing anomaly.'

'Psychologists do like a label,' Warlow muttered.

'I'm not dissing it. Just saying. Therefore, we've made our own executive decision chez Jones that while the little ones are with us, they will be treated as I was.'

Warlow flinched and sent Gil an anxious glance. 'Take care of what you say next. I am an officer of the law and think I have social services' number on my phone.'

'They read,' Gil said loudly. 'Or catch a ball, or go outside to play – weather permitting – and only watch TV under supervision and so long as it's sport or a film with many explosions. I mean, what harm did it do me?'

'The number's under, H, for help.'

Gil ploughed on, 'You wait. Your turn is coming. There'll be a book about when they should eat carrots and how big the pieces should be, Grandad. And, for the record, I have nothing against causes. As we well know, as a species, we have a gift for buggering everything up. Fran and Lizard were what, early twenties? Making me eat wind-heated tofu will not help the three hundred million malnourished in Asia. And they're the ones who don't give a stuff about CO2. Why the hell should they, when burning anything they can grab hold of is the only way they can keep their kids warm or cook food?' He paused to consider his outburst. 'Having said that, I like a tree as much as the next man, I really do. But *Iesu*, instead of complaining, get off your arse and work to find a sustainable answer for those poor buggers in the third world. Let's get them out of poverty so they can afford to care instead of building a tree house or throwing eggs. Because it's that three hundred million and the rest who'll determine the planet's destiny.'

Silence ballooned in the car until eventually, Warlow said, 'Come on, Gil, get off the bloody fence and tell me how you really feel.'

The balloon ruptured as both men laughed out loud.

'By the way, you had me at wind-heated tofu,' Warlow said when they'd calmed down.

'You may well mock,' Gil replied, but there was no malice in it.

'I'm not mocking. But I'm giving the Oxford Union a ring when I get home. See if we can get you a slot in one of their debates before you're cancelled.'

'*Argwlydd Mawr*, I'd be stoned as a heretic before I crossed the threshold.'

'Not if you take it easy for the first few puffs.'

Gil sighed. 'See, that's the trouble. Everyone's a comedian, these days.' The DS pressed the button and dialled Povey's number. 'Ah Alison, Gil Jones, here. Tell me, what had you planned for the rest of the day?' He pulled the phone away from his ear to let Warlow hear Povey's reply, which was not short of the odd expletive.

Foxtrot foxtrot sierra indeed.

THE TROUBLE with having been named as one of, if not the, best place to live in Wales by the Sunday Times was that it made people want to come and have a look. And that meant traffic. The absence of a bypass – a bone of contention that was set to run and run like one of those interminable Netflix series about walking zombies – also meant parking in Llandeilo was at a premium. King Street leading to Market Street had parking on both sides of the road as angled bays with a maximum of an hour before a warden swooped down and slapped a ticket on your windscreen. And though it was only a Tuesday, the fact of it being this close to the 25th and with the icy weather now having done its worst, to be replaced by milder wetness, the town was filling up.

Warlow eventually found somewhere to park on the A40 outside the church, near the bus stop. He locked the Jeep and he and Gil crossed the road that bisected the old churchyard. Gil used a gate in the graveyard wall and took the path through the churchyard to emerge at a kissing gate on Bank Terrace. The eponymous building in front of them, no longer a bank per se, was now a repainted wealth planning office.

Charlie Brewer and John Napier stood on the bend where King Street became George Hill. The corner building had John Napier Solicitors etched on the glass window and the man himself, still in his brown suit under the waxed jacket, hailed the officers as they emerged through the churchyard wall. Warlow looked back down the valley at distant hills forming a backdrop for the Church Tower with its clock framed by fir trees.

Chocolate box stuff.

'Ah, officers, we are pleased to see you. Though the

circumstances could be better,' Napier said. His comb-over wafted mesmerizingly in the breeze.

Warlow, however, turned his attention to the younger man at Napier's side. 'Tell us what happened, Charlie?'

'After I left you, I dropped off Mrs Roach and Roger Hunter, then came straight back here. That must have been around ten. As I explained, Mr Moyles has a small office above Mr Napier's. I thought I'd better attend to… things.'

'Peppercorn rent to keep it official,' Napier said. 'He's been there for years. We would only have used it for storing files otherwise.'

Warlow walked to the front of the building. 'So, you came in this way?'

'No,' Charlie explained. 'It's been my habit not to interrupt Mr Napier.'

'I wasn't here, but Caroline, that's my secretary, she was in.' Napier's clipped voice had taken on a military edge.

Charlie took some steps up the hill. 'There's a covered alleyway here that leads to the back of the building.'

The alleyway was a covered throwback to the previous need for stables. Warlow passed under a room in the building above to a small courtyard and galvanised steel steps that ran up to a door on the first floor.

'I use the fire escape to get in and out. It's convenient. Have done ever since I began. As soon as I let myself in, I could see that someone had been here. That's when I rang you.'

Warlow fished some gloves and blue plastic overshoes out of his pocket and, staying close to the banister side of the steps, ascended on metal treads next to vertical bar balustrades. His footfalls rang out a dull note on the metal as the stairs took a right-angle halfway up and ended in a balcony big enough for two people. There, Warlow paused outside a glass-panelled door stained a dark brown. Glass shards lay on the metal fire escape balcony floor and the door itself was ajar.

Warlow pushed it open with one finger. The room he entered was not big. A coat stand in one corner and an old-fashioned filing cabinet were all it contained. The cabinet had all three drawers open, the contents strewn across the floor. Beyond, through an open doorway, a second room beckoned.

Warlow took two steps and stood on the threshold, much as Charlie Brewer would have done. This room had, as Charlie had said, been well and truly trashed. Every drawer was open, every piece of paper riffled through. A monitor on the desk had been tipped over, wires trailing from the back but connected to nothing. On the far side, a window covered by slatted blinds faced King Street. Warlow picked his way across and lifted a slat to stare out at the road below, with its cafés and shops leading back towards the A40. A trunk road that cut through the town to all points northeast.

The sound of glass being crunched underfoot made him turn to see Gil filling the doorway. 'Think they found what they were looking for?'

'Whatever this monitor was attached to isn't here anymore. Charlie needs to wait for Povey and then give us a list of what's missing.'

'But that would have taken minutes. This mess speaks of them looking for something else, doesn't it?' He wafted a hand across the paper-littered floor.

Warlow had his phone out, taking photos of the scene.

'I had a word with Caroline, the secretary,' Gil said. 'She got in at nine-ish and she does not recall hearing anything.'

Warlow glanced across to another door. From beyond it, the noise of someone walking up a wooden stair came to them.

'Okay if I open this door?' Charlie's voice came through.

'No. Stay where you are,' Warlow ordered. 'We have crime scene officers on the way. But the stairs you're on links the offices downstairs, does it?'

'It does.' Charlie's voice came through the door.

'Then go back down. I'd rather not contaminate this any further. We'll meet you downstairs.'

Napier's office looked in need of a makeover. Caroline, a neat mid-fifties with dark-rimmed glasses and thinning hair – maybe it had something to do with the job – explained how she'd done everything as normal and only knew something was wrong when Charlie had burst through the door looking highly upset. By that time, John Napier had arrived back from coffee with a client in the town and was in his office at the back of the building. The other member of the firm, Enid Morris, was not working today.

Gil went through the motions of quickly assessing the office space and all the rooms. They had an alarm system downstairs, CCTV inside, but none outside and none at the back.

Warlow walked out and around to the fire escape once more. The yard gave way to a patch of lawn ending in a low wall and, beyond that, the higher ground of a park.

'What's up there?' he asked Gil.

'A park. Penlan Park. There's even a bandstand. I take my daughter's dog up there sometimes.'

'Easy way for someone to slip in and out of here, then.'

Gil thought about it before answering, 'Not easy, but doable. And beyond that is an unused church straight out of Harry Potter, and then Dinefwr Castle. Lots and lots of parkland that's never that busy.'

'Charlie was here on Friday. That was when he last saw Moyles. Between then and now, Moyles is murdered and the office ransacked.' Warlow squinted up at the grey January sky but found no answers there. 'Right.' He turned away and started back towards the alleyway. 'Let's gather the troops and try to get some flesh on the bones of this case.'

CHAPTER FOURTEEN

WARLOW WALKED through the Incident Room door at Llangunnor, Dyfed Powys's police headquarters, a little after midday. Gil had insisted on picking up a team packed lunch prepared by his wife. Despite Warlow's protestations, Gil persisted on the grounds that the weather had resulted in a book club meeting cancellation the night before and she already had all the necessary "stuff".

There'd been quite a lot of it, too, judging by the size of the silver insulated cool bag she handed over to Gil when Warlow dropped him off to pick up his own car. The Lady Anwen had made enough for a small army – or book club – or so it appeared.

Warlow had the sense to phone through and tell the others not to get any lunch because he and Gil were providing. He'd spoken to Jess, but in the background, he'd heard an unmistakable shout of delight.

'Yesss. A picnic.'

If he were a betting man, Warlow would have put his shirt on that voice belonging to Rhys.

At 12.40 on that Tuesday afternoon, Catrin stood in front of the team who'd arranged themselves in the customary semi-circle, close to a desk to facilitate easy access to the sandwiches. Catrin had taken the lead, given that Gil had been out of the office providing local knowledge for Warlow at the scene. She wore a grey roll-neck sweater over darker trousers and the kind of in-vogue chunky Chelsea boots that would not, in Warlow's opinion, have looked out of place on Buzz Aldrin as he stepped onto the moon. But then, what the hell did he know?

'What's unusual, apart from the way the body was trussed up, is the time frame,' Catrin said. 'Change-over days for rental properties, Airbnb, or NONs are normally Saturdays. In fact, the Sadlers had rented from Saturday but only got there on Monday.'

'Why is that?' Jess asked. On the desk next to her, as with the others in the team, several packets of foil-wrapped rectangles, some open, some still not, lay next to packets of crisps, tomatoes, radishes, and the inevitable mugs of tea.

'They got married on Saturday, spent two nights in London and then travelled down to Wales,' Gil explained.

'So, they'd planned to stay over Christmas?' Rhys asked.

'Until Monday. Boxing Day.'

Catrin had borrowed Rhys's laser pointer. Mainly to stop him from using it like a manic lightsabre whenever he asked a question. He usually encircled the image or name he was asking about with the red light until it made everyone dizzy. She used it now to briefly highlight Moyles's photograph. A posed image of him sitting, half turned towards the camera, in some kind of ceremonial garb complete with a chain of office.

'Right, starting with the victim. Royston Moyles, age sixty-two. Ex town mayor. Ex councillor. Found dead at *Cân-y-barcud* cottage, a rental property managed by Moyles on behalf of his wife, who is the owner. DI Allanby has already interviewed Janet Moyles, am I right, ma'am?'

Jess put down the sandwich she was holding and wiped a crumb from the corner of her mouth with a thumb, which she then put up to indicate Catrin was correct. 'Does Anwen make her own bread?' she whispered to Gil as she got up.

'Yep,' Gil said. 'She has a gizmo on her food processor thingy that mixes the dough.'

'Was it a deer, sarge? You know, the thing that made dough, as in doe a deer?'

Everyone turned their gaze on Rhys, who had already demolished a round of egg and cress and was now into a round of coronation chicken.

'Did you eat any biscuits before we arrived?' Warlow asked.

With his mouth full of bread and creamy poultry filling, Rhys wisely opted to keep his mouth shut, and held up two fingers with palm side out, by way of answer.

'Thought as much,' Warlow said. 'Way too much sugar.'

Jess joined Catrin at the board. 'Janet Moyles was obviously in shock when we talked, but I did not get the impression she was hiding anything. They have no kids and a nice house. Didn't look like they were struggling for money. She denied all knowledge of any ongoing disputes.'

'So, she didn't mention the little feud over rewilding up at Llanfynydd?' Gil asked.

'I've asked that we get access to his study and whatever papers might be at their house and she was cooperative. We'll need to go back at some point. But how did it go in the forest?' Jess asked.

Gil didn't bother standing, not wanting to crowd the female officers. 'There is a wild card up there called Lizard.' He caught Rhys's sceptical, chew-frozen look and shrugged. 'Probably a name he called himself.' He paused, frowning. 'Doe as in deer, name he calls himself. *Arglwydd*,

I'm in a remake of *The Sound of Music*. Where's Maria?'
His gaze settled on Catrin.

'I'm no Julie Andrews,' Catrin said.

'You should have said nun-taken, sarge,' Rhys
mumbled through his sandwich.

Gil shook his head as if to clear his thoughts. 'Anyway.
No love lost between the eco-crowd and Moyles, obviously.
So far, they are the only people we've come across with a
motive for doing Moyles harm.'

'Enough of a motive for murder?' Jess asked.

'Hmm,' Warlow muttered with a questioning tilt of his
head. 'And now we have the little wrinkle of Moyles's office
being ransacked sometime between Friday and this morning. And before anyone asks, yes, I think the two incidents
are tied together. No question of a "c" word here.'

They all nodded. No one wanted to mention coinci-
dence and get a glare from the DCI. Warlow took a last
bite of a ham and mustard, washed it down with a swallow
of tea, and stood up.

'Povey is waiting for the HOP to visit *Cân-y-barcud*.'
He glanced at his watch. 'Someone text her to find out if
he's been. She's going to go over the scene without the
body present. Then she, or someone from the team, is
also going to look at Moyles's office. See what she can
glean from that. In the meantime, there's the donkey
work. Let's get hold of Moyles's bank statements, chat
with other tenants, the usual. Oh, and the list of people
stranded at the hotel. Someone might have been around
when Moyles's office was done over. You never know
unless you ask.' He turned to Rhys as another thought
struck him. 'Get hold of his wife and maybe you can get
out there and have a look through his study for anything
relevant?'

Rhys got to it.

'Catrin, you work on the timeline. Chat with the cleaners. Find out what Moyles was doing at the property if you can.'

'His wife says he liked to put finishing touches occasionally. The Sadlers were a honeymoon couple, after all,' Jess said.

Catrin wrote on a Post-it note and stuck it up on the Job Centre. 'I've already contacted the provider for his phone records. But did they find a phone at the scene?'

'Good question,' Jess said. 'Add that to the list for Povey. They've been hamstrung by the HOP being delayed, but a phone would be useful.'

'Gil,' Warlow said, 'chase up Lizard and the other names we got from the tree-hug—' Warlow backpedalled. Gil's tirade in the car had been for personal consumption, just two seasoned coppers chewing the fat. But in the office, a touch of decorum was called for. '—protesters. Find out who the rest are and if any of them might be capable of this.'

'Will do.'

'Jess, we need to brief Buchannan. One of us will need to go to the post-mortem, too. I'm—'

'Catrin and I have talked about it. We'll go.'

'Oh, what?' Rhys, half a sandwich already on the way to his mouth, stopped to register his objection.

Jess answered, 'You've been to half a dozen in the last year. Not that it's top of my list of a fun day out, but Catrin needs some experience, too.'

'Thank you, ma'am,' Catrin's reply was anything but enthusiastic.

'Very magnanimous of you, DI Allanby,' Warlow said.

'I have my moments.'

'Can you spare one for the Buccaneer?'

'After you.'

CHAPTER FIFTEEN

SUPERINTENDENT SION BUCHANNAN's office was on the floor above the Incident Room. Warlow and Jess took the stairs, and the DCI took the opportunity away from the Incident Room to check on the kids. Not their own children: Warlow's sons and Jess's daughter. The ones on their team. After all. Jess had spent the morning with both younger officers.

'Rhys seems preoccupied by trying to keep everyone happy over Christmas. For that, read Christmas dinner.'

'Of course.'

'He's even toying with eating two.'

Warlow winced. 'Two Christmas dinners. Even he would struggle with that, surely?'

'I wouldn't put it past him to try,' Jess said. 'If I was Gina, I'd suggest making my own, but Rhys is a people pleaser.'

Warlow snorted. 'One of his many faults. What about Catrin? I keep meaning to ask her about the IVF stuff, but it isn't the sort of thing that's easy to drop into a conversation. At least, not the conversations she and I usually have.'

'You know Catrin. Keeps her cards very close to her chest, but if we go to the post-mortem, I'll probe.'

'Not the corpse, I hope?'

That earned Warlow a slow shake of the head from the DI. 'No need to ask who you spent the morning with.'

'It rubs off, does the Gil charm.'

'That's one word for it.'

'But using a Cardiff trip to quiz our enigmatic Detective Sergeant Richards…' Warlow narrowed his eyes. 'What a cunning person you are, DI Allanby. I always thought there was a touch of the wiccan about you. Clever. Looks great in a pointy hat. Good with a broom. That sort of thing.'

'Careful, or I'll turn you into something slimy that croaks.'

'Talking of which, have you seen Two-Shoes, lately?'

Jess giggled. 'No. She's kept well clear after all that crap with Hopper. The internal investigation is still pending. Am I right?'

Only a couple of months ago, Superintendent Goodey, aka Two-Shoes, had mentored and tried to introduce a detective sergeant named Hopper into Warlow's team. He'd proven to be a very bad apple who'd gone over to the dark side and become as bent as a boomerang. Warlow sometimes still woke up in the early hours waiting for the shot from Hopper's gun that would have ended everything as he lay on the floor. He still heard the report of that pistol, still felt the debris from where the bullet hit the skirting board caress his cheek.

Those were tough nights.

Buchannan's bass voice bade them enter his room after only the one knock. The place was neat and tidy. As was the tall man sitting on the far side of the desk.

'Nasty one,' he commented as Warlow and Jess sat.

'Aren't they all?' Warlow brushed a sandwich crumb from his sleeve.

'How do you see it?'

Warlow turned to Jess for her to answer. He had the utmost confidence in her as a fellow officer and they sang from the same hymn sheet. She was astute and had a nose for this stuff.

'The way he was trussed up suggests vindictiveness. There's a chance that it's a sex game gone belly up. But no way self-induced. My feeling is it reeks of anger.'

The Buccaneer arched his long neck. 'And just before Christmas, too. Shite. Well, as always, the ball is in your court. You need me to shout at someone. Let me know.'

'Oh, so, you're not away on a Christmas cruise, then, Sion?' Warlow threw the question up, waiting for the superintendent to catch it.

Buchannan had been away during the catastrophe that had been the last case involving Hopper and had avoided the shit storm by conveniently being on the other side of the world.

'Low blow, Evan. No, I am here for the duration. And anyway, you can talk. Aren't you away soon?'

'Mid-January.'

'How are they all in… argh, you did tell me… Perth, is it?'

'Yep. The one with 38-degree heat, not the one in Scotland that's never heard of 38-degree heat.'

'Always wanted to go to Freemantle. They say the prison tour is a laugh.'

'On my list,' Warlow said.

Buchannan's smile faltered. 'But they're all okay, are they? Your granddaughter and daughter-in-law? Jesus, that was a nasty one.'

There'd be no argument from Warlow on that score. Reba had ruptured her uterus during labour and Eva, his granddaughter, had been delivered via an emergency caesarean. Not a forty-eight hours he was likely to forget in a hurry. And right in the middle of the Hopper debacle as well. Still, they'd got through it and were thriving. He told Buchannan exactly that.

'Be sure to give them my regards when you go.' Buchannan steepled his fingers. A sure sign that the meeting was ending. 'It would also be great to break the back of this case before you flew off.'

'If I don't, Jess will carry the baton, you know that.'

'I know she will.' Buchannan turned his grinning face to hers. 'I bumped into one of the examiners from the Hydra course last week, Jess. He said you were miles ahead of the others.'

Jess raised an eyebrow. The Hydra course was a mandatory assessment for Senior Investigating Officer accreditation, which she had attended a few months before. 'I enjoyed it. Not everyone does.'

'How's Molly?'

'Growing up fast,' Jess said with a grin. 'University next year.'

'Hard to believe. Right, I'll leave you to it. Report to me on this one.'

Warlow was tempted to ask after Two-Shoes, but why poke the bear's cage? He'd underestimated Buchannan's perspicacity, though. 'Before you ask, she's been shifted sideways again into recruitment. We need more inclusivity across the board, especially female officers. Though I'm pretty sure we'll be abandoning that term before long.'

'What are we meant to call each other, then?' Warlow shifted in his seat, his irritation thermometer rising.

'Whatever the hell takes your fancy probably, and depending, as far as I can see, how you feel when you get up in the morning.' Buchannan suddenly had the expression of a man lost in a maze.

'This isn't Scotland, man,' Warlow said.

'Very Mcfunny. But all this reminds me of that TV programme… you remember, you went through a curtain as one person and came back togged up as another. It's the way of the world, and I get that. But Christ, it makes it hard to bloody police.' He paused, before adding, 'And, if you've been affected by anything that I've just said, I can give you a number to ring.'

Warlow grinned. 'That cruise did you good, Sion.'

Buchannan grinned. 'Jess, apologies if my blathering offends you.'

'It takes a lot to offend me, Sion. And if you think that did, you need to try harder. I'm having to guide my daughter through these choppy seas, don't forget.'

CHAPTER SIXTEEN

THE AFTERNOON'S DONKEY WORK: phone calls, staring at monitors, telephoning, held all the glamour of a faded copy of the Beano, with a lot fewer laughs. The HOP, Sengupta, though thorough, was not the quickest, and Gil learnt from Povey's 3 pm text, that the body had just left, the post-mortem was scheduled for first thing next morning in Cardiff, and she probably wouldn't have anything useful to tell Warlow about the crime scene or Moyles's office burglary until at least midmorning the following day.

Happy days.

They held a mini vesper. Nothing more than a cup of tea and a chat, at around four. Rhys phoned Janet Moyles, but her sister remained firmly of the opinion that now was not the time to bother the widow about her husband's study. And phone records had not yet come through, much to Catrin's irritation.

'It's that time of year,' Gil said. 'People's minds are on turkey dinners and TV reruns. Best you kick some backsides.'

Buchannan did the needful. Confirming Moyles's identity as the victim in his statement to the press. Standard fare as it appeared on the WalesVoiceOnline site.

———

Detective Superintendent Sion Buchannan, of Dyfed Powys Police, said: "This is a devastating time for Mr Moyles's family and our thoughts are with them as they attempt to come to terms with the events on Monday. We are treating his death as suspected murder. We continue to offer all support possible and the family deserves tact and privacy at this most difficult time. But we, as a police force, are determined to get them the answers they deserve. We have a range of inquiries we are pursuing to get a clearer picture of events. But I can now say that at some time on Monday, Mr Moyles was seriously assaulted by a person or persons unknown. No arrests have been made in the case yet."

———

Catrin had been luckier with the cleaners. A mother and daughter operation who sorted the clutter and did the laundry on Saturday mornings.

'They said that Moyles could be a bit of a fuss-arse—'

'Fuss-arse? Actual words?' Gil asked.

'Actual words,' Catrin confirmed.

Gil got up and wrote FUSS-ARSE, in capitals, on the Job Centre. 'That's a phrase I'll be using every day from now on.'

Catrin ignored him and continued, 'A fuss-arse who liked to know who was going to stay. And since the Sadlers were a honeymoon couple, he'd probably have taken some chocolates and a bottle of Prosecco to the flat.'

'He did,' Gil said. 'They were on the kitchen peninsula.'

'Nice touch,' Jess said.

'Be lovely to think he did it out of the goodness of his heart,' Catrin added. 'But I doubt that. All to do with maintaining the five-star rating on the NON site.'

'He didn't do it for everyone, then?'

'Honeymooners definitely. Some others, too, but they didn't see a pattern.'

'Fickle, then.' Rhys, digestive in his hand, appeared ready to dunk.

Gil was awaiting a call-back from a West Mids sergeant who'd been the Officer In Charge in a case of GBH involving Lizard, and Rhys had checked off half a dozen of the stranded motorists who'd been rescued by the hotel and drawn a blank in terms of them having seen anything odd.

Warlow threw in the towel at five-thirty. Return calls and third-party cooperation seldom came after half five. As they left the building, Jess confirmed that she'd ordered some flowers for the Lady Anwen on their behalf for putting them up and almost killing them with food, and Warlow promised to bring in a bottle of good Sicilian wine as a thank you to Gil the next morning.

'Anything planned this evening?' Jess asked.

'Nothing more than to see my dog and cogitate about this case. You?'

'I'm hoping the Amazon man will have left some parcels for me out of Molly's view. Just a few stocking fillers, but she sees anything with a little black curvy arrow as fair game to open.'

'In which case, I'll see you lunchtime tomorrow. Have a wonderful trip to Cardiff,' Warlow said as they went to separate cars.

'Can't wait,' Jess replied.

He sat in the Jeep to watch her leave and pondered, not for the first time, how lucky he was with his colleagues. Gil had become a friend, and so had Jess. As regards the kids, Catrin and Rhys, he considered them friends too, but in a more paternalistic way. He let out a cynical cough. Bloody hell, here he was, single white male with a sell-by date that had come and gone, perpetuating the patriarchy.

Ah well, here is my head above the parapet. Take your best shot why don't you?

His thoughts drifted back to last night when he'd lain in a bed, a few short steps away from Jess. He'd be lying to himself if he denied wondering what might have happened had he taken those steps. Such thoughts were no strangers. They'd preoccupied him for a good half hour prior to sleep. Of course, there'd been opportunities over the months. When Molly had gone to London for the odd weekend with her boyfriend and he and Jess had shared a meal at a pub or a walk with the dog. But he'd never pushed his agenda, even though he'd felt the inclination more than once. Jess was aware of the fact he was an asymptomatic HIV patient. She, along with his sons, his doctors, and everyone else who had any knowledge of the matter, had reassured him he was not a danger to others, given that his viral titre was zero, more than once.

And yet, there remained obstacles. One, the big one, was the psychological barrier he'd struggled to overcome in terms of being a risk to others. He knew the stats. He had the evidence. But he dealt daily with worst-case scenarios. And such things coloured his judgement.

The other obstacle was an unknown, too. He and Jess made a great professional team. If their relationship ever changed, what effect might that have on how they worked together?

'Come on, Evan. Get a grip.' He muttered the words with one eye on his cut-off face in the rearview.

What he needed to do was run all this past someone with a sympathetic ear. He thought of Cadi, his black lab, who had the softest, blackest, and most sympathetic of all ears. She'd listen, gaze at him with eyes that said, "I don't care if you haven't shaved for four days and wear a T-shirt with holes in it. I'm still your pal." And lick his hand.

Not exactly an impartial voter when it came to decision making, was Cadi.

Thoughts of the dog galvanised him, and he started the engine and watched Jess's taillights disappear out towards the entrance.

'Let's see a man, and a woman, about a dog, and stop this mithering, eh, Evan?' He spoke the words out loud, but in a Mancunian accent.

———

TUESDAY NIGHT in The Farmer's – the shortened name everyone in the town used for The Farmer's Arms – was hardly ever rip roaring. If you excluded the evening Nadia Prentiss got engaged, which was a night hardly anyone would forget. Three tons of manure tipped on said Miss Prentiss's open-topped Mazda convertible by a jilted lover stuck in the mind, let alone the glove compartment, between the seats, and in every cup holder.

The Farmer's had resisted all the breweries' efforts at "thematic manipulation". What people wanted was a dim interior, a pool table, darts, and a snug. And that, in the case of The Farmer's, was exactly what you got.

No one cared about photographs of the town in 1901, sheep drovers or celebrities on the wall. At least, none of the regulars did. And summer visitors, seeking a little taste of the real West Wales, got their money's worth in the form of smoke-stained wood (from times when it was still possible to light up) rickety chairs with decades old chewing gum hardened under the seats, and small round, beer-ring-stained tables. And in the back, in the snug, there were even faux leather banquettes – for ease of wiping.

It was on their usual banquette, at a corner table, that Dan Hughes and John Napier sat having a pint in memoriam. They spoke, this evening, in whispers.

'Are we in trouble, John?' Hughes asked.

'Why? Did you knock him off?'

Hughes looked around. There was no one else in the room. 'Don't.'

'Too soon?'

'The next millennium would be too soon.'

Napier sighed. 'So, why would we be in trouble?'

Hughes dropped his head in a little shake.

'Look,' Napier said, 'there are a dozen people in this town with reason enough to want to see Roy dead. He owed some people thousands. You weren't one of those people and neither am I.'

'But the police, they're bound to dig into stuff.'

'Let them dig. What are they going to find? I'm going to give them everything I have. And so should you.'

'I have nothing.'

'Good.'

Hughes ran his finger down the condensed water on the outside of his glass. 'But I'm worried that things will come back to us. Bloody Roy.'

'Look, whatever his recherche tastes, it had nothing to do with you or me.'

'But we knew.' Hughes pushed the words out through clamped together teeth.

'Did we? I knew he liked to brag a bit, but half of what he said was bullshit.'

'But doesn't knowing make you complicit?'

'Are you culpable if you suspect a crime and don't report it?' Napier asked. 'I would argue that Roy was grandiose. You could only ever believe half of what he said.'

'Yes, but—'

'Forget it. We did nothing but listen to his crap.'

This time Hughes's whisper was a low slow lament. 'What about the stuff he showed us?'

Napier dismissed this with a noise like air leaking from a ruptured tyre. 'That could have come from anywhere on the internet. You know that. It's a bloody cesspit.'

'God, I hope you're right.'

Napier picked up his pint and held it up. 'To absent friends.'

'And Roy Moyles,' Hughes added.

They clinked glasses and swallowed the bitter liquid.

CHAPTER SEVENTEEN

'So,' Warlow said to Rhys at a little after eight-thirty the following morning, 'I hear you're going to have to cancel Christmas.'

They'd left HQ and were now heading up the Towy Valley on the east side of the river towards Llandeilo, where they'd pick up the A40 before taking the Talley road. Warlow wanted a look at the area in daylight.

'Don't say that, sir. I love Christmas.'

'And what is it about Christmas that you love so much, Rhys?'

'You mean apart from the food?'

'Food is a given. I mean, what else?'

'Presents, sir. I like presents.'

'The giving or the receiving?'

Rhys didn't hesitate. 'Funny you should say that, sir. Because I do like the giving. When you get it right. I bought my cousin, Cai – I told you he had Down's, right?'

'I remember.'

'Anyway, he is Star Wars obsessed. I bought him a Mandalorian Bounty Hunter Hoodie last year. I don't think he's taken it off yet.' Rhys grinned and gave a little shake of his head. 'But I do like the odd surprise myself, too, sir.' He reached forward to turn on the radio. He'd been a passenger in Warlow's Jeep enough times to be familiar with the entertainment system. But, with the enthusiasm of youth, liked the random press of a button, too. This time, Cliff Richard's *Mistletoe and Wine* whined out of the speaker.

'You can turn that off, pronto,' Warlow muttered.

'Sorry, sir. So, no Christmas stuff, I take it?'

'You take it correctly, detective constable. There's a time and a place. Christmas Eve from midday to midnight Christmas Day. More than enough.'

Rhys found radio six and Warlow bounced his neck in time to Crosby, Stills, Nash, and Young. Even the oldies on this channel were good ones. 'What have you bought Gina?' he asked.

'Ah, well, we both decided on a spending limit this year, things being a bit tight, what with the new place, rent, cost of living, and stuff. Plus, we told each other what we wanted. Useful gifts, you know. No frippery.'

'Frippery? Where did that come from?'

'DS Jones, sir. He says it's the slope you end up on when you can't decide what to buy someone and spend it on tat. A frippery slope, sir.'

Warlow chuckled. 'So, no frippery and no surprises for you and Gina, then.'

'Well, no… theoretically.'

Warlow grinned. 'But you're going to anyway?'

'Yes, sir. I thought a weekend away. Antwerp. I read about it last month. They say the brewery tour there is brilliant.'

Warlow twitched an eyebrow. 'Is that a present for you

or for her?'

'Her, sir. Definitely. She loves the Eurostar. And we've never been to Antwerp.'

'Famous for diamonds,' Warlow said, letting the inference hang.

Rhys's face fell. 'I'll try to keep her away from that section. To be fair, she's pretty good. Practical and smart.'

'Did I ever tell you she was a keeper?' Warlow asked.

'You did, sir. About fifty times.' Rhys reached for the lidded mug of tea he'd brought with him. Warlow had a similar one sitting in a holder in the centre console.

'Have you decided on dinner arrangements? Your parents' or Gina's.'

Rhys sat up. 'That's the problem. How to keep everyone happy. We're toying with going out for Christmas lunch. Our treat for my parents and Gina's.' The forced enthusiasm in his voice was almost pathetic.

'Very diplomatic.'

'And expensive, but the easiest way. My mother doesn't drink, so she'll drive. Win, win.'

'Good way to kill three or four hours, too.'

'Exactly, sir,' Rhys said. 'Then it'll be back to my parents for turkey sandwiches and Gina's on Boxing Day. Her mum does a brunch.'

'Christmas can be complicated.'

Rhys gave a wistful sigh. 'Remember when you could just jump out of bed in your PJs and dive into your prezzie sack?' His eyes glazed over.

Warlow gave him a side-eyed glance, grinning at his expression. 'When was the last time that happened?'

'Last year.' Rhys's eyes, still shut when he delivered the memory, sprang open, realising what he'd just said. 'I mean, we'd just cleared that case in Llanelli. Gina wasn't around then and I was knackered. I didn't get in until midnight Christmas Eve. I didn't even get up until half ten Christmas Day…'

'Right, enough of this frippery. You've got the map. It should be easier in daylight.'

'Are we looking for something specific, sir?'

'We'll know it when we see it, I reckon. Bring the file with the crime scene photos?'

Rhys reached down between his legs to a backpack and removed a folder.

'Good. So, once we get up past the Abbey, it's eyes peeled.'

———

JESS AND CATRIN listened and watched as Sengupta outlined her findings.

'The petechiae and subconjunctival haemorrhaging all confirm strangulation as a cause of death. The arrangement of the binding meant that it would have been impossible to maintain a position whereby he would've been able to breathe.' She looked up, her dark eyes almost sorrowful under the theatre cap. 'Death would have been slow and painful.'

Jess threw Catrin a glance over her mask. The DS's freckled face, winter pale, looked even paler under the hard mortuary lights. Still, the notebook in her hand was steady as she jotted down the pearls Sengupta offered up.

'There are some bruises over the side of the face. Blunt instrument injuries, but in some places the skin is torn as well.' Sengupta pointed out the areas as she referred to them, paused and glanced up. 'Whatever was used had some sharp edges.'

'What's your interpretation of that?' Catrin asked.

'The tears have consistency.' Gupta pointed to the flesh on the right cheek and temple and flicked her finger at an angle. 'They run in the same direction. My guess is that he was struck several times across the face.'

'While he was bound under the eaves?'

'Doubt it. The angles are wrong. I'd say they were inflicted while he was sitting up. There's evidence of white material on the wrists. Duct tape residue would be my best guess. Obviously, the lab will confirm. So, he was taped first, perhaps in order to subdue him. So that he could be bound up. It's feasible that he was forced into allowing himself to be tied up. In which case, being struck across the face is a likely compliance injury.'

Jess tried to pin her down. 'Are you thinking gun?'

'Hard to say. A handgun would explain the tears, and the facial injuries. But that's conjecture.'

'And no gunshot wound?' Catrin asked.

'None. But we'll test the skin for powder residue. If we're lucky and it was a gun that had been used recently, we might find traces.' Sengupta moved down the body. 'As you can see, he was overweight. He'd had a meal a few hours before, but that's all we can say. Tox report will come in due course.'

'We think he was killed in the morning,' Jess added.

'So, held at gunpoint and struck a few times to make sure he cooperated,' Catrin said. 'Taped first, then tied up and left to die.'

'Any evidence of sexual assault?' Jess asked.

Sengupta looked up. 'No tears or lacerations around the genitals or anus. Nothing in the throat. We'll swab, to make certain.'

The officers left shortly after that. They'd await Sengupta's formal report. But they had enough to be going on with.

Catrin, never one to waste time, worked up her notes on her laptop as Jess drove out of the city.

'Brutal way to die,' Jess said.

'I don't think there's ever a good way, ma'am. But I agree. That looked… unpleasant.'

'And deliberately so,' Jess added. 'Whoever did this was—'

'Vengeful and angry,' Catrin said.

They drove on for a few minutes in silence as Catrin typed quietly. By the time they reached the A48 turn off, she'd completed a brief *précis* and shut the laptop.

Jess glanced across. 'I've been meaning to ask. How's it all going? The IVF?'

Catrin sent her a toothless smile. 'It's going okay. The first tranche didn't take, but we're going to try again. In the new year.'

'How many goes do you get?' Jess winced. 'Sorry, that sounds like I'm asking about a fairground ride.'

'Feels like it is, some of the time, ma'am. But to answer your question, three goes at the whole thing. Of course, if it hasn't worked after three, there is always the option of private treatment.'

'Is it not expensive?'

Catrin smiled. 'My mum and dad said they'd help.'

Jess oozed sympathy. 'It's bloody tough, though, isn't it? For us. You especially. No sooner do you get a foot on the career ladder than that sodding clock inside starts ticking.'

Catrin's little smile faded. 'But you were young, having Molly, weren't you?'

'Mid-twenties. And, truth be told, it was unplanned. I was a DC, and it did not go down well because I had not been there that long. Things are a bit better now, I'm glad to say.'

'I know what you mean, though. I wasn't sure how DCI Warlow would take it when I told him about the IVF.'

'Don't worry about him. He'll be the first to cheer when it happens.'

'If it happens.'

'It will. Trust me. Evan says I'm a bit witchy. I can see things other people can't.'

'Did he say that, ma'am?' Catrin grinned.

'In his own way. Clever. Looks great in a pointy hat. Good with a broom. And I quote,' Jess said.

Catrin laughed, but it petered out into a heaved sigh full of mingled concern and anxiety. 'Thing is, I really love this job, ma'am. I'm worried he won't want me back.'

'He'd be a fool not to,' Jess said.

They arrived at the Culverhouse Cross exit. Jess, instead of heading straight on to the M4, took a left to the A48.

'We taking the back roads home, ma'am?'

Jess signalled left to the retail park. 'No. There is a gigantic M&S here. This is as good an opportunity to stock up on bits and pieces for the big day as we'll get. Are you up for it? Half an hour won't be missed. Will get some mince pies for the boys that should keep them quiet.'

'Mmm. Christmas retail therapy.' Catrin grinned. 'Don't mind if I do.'

'Too right, sergeant. Nothing like it after a hard day with the dead.'

CHAPTER EIGHTEEN

WARLOW PARKED against the wall at the entrance to Talley Woods opposite the church.

'We came here on a school trip, sir,' Rhys said as they slid on coats and changed into walking boots. 'I think I might even have my name for the chap who built it. Rhys ap Griffith.'

'Did your parents tell you that?'

'They always liked the name Rhys. It's an old name meaning ardent, or fire, sir.'

'Have you ever been up here before?' Warlow pointed up the hill towards the forest.

'No, sir. Just the Abbey. You?'

'Sergeant Jones and I have strolled here. Him with the occasional granddaughter, me with Cadi.'

'Easy walking, then, is it?'

Warlow ignored the cheeky little jibe. 'Don't forget your phone. The views are spectacular. And save your breath. You're going to need it.'

A stroll it was not.

The map posted up on a board at the entrance to the hill opposite the Abbey had several colour-coded paths. All circular, but where the circle had been tilted on its axis such that the first half was almost vertical.

The quick way up went through the centre of the horseshoe-shaped escarpment on the slopes of which the forest had been planted. This was a business trip, so Warlow did all the talking as they took the steep zigzag up the middle, which saw them climb above the hamlet of Talley within minutes of leaving the car park. It took twenty minutes to get to the apex, and a picnic table next to a forestry road. But it was here that Rhys, after a few seconds of puffing, stood, goggle-eyed, on the picnic table with his phone held out in front of him in both hands, one finger pressing the camera button to capture the views.

Beneath him, the bare trees and fields that made up a winter landscape spread out in every direction. East towards the Black Mountains with Pen Y Fan clearly visible in the distance, north to the rolling Cambrian Hills. A few yards away to the south, their way down beckoned through the forest back to the ruined Abbey. Behind him, if they kept walking west in a straight line, they'd end up, after a good fifty miles, at the sea in Newport, Pembrokeshire. Not that Warlow had any intention of doing that.

'Did we bring any food, then, sir?' Rhys sprang off the table like a cross between a mountain goat and a stick insect.

'No, we did not.' Warlow studied the terrain. 'Now we head cross-country.'

The circular route led back down to the trees to the car park, but at the forest gate, Warlow turned right through a kissing gate to head southwest.

'Orientation is the key here. Get Alison Povey to drop you a pin. She should be still at the scene.'

'Are we walking to it, then, sir?'

'This is higher ground. Coming in by road, I lost all sense of direction. As the crow flies, by my reckoning,

we're probably only a mile or so from where Povey is.'
Warlow took out his phone and scrolled to a compass as
Rhys sent a text. A minute later his phone pinged, and the
DC used his thumb and middle finger to enlarge the map
with a red inverted teardrop pin at its centre.

'We'll head for this trig point.' Warlow pointed to a
little triangle on Rhys's phone map.

They stuck close to the forestry fence for a while, but
after a few hundred yards, they struck out south across
open moor. The land rose gently, the grass underfoot
brown from the winter cold.

'This is a Marilyn, Rhys.'

'Who is she, sir?'

'You've heard of the Munros in Scotland?'

'The hills, sir?'

'Of a certain elevation, correct. Someone with a
sense of humour called the next lot of hills above one-
hundred-and-fifty metres, Marilyns.' Warlow wore a wry
grin.

'Why is that funny, sir?'

'Marilyn Monroe?'

Rhys pondered for a moment or two before the penny
dropped. 'Oh, she's the blonde in that dress over a hot air
grate, right?'

Warlow didn't stop walking, but he squeezed his eyes
shut in horror. For someone of Rhys's meme generation,
Norma Jean's troubled life might well have been encapsu-
lated in that iconic photograph, though he doubted Rhys
would know the photograph itself would later fetch four
million plus at auction. 'Yes, that's her. Probably warm
where that photo was. She liked it hot.'

Rhys, aware enough now that Warlow's throwaway
remarks were never wasted bait, intrigued but ignorant,
stayed quiet for all five seconds. 'Is that a reference I'm not
getting, sir?'

'Of course, it is. But life is too short. Now, there's the trig.'

It wasn't much of a trig. Just a narrow pyramid-shaped stone with a flat top which Warlow didn't even stop at. Instead, he kept walking, using his compass as a guide. They continued across the broad swathe of open land known as Mynydd Cynros, until it fell away to a point where Warlow called a halt.

Rhys glanced again at his phone. 'It's less than half a mile from here, sir.'

Warlow squinted across to where the fenced fields once more marked usable farmland, consulting the compass until at last he pointed. 'There. See the white vehicles?'

Rhys followed Warlow's gaze. 'Yes, sir. You're right.'

The presence of telephone poles and hedgerows showed where roads might have been, but they saw no traffic movement. Warlow was struck again by how truly out of the way *Cân-y-barcud* was.

'Take some more snaps, Rhys.'

'Are we going down, sir?'

'No. There's no point. I just needed to know if it was accessible, that's all.'

'Why is that?'

'Because the way in by vehicle is difficult. The road is narrow. Anyone coming the other way would mean that you or they would have to stop, reverse, and find an awkward passing place. That meant more than just a few seconds of contact. It meant several moments of interaction. People remember that sort of thing. And if you are trying to get away from a crime, especially one where you've killed someone, you don't want your vehicle being clocked by a white van driver, or a farmer in a big tractor, whose only source of entertainment might be making your life difficult on a very narrow lane.'

'So, you think he might've come in and out this way?'

'How easy would it be to park your car at the Abbey? No one would bat an eyelid. There's no CCTV. People come and go. It's hiding in plain sight that way.'

Rhys, however, was not convinced. 'But you can't be sure, sir.'

'I cannot. But it's what I would've done.'

Rhys's laugh was more a loud bark. 'You, sir? Have you got a list of people you'd like to kill, then?'

Warlow dropped his voice. 'Of course, I do. And it's a bloody long one.' With a quick wink, he walked away from a slightly baffled Rhys. 'Right, let's get back. Ever had a custard slice from the bakery?'

'No, sir.'

'Well, DC Harries, your luck is in. We'll make a quick stop at Llansawel and then head for Llandeilo.'

Rhys's face broke into a beaming smile of delighted anticipation. 'I always like a walkabout with you, sir. You know all the best places.'

'I'd like to take credit. But this is Llandeilo we're talking about. The custard slice expertise in this instance comes from one source and one source only.'

———

GIL HAD his desk arranged just as he liked it. Photos of his granddaughters were on the left of the keyboard and just under the bottom of the monitor. Pens, two of, pencils, one of, highlighters, two of – one green, one yellow – blue Post-it notes, one square of. All neatly arranged, with a cup of tea off to the right. He was looking at the screen and waiting for it to download a request he'd chucked at the PNC, but his attention was on the phone held to his ear.

'I understand congratulations are in order?'

'Thank you, sarge,' Hana Prosser said, sounding delighted. 'How did you know?'

'A little bird. Though if she heard me calling her that, I'd probably get one of her looks, and a look from DI Allanby has been known to turn people to stone. Let's just say I know.'

'Aw, she's lovely, is DI Allanby.'

'You'll get no arguments from me.' Gil, like Warlow, had a soft spot for the PCSO, who was not that much younger than Gil's youngest daughter. 'Right, to business. The rewilding dispute between Royston Moyles and the protesters up at Llanfynydd.'

'Ah, yes. We've been up there a few times. Funnily enough, at the request of the protesters, not the landowner.'

'Guns?'

'Yes. Gosh, you are well informed.'

'We do our homework.'

'But there was nothing to do. Everyone had a licence, and they were there with permission to shoot rabbits.'

'Did you get a list of who lives on site?'

'We did. There's a bit of coming and going with Tipi Valley, but there are six hardened protesters who cut their teeth elsewhere.'

Gil didn't need that explained. As eco-communes went, Tipi Valley near Cwmdu was one of the oldest. Some residents had been there for thirty years or more. 'Vehicles?' he asked.

Hana laughed. 'Only the one and it is as per the script. A rickety VW camper van in blue and orange, orange being the hand-painted psychedelic swirls on the sides. You'd spot it a mile off.'

'Of course. What else could it be?' He was amazed they hadn't called the dog Scooby.

'It's owned by a Marit Dekker, one of the females on site.'

'Can you send me the list?'

'I will. How's it going with the Moyles thing, anyway?'

'Slow to crawling.'

'Well, if you need anything, just shout.'

Hana was as good as her word, and the six names came through immediately. Gil sipped his tea and ran the names. He'd already spoken to the sergeant in Lizard's GBH case, which turned out to be more of a hothead-drunk-after-provocation case. But it confirmed that Lizard was the loosest of cannons. The three females on Hana's list, including Fran, had no record. But one of the other men looked like a diehard activist. His was an impressive arrest record. Wilful damage, trespass, and a drunk and disorderly times-two. This was a chap, a bit like Lizard, not averse to painting slogans on the side of buildings, throwing eggs at anyone important, pouring oil over carriageways, and being a general nuisance.

Gil had opinions of his own as regards "causes". Most of them sympathetic to an extent. Most of these thoughts were not for public consumption because they were his and no one else needed to know them. Not even little blue birds. Yet, he often had to hold his tongue sitting of an evening with the Lady Anwen, especially if one of his daughters was around, watching the latest TV drama dripping with insidious bias and a manic need to disregard any kind of accuracy in favour of blatant political flag waving, which he could do without at that time of night. It was one thing to argue the themes of the day over a pint in the pub, another to have it rammed down your throat in the guise of entertainment. What Gil wanted was something gritty with real people that made him feel something. He could count on one hand those that had gripped him over the last few years. And the last thing he wanted at nine o'clock every night was a polytechnic lecture.

Polytechnics.

Did anyone under forty even know what they were anymore?

He glanced at his tea mug. Another present from his daughters, well used to their reactionary, grumpy old dad. This one had a handwritten font in black on a white background.

If you're happy, and you know it, just shut up.

They were probably right.

Still, 1984 seemed to creep closer every day.

The media's belief that they were on the planet to re-educate the population (and good luck with that) had not escaped him, yet the nuances of the protest up at Llan-fynydd had. They were trespassing and breaking the law. Admittedly, that law could be a bugger to apply and enforce, but you did what you could to make it stick where it was needed.

Gil noted the name again from Hana's text:

Andrew Gachot, aged twenty-eight. Goes
by the name of Gatch

So, Lizard and Gatch.

He downloaded the last arrest photo, printed it off, and stuck it up on the Gallery. Gatch had even more ironmon-gery in his face than Lizard.

'Must be a bloody nightmare going through airport security,' he muttered. But then, the chance of either of these two getting through any country's border control was minimal, so it would never apply. He turned back to his desk. Next on his list was seeing what CCTV might be around in the town.

Gil had a cunning plan.

CHAPTER NINETEEN

GIL WAITED for Catrin and Jess to return from Cardiff. Upon their arrival, he graciously accepted the mince pies, still wrapped in their festive packaging. Instead of opening them, he stashed them away in the "Human Tissue For Transplant Box," his not-so-secret hiding place for baked goods that often made an appearance during briefings.

'Tidy,' he said, and proceeded to brief Jess on how his enquiries into Lizard and Gatch were progressing. When he outlined his ideas for following it through, she approved with:

'Good idea, sergeant.'

And so, mid-afternoon on a cold December day clouding over after such a promising start, Gil parked in the Co-op on Rhosmaen Street in Llandeilo and walked the thirty yards to the primary school. Weirdly, there were two, one an English medium, the other a Welsh medium. For his purposes, it really mattered little which one he chose, but opted for the one where his face would be best known. Where he'd stood in the yard on more than one occasion to pick up one of his grandchildren.

Not ideal having two schools whose main entrances

stood on a very busy road. Traffic lights and a manned crossing during opening and closing helped. But the speed restrictions and traffic calming measures had been bones of contention for years. The good thing was that the schools had CCTV cameras pointing out onto that busy road. There would have been CCTV in the Co-op, no doubt, but he'd have needed to jump through hoops to access that. Whereas the school knew him. He'd even helped to arrange a couple of visits from Uniforms as little talks to the children about not talking to strangers and road safety.

He was met in reception by the deputy head. Megan Roach was in her mid-fifties and had gone through, for want of a better cliché, a bit of a midlife crisis. At least, that was what the Lady Anwen had put her drastic change of hair colour, having her eye bags done, and shedding her glasses in favour of contact lenses, down to. The comfortable, if not downright frumpy, teacher of a few years ago had certainly... changed. He put it down to the plethora of makeover shows bombarding viewers touting a "be your best you" mantra that even the Lady Anwen dipped into now and again with a sudden change of nail varnish in the form of maroon or, once, startlingly, baby blue.

Mrs Roach met Gil in the reception area of the school. She still wore a surgical mask, explaining it away as her attempt at avoiding yet another dose of Covid from the children. Vulnerable people were still careful.

'*Diolch am hwn,*' Gil said, a simple thanks for her cooperation. The conversation that followed continued in Welsh. Megan Roach led the way to the secretary's office while he explained what he required.

'None of this involves the pupils or staff of the school,' he said.

'That's good to hear,' Roach said.

'It's early Monday morning I'm after. Maybe late Sunday evening.'

'Just as well because school was shut on Monday. Because of the ice,' Roach explained.

'I only want a view of the traffic.'

The office had a simple single monitor split screen arrangement for the CCTV. Three views, one at the rear of the school, one on the side facing the gate leading to the car park in the Co-op, and one out onto the road. The secretary quickly showed him how to access footage and, armed with a cup of school tea, Gil sat down and began to view the recordings. He accessed three days' worth and decided to go through it all quickly.

He found what he was looking for after forty minutes of times 2.5 speed. He made copies of the relevant footage on a USB drive he'd optimistically brought with him and thanked the secretary and Megan Roach for their coop-eration.

'And you got home okay on Tuesday morning?' he asked the deputy head as he made to leave.

'Yes,' she replied. 'I only popped in on Monday evening to a church meeting.'

'St Michaels? Anwen goes there. Spends most of her time praying for me, she says.'

'No, it's a group involved with the restoration of Llandyfeisant. We're trying to raise funds. There's a lot of history crumbling away.'

An image of the little stone church tucked away on the valley floor with a sloping graveyard on the edge of the estate now known as Dinefwr Park sprung to mind. His granddaughter, Eleri, had even been on a little jaunt there, which the school had arranged in combination with a nature walk. He remembered her painting it as homework.

'That frozen rain was freakish,' she said. 'I've never been so scared. People were driving like lunatics.'

One glance at his watch told Gil he had ten minutes before the school bell.

'Are you picking up Eleri?' Roach asked.

'No. That'll be her mother today. I'd better make myself scarce before either of them sees me. Eleri will want me to take her home and I am still on the clock.'

He left his car in the Co-op and headed back towards the town. This time taking Carmarthen Street and heading towards the two pubs that were not Moyles's haunts. Time for a quick half and a chat with regulars who would, by now, no doubt have heard about the death of one of the town's more colourful characters.

———

AT THE SAME time as Gil was ordering half a bitter and staring around at the tables in the Salutation Inn for likely people to chat to, Warlow stood in Royston Moyles's study at his house in Llansawel.

As the SIO, he needed to meet the victim's partner. Far better that they see a face, and not just hear a name. Janet Moyles had seen Jess's pleasant visage, and how much more acceptable than Warlow's it was. But that wasn't the point. He had a way of doing things and establishing a relationship, albeit a transient one, which was important in a case like this.

Her sister, the self-appointed gatekeeper Lois, had given them a frosty reception. But Warlow did what was necessary to ensure Janet Moyles was aware of how seriously Warlow and the rest of the team were taking this investigation. Finding out who killed her husband was his priority. Once that "I" had been dotted, he'd asked to see the study.

It was a small room looking out into the garden with a desk and easy chair and a more comfortable reclining chair where, Warlow suspected, Moyles might catch a few power naps. On the desk, which was polished wood, sat a silver-backed monitor and a small, white box, which he recognised as a Mac mini. Behind all that, one wall had box files stacked one above the other in a dedicated space. Against another wall was a small bookshelf. Moyles clearly had a thing for Reacher and McNab, it appeared. Above this, images of Moyles and his wife, Moyles with John Napier, and Moyles on his own adorned the walls. Those involving Napier were shots of them fishing. The ones of Moyles on his own showed him with a gun at his shoulder against a bruised sky with a gundog at his feet.

Warlow sat at the desk and pulled out a drawer. He'd often wondered what people would make of his own drawers if they ever ended up being pulled out for examination. Some people might know exactly what theirs contained. Were he to look at his own, he'd be able to tell what everything was. Probably what everything did. But whether they all needed to be there was a different question altogether. In Moyles's case, nothing odd jumped out at him as he looked at the flotsam. Unpaid bills, pens, pencils, stapler, letters to the council, a plumber's invoice, electricians' business cards. All related to the rental business that he ran. Nothing looked even vaguely threatening or suspicious. Someone else would go through this and index it all. But from what Warlow could see here, this was an annexe of the space Moyles shared with Charlie Brewer above Napier's office.

He left the study and joined Rhys, who'd been tasked with checking out the vehicles in the garage. Apart from the Land Rover they found at *Cân-y-barcud*, the Moyles had a Mercedes. Other than those, Rhys had found nothing of interest.

'Right, I think we're done here. Let's get back to the Incident Room for vespers.'

Warlow thanked the still distraught Janet Moyles and her disapproving sister, with a warning that they would want to remove Royston's computer for analysis and that someone would be around to collect it. But, as they reached Manordeilo, a few miles from Llandeilo on their way back to Carmarthen, Povey rang.

'Evan? Where are you?'

'Not one hundred miles away. Why?'

'We found something.'

'By the sound of it, you're suggesting it's something I ought to see?'

'Oh, yes. I could send you a snap, but on balance, I think you'll want to look at it yourself.'

'Twenty minutes,' he said and glanced at Rhys whose delight at the promise of vespers had evaporated on hearing they were bound for another trip to the crime scene.

'Is she always this secretive, sir?'

'No. But if she doesn't even want to tell me over the phone, I generally accept that it's something I need to see.'

In the passenger seat, Rhys nodded. The kind Warlow had come to recognise as his waning enthusiasm, low blood sugar nod.

'I realise it's coming up to teatime,' Warlow said. 'We could stop off at the bakery and grab a quick cup of tea and a sticky bun for you.' It would add five minutes to the journey, but if it meant a fully functioning, non-hangry Rhys, it would be worth it.

'That sounds good, sir.' Rhys perked up at that.

'Mind you, I'm still suffering the trauma of watching you eat that custard slice at lunchtime. While you were in Moyles's garage, I googled it. YouTube says you're meant to put it on its side on a plate and cut it into slices. That's not what you did.'

Rhys looked horrified. 'A custard slice needs to be held in the hand, sir, and eaten all in one sitting.'

'What, while your other hand hovers underneath to catch all the yellow stuff oozing out the side?'

'That's custard, sir.'

'Dis-custard more like.'

Rhys grinned. 'Good one, sir.'

'How come I'm always reduced to food puns when I'm with you? I'll get the teas, you go to the bakery. But I don't want you eating anything in the car that oozes.'

Warlow could see Rhys frantically ticking off his new limited options.

'How about you, sir? Can I get you something?'

'No. Tea'll be fine for me. I'll hang on. Gil says there are mince pies back at HQ. I'll wait.'

Rhys seemed perplexed at this. 'Can't you have a bun now and a mince pie later?'

'We don't all have your metabolism, constable. One day, you'll have to start taking it easy on the old calories, too.'

'Not looking forward to that day, sir.'

'No, I'm sure you aren't.' Warlow pulled into the car park opposite CK's supermarket. 'Right, meet you back here in five.'

Rhys was out of the door before Warlow had finished the sentence.

CHAPTER TWENTY

'FIRSTLY," Povey said, 'I want you to go upstairs to the crogloft bedroom and look around. We've put things back.'

'What do you mean, put things back?' Warlow asked.

'As it was when you first saw it. But without the body.'

'Why?'

'It's important,' Povey insisted.

With Rhys behind him, head bowed against the angled ceiling, Warlow took the steps. They'd removed the covers from the bed and the mattress looked remarkably unscathed. The room, otherwise, looked as twee as a loft bedroom ought to. Warlow scanned the space. 'What am I supposed to be looking at?'

'I'll give you a clue. It's not at eye level.'

Warlow regarded the bedroom furniture. A couple of low bedside tables with magazines, a bedside lamp, a blanket box. Beneath him, with his head just above the mezzanine floor level, so did Rhys. After a while, Warlow let his eyes stray upwards, to the boarded ceiling and the exposed A-frame with the cross-tie beams pegged to the rafters. The style was rustic with the warts and all construction on show, except at the centre rafters where, at the apex, a boxed-in area of about a foot either side had wooden panels with the shapes of love spoons cut out of them. A nice, decorative touch. Probably hiding a smoke sensor was Warlow's original thought.

'Are we talking about the love spoon panels?'

'Well spotted. Now come down,' Povey said.

Warlow complied and stood back while two techs in snowsuits and armed with pry bars, a hammer, and a couple of screwdrivers went up. A few minutes later, after some power tool whining and a noise akin to wood groaning under pressure, they came back down holding the love spoon panels and some long pieces of white-painted wood that, Warlow presumed, had been part of the match-board ceiling.

'Right, up you go.'

Warlow went up again and shimmied around to stand at the bottom of the bed. The only place you could stand completely upright. Rhys stood with his feet on the top two steps of the stairs, his mouth open.

'Wow,' he said.

Wow indeed. Warlow had been right about the smoke alarm. But what he had not anticipated was the other electronic devices arranged around the white housing of the sensor. Two small – no more than an inch in diameter – round, black objects had been screwed to the ceiling: one pointing to the bed, the other to the small area behind the stairs towards a low cushioned seating area.

'Cameras,' Warlow muttered.

'Indeed.' Povey's voice came up from beneath. 'There's another one, much more subtle, hidden in the digital clock on the mantelpiece downstairs.'

'No cabling?' Warlow asked.

'No. These cameras work through a sync module linked via wi-fi. The sync module has a USB slot. Depending on the wi-fi setup, it could be streamed remotely or, just as easily, video could be stored on a USB drive attached to the sync module.'

Warlow didn't understand all of the jargon. But he understood enough to know that these cameras had been deliberately hidden.

'And, before you ask,' Povey said, 'it isn't illegal to have security cameras in a rental property. But it is required that owners inform renters of this fact.'

'Had Moyles?'

'There is no mention of it on the NON site. Also, the wi-fi here had been disabled. We've checked and it does function. But the modem was off.'

'Sir, does this mean he was filming people? Guests?'

'It looks like it, Rhys.'

The DC shook his head.

'Nothing is stored on the cameras themselves I take it?' Warlow asked.

One of the techs answered from the bottom of the stairs. 'That's not usually the case, sir. Images are either transmitted via wi-fi to apps or stored locally, as Alison says. The setup here would suggest local storage.'

'But there's no drive plugged in, right?'

'No, sir.'

Warlow recalled Charlie Brewer's words. The fact that his girlfriend thought Moyles was a bit of a letch. If he'd been recording people without their knowledge on the one and only bed in the place, he was more than just a letch. Warlow moved away from the bed and went back down the stairs.

'Thanks, Alison.'

'I could have just told you, but I knew you'd want to see the setup.'

'You're right. Is there any way we can check his other properties without tearing the places apart? People might be staying there for the holidays.' On the one hand, they ought to know, on the other, he didn't want to ruin people's Christmas.

'We can access RF sweepers. In other words, we can run scans to find out if there are any cameras hidden. We'd need to get into the rooms, but we could get that set up by tomorrow.'

'Good. Let's do that. Rhys ought to go with whoever runs the scans. If we find any cameras we'd need to tell the guests.'

'Shouldn't be difficult to find the sync modules and disable them without disrupting wi-fi, etc,' the tech who'd answered Warlow's original question added.

'Rhys will have a list. I think there's another four properties. All dotted around the area,' Warlow said. He grinned at Povey. 'This is bloody good work, Alison. Or should we start calling you, Q?'

'I've been called a lot worse things.' She shrugged.

'Little one excited?' Warlow asked as they walked back out of the tiny cottage. She and her partner had a four-year-old boy.

'He is as wound up as a guitar string, but Meena's worse. She goes OTT on decorations and this year we've even got a lit-up reindeer in the garden.'

'Nice.' Warlow kept a straight face straight but his eyes suggested otherwise.

'No, it's tacky as hell. But it keeps her and Ollie happy. So, who am I to deny them that? Oh, and the burglary report should be with you tomorrow. I haven't been across but we've had a team over there.'

Warlow thanked her again and got into the Jeep.

It was well after five-thirty by now and his rule of getting anything really useful done after six would kick in shortly. He called it a day and suggested an early run-through in the a.m.

'Want me to tell the others, sir?' Rhys offered.

'No. Let me think about all this first. We can brief them in the morning.'

Once they'd got through Llandeilo, Warlow crossed the river at Nantgaredig and took the lesser travelled road towards Llangunnor and HQ. Rhys, unnaturally quiet, hadn't even asked to have the radio on.

'Right, come on, what's troubling you?' Warlow demanded.

'Those cameras, sir. It's not right.'

'No, it isn't. It's an infringement of privacy. Of the worst kind.'

Rhys turned back to the window. After a minute of cogitation, he turned back to face front, finally finding words to express what it was that troubled him. 'Gina and me, we stayed in a place a couple of months ago. I hope to God they didn't have any hidden cameras.'

'Why? Apart from the obvious.'

'You know, sir. We spent quite a lot of time there. In the bedroom.'

'Don't tell me you were doing role play. Batman and Catwoman?'

Rhys looked aghast.

'Don't tell me you were *Catwoman*?'

'No, sir. We don't do *that*... but, you know, we do, are still... experimenting.'

Warlow couldn't resist. Rhys's expression of discomfiture was too much of a temptation. 'What, you had test tubes and a Bunsen burner?' Gil would have been proud.'

'No. No test tubes. But Gina... she's more adventurous than me, sir. And—'

'Say no more, Rhys. I'll spare you your blushes. But I've said it once and I'll say it again. She's a keeper.'

'I think you're probably right, sir.'

'Now, put on some music so we can distract your brain

from thoughts no self-respecting detective constable should be having whilst on duty.'

Rhys turned on the radio. Chris Rea's *Driving Home for Christmas* purred out of the speaker. Rhys shut it off instantly. 'Sorry, sir.'

'No, no. This is the only Christmas song worth listening to. The old Rea is a king. Turn it up if you want to.'

Rhys did. Both DCI and DC tapped along to it as the night closed in around them and their thoughts drifted towards a day in the calendar that, love it or hate it, loomed ever closer.

———

WARLOW HAD a walk he could do in the dark with Cadi a couple of miles from Ffau'r Blaidd. Only five minutes by car. As soon as he got home, he changed, stuck on a powerful head torch and wandered out to look at what the workers had done that day. He had Bryn Davies and his man Alwyn at the property attacking his garden room. When they'd finished off the cottage, Alwyn had suggested using a load of concrete they had left as a base for a shed. That shed had become a fully insulated, double glazed, garden office cum summer house, cum... whatever he might want it to be. They'd had materials that needed using up. Enough for the wooden frame, enough for the slate roof and insulation. All he'd had to splash out on was some tanalised shiplap cladding. The boys had made it watertight a few weeks ago and now were sorting out electrics and the fittings inside. Warlow opened the door and looked in, The place smelled of sawn pine and sealant. But it looked good. It looked really good.

They'd promised to have it finished by the time he got back from Oz.

A builder's promise, then, but at least they'd be around to keep an eye on the place while he was gone.

He bundled Cadi into the Jeep before driving west towards the estuary. The rain might hold off for another hour or so. More than enough. He needed to clear his head. And Cadi needed to do what dogs needed to do. Sniff a bush every ten yards, mark her territory every thirty or so, and make room for more food by emptying her bowels. Always hunched over, pointing north which was the adopted position of choice.

Warlow scooped up the products of this little exercise a minute in and walked on. In daylight, the River Nevern and a view over water towards medieval Newport —*Tudraeth* in Welsh— would be on his left, Newport Bay directly in front over the dunes. That view, and the water, were still there of course but night had stolen them from sight. It didn't matter. Being out with the dog doing something not work-related was what helped.

He'd had an email from Tom containing a forwarded copy of his E-ticket to Australia. As usual, he'd not given the trip much thought while at work, but opening the email and seeing the ticket brought the forthcoming visit to see his grandson and new granddaughter into focus again. He was off mid-January. Mid-winter in the UK, not far off the middle of summer in Australia. He was beginning to look forward to it.

But first, there was Christmas and before that… Royston Moyles.

The hidden cameras at the property, he was convinced, a significant factor in all of this. Just how much of a factor he had yet to decide. But the familiar, barely audible internal buzzing had begun in his head and, until this case was cleared, like an insect insistently drawn to the light, it would remain. Until he caught it in his fist and threw it out of the window.

They were on a stretch of the estuary where there was hard sand. Warlow had a pale white glow-in-the-dark ball with him. He launched it and heard Cadi sprint off in pursuit.

'We could probably do this on the moon, eh girl?'

No one was listening as the dog brought the ball back and deposited it in his outstretched hand.

'Okay. Two more. Then home for supper.'

Cadi watched the ball arc away into the darkness and set off after it.

CHAPTER TWENTY-ONE

A PALPABLE SENSE of urgency permeated Dyfed Powys Police HQ the next morning. Everyone in the team, as well as the co-opted CID officers and staff involved in collating information, indexing it, and uploading it, were aware the 25th was only three days away. Though Warlow had not mentioned the day itself, it loomed like a great big garish bauble on a Christmas tree. The hope in everyone's head, if not their hearts, was that they might put this case to bed quickly. No one wanted to be manning phones or knocking on doors on Christmas Day. And this year it fell on a Sunday, which meant bolted on bank holiday on the Tuesday in lieu.

The overtime would be crippling.

Some secretaries had wanted to make an effort at Christmas cheer by dangling some tinsel over notice boards. Though not across the Gallery or the Job Centre. That would be crass. And with the number of people flitting in and out of the Incident Room bringing in, or taking out the myriad bits of information this stage of the investigation always generated, all it took was one insensitive, or deliberately mischievous, individual to take a snap of that tinsel and send it out into the ether, for the Christmas crap to hit the fan.

Police find time for festivities in gruesome murder case.

Warlow could just see it.

Better that Christmas was kept outside the room for now.

This morning was a full briefing. Not only the team, but everyone involved needed to be brought up to speed. And so Warlow had a pre-brief chinwag with the team in a conference room. They sat round a table that would seat another ten, with chairs around the edge to double up that number. But first, he wanted a catch up before everyone else arrived.

'Right, we've got ten minutes.'

Rhys had brought the teas. For now, there'd be no baked goods.

'Rhys, you start off. Tell everyone what Povey found.'

The DC, put firmly on the spot by his boss, swallowed loudly before delivering his bombshell. 'There are hidden cameras at *Cân-y-barcud*.'

'What?' Jess barked out the question.

Catrin had gone pale, which, in someone of her colouring, was quite a feat.

Warlow confirmed it. 'Povey showed us last thing yesterday. Once we finish here, Rhys is off to visit Moyles's other rental properties. See if it was a one off.'

'You don't think it is, do you?' Gil asked. 'A one off?'

Warlow lowered his head. 'Let's just say I'd be very surprised. The setup looked quite… sophisticated.'

'Can we get footage?' Jess asked.

'No,' Rhys said. 'The setup is self-contained. Whatever's recorded is stored on a local drive that can be detached from a sync unit. All wi-fi. No cables.'

'But the cameras, they were still at the scene? I mean, they hadn't been disturbed by the killer?' Catrin asked.

'No. They were found by a vigilant tech poking into every nook and cranny. He spied a hidden lens behind a panel used to cover a smoke alarm.'

'Bloody hell,' Gil muttered. 'So Moyles really was a perv.'

No one commented on that. There didn't seem any need. 'Let's wait for Rhys to check out the others. Then we can draw conclusions. Jess, any surprises in the post-mortem?' Warlow asked.

'Nothing. He was trussed up and choked under his own weight. Full report should be with us this morning. But there were some wounds on the head and face. Blunt trauma. A few tears. Sengupta's going to run some tests, but the discussion was around whether it could have been the barrel of a handgun.'

'There was white gum residue on the wrists, too, sir. So, he was taped up. If there'd been a gun, used as a threat to subdue, it would do as the blunt instrument,' Catrin added.

'That would make sense. He wasn't a small bloke. Some threat would have been needed to get him to do what was asked of him. There was otherwise no sign of a struggle?'

'No,' Jess said. 'No defensive wounds. No sign of any other trauma.'

Catrin flicked through her notes. 'We know he visited the properties now and again, but there was no discernible pattern. No set days. The Sadlers were a honeymoon couple. The cleaners said Moyles made a point of visiting rental properties when he knew they were young couples.' She looked up and flicked her gaze from one face to the other. 'The cleaners wondered if he visited to sprinkle rose petals on the pillows. But now we know better. He went there to switch on the cameras.'

'Ugh,' Jess said.

Warlow turned to Gil. 'I hear you had a day out in Llandeilo yesterday afternoon. Skiving again?'

'Indeed. but before that, I got some intel on our friends at the rewilding site. Lizard, our many piercings friend, has a like-minded eco-warrior in the forest with him, by the name of Andrew Gachot. Another stand-up citizen if ever there was one. But he, aka Gatch, has the group transport. A Scooby Doo-style camper van. And yesterday, using a covert surveillance technique – my granddaughter's school's CCTV – I spotted that same van entered Llandeilo late Monday night.'

Rhys made a noise in his throat that might have been an impression of Scooby Doo saying, "Well done, sarge", but sounded a lot more like someone strangling a yodelling cat. The scathing looks he got made him mouth a silent. 'Sorry.'

'And, since the freezing rain hit that night and the van hardly looks capable of driving up a hill even when it isn't a skating rink, my guess is they stayed the night somewhere in town.'

Warlow tilted his head. 'You think they might do for the office break-in?'

'It's something to consider. The town was locked down. Hardly anyone was about. And we know Moyles had been using scare tactics with his shotgun toting friends up there at the rewilding site.'

'Motive and opportunity, then,' Rhys said.

'I think we ought to get them in, old Lizard and Gatch,' Gil said. 'Have a little chat under caution.' Gil smiled. 'Having spoken to some locals in the pubs Gatch and Lizard sometimes frequent, they've not been shy in expressing their dislike for Moyles publicly. And the good thing is that Gatch's partner has a son who attends the local primary school. He's brought to school every morning in the camper van. More often than not by the good Gatch.'

Warlow looked at his watch. 'Right, let's move on that. Let's get them down here for questioning. Is it too late to get a response car outside the school to wait for him this morning?'

'Already sorted it,' Gil said. 'I'm a mind reader, me.'

'Mystic Meg?' Rhys said.

'Guesswork Gil, more like,' Catrin muttered.

Rhys grinned his approval at her swift wit.

'We've got five minutes before things start here. Anything else?' Warlow asked.

Catrin flicked through some more pages of her note-book. 'I'm chasing up the names of the people brought to the hotel on Sunday night I'm yet to contact, sir. If I'd have known Gil was visiting the school, he could have talked to the deputy head, um… Roach?'

'I'd offer to help, too, sarge, but I'm on a road trip,' Rhys's pseudo apology drew a scathing look from Catrin.

'Doesn't matter. Half of the ones I've contacted are local, half not. Besides, when I told Craig that one of the names on my list was Roger Hunt, his eyes lit up.'

'Why?' Rhys asked.

'Believe it or not, Craig has hidden depths.'

Rhys's guffaw was stifled by one of Jess's warning looks.

'Craig is a bit of a wildlife buff, I'll have you know. He watches all those *Wildscene* programmes.'

'When he's not watching *Top Gear*,' Rhys muttered from behind a hand.

'People are allowed to be eclectic, Rhys,' Warlow said. 'And don't say you can have pills for that.'

'Anyway,' Catrin said. 'Craig's a fan of Hunt's. He says

his wildlife photos are stunning. He used to have a slot on those programmes advising amateur photographers.'

'Used to?'

'Yes. No longer, apparently. Craig said something about him stepping down. Breakdown, or more money elsewhere, were the whispers.'

'Who knows what goes on behind closed doors,' Jess said.

Everyone there had the sense not to comment.

'Anyway, Hunt has books out. Lovely books with amazing photographs of birds and animals. A lot of them are shot here in Wales. I thought I'd get one for Craig as a stocking filler, and then I'd ask Hunt when I get through to him to sign one.' Catrin wrinkled her nose. 'Or would that not be professional?'

'Go for it,' Gil said.

'Nothing wrong with that,' Warlow added. 'Besides, how can he object? You're putting money in the man's pocket.'

Catrin beamed. 'I'll take that as a seal of approval, then.'

Someone knocked on the door and Warlow shouted, 'Come in.' He had just enough time to say 'Vespers,' by way of fixing up another point of contact in time before the room started to fill.

Within ten minutes, there were another sixteen officers jostling for seats. Two were left standing. People took notes, Warlow and Jess fielded questions. But Warlow had made the executive decision not to mention the hidden cameras yet. Not until they'd checked out the other properties. Rhys outlined Povey's findings, and it was the search coordinator who suggested they take a look at exploring access to the property from the Talley Woods direction.

Catrin issued actions. They needed officers knocking on doors in the town to establish Moyles's movements over the days before his death and after the meeting in the office with Brewer. It all needed coordinating.

'We also have a breakdown of his phone records. If someone could get in touch with the people he contacted and do the necessary. I'll post the action on the board once we finish here.'

More donkey work.

More noses to the grindstone.

When the briefing finished, Sion Buchannan, who'd also sat in, stayed in the room after everyone else had left. Warlow briefed him on the camera situation. He listened in shocked silence.

'What do you make of that, Evan?'

'An unpleasant surprise, but from the picture we're building up of Moyles perhaps we should not have been surprised.'

'This could be a very ugly twist,' Buchannan said.

'God knows how many people he could have filmed just in that one property.' Jess said.

'We've got someone making lists of previous guests, though, yes?' Buchannan asked.

'We can get all of that from his assistant, Brewer,' Warlow said.

'What about the other angles?'

'Gil's on it. He is our man in Llandeilo and has his ear to the ground.'

'It'll be interesting to hear what the eco-warriors have to say for themselves,' Jess threw in a thought.

'I'm sure it'll be colourful, whatever it is.' Buchannan sucked in air through a couple of flared nostrils.

CHAPTER TWENTY-TWO

DANIEL HUGHES DID NOT CONSIDER himself a superstitious man. That was not to say he'd deliberately tempt fate. He did not walk under ladders, for example. Mainly because one leaning against a wall or disappearing up into scaffolding usually had someone on the top rungs, and walking underneath increased your chances of being hit on the head by a fumbled screwdriver, a dropped hammer, or a loaded paintbrush, one hundred percent. That sort of superstition he was all for because it had tangible benefits and came with a dollop of common sense. But seeing black cats cross your path as an omen of bad things? Or thinking that getting a shoulder's worth of crow or seagull guano was lucky?

Really?

His wife, on the other hand, a stalwart of many a town committee, read her bloody horoscope each day. She would shriek if you ever put new shoes on the table or open an umbrella inside, even if the logical thing to do would be to stick it, unfurled, in the mudroom to dry. And God forbid she should ever see one magpie. Dan Hughes thought it was all nonsense.

And yet, after the drink and chat with John Napier to mark Roy Moyles's passing, he'd been left with a kind of nameless dread. His conscience was clear. Or so he kept telling himself. Whatever business schemes Roy had been up to, and he was always up to something, Hughes had kept well away and kept his mouth shut. Even when, in his cups, Moyles shared the odd toe-curling anecdote that would have been best kept private. And that silence had become his greatest fear now. He'd not been convinced by Napier's dismissal of guilt by omission.

Since getting up that morning, he'd been unable to shake a vague feeling of unease. Nothing good was going to come from Roy Moyles's death. He'd employed builders, no local ones, as they all stayed well clear, to renovate at least one of his properties this winter. Would they get paid now? Would Janet do the right thing by them? And those hippies up at the forest in Llanfynydd, the ones Moyles had taken so much pleasure in trying to scare with his double-barrel shotgun cronies. They would not be shedding any tears. Neither would the many people who crossed the street when they saw him coming into town for fear of losing control and giving the smug sod a good slap for the money they'd been cheated out of during his bankruptcy.

His more than one bankruptcy.

At least the other thing, his sleazy little hobby, would die with the man.

Christ, he'd had the thickest skin Dan Hughes had ever come across. John Napier came a close second. They could dismiss the unpleasantness Moyles generated as nothing more than poor luck. Yet, Dan had woken in the early hours with his mind churning. All very well to chalk it up to "business" but that "business" had triggered someone enough to commit the ultimate crime. And there were a load of rumours flying around about the actual deed.

That Roy Moyles had been crucified, or stabbed fifty

times, or trussed up and left to die. But there was no point asking that nice-looking DI because she was as hard as nails underneath her looks. No doubt the inquest or trial or whatever the hell this ended up as would reveal all the dirty laundry in due course.

Hughes sat in his office at the bakery, looking out into the shop floor at the ovens and production line. His wasn't a big concern, but he had a good name, and the bakery on Station Road, within sight of the heart of Wales railway line and the river, was an institution. His father and his uncle had baked bread here just after the war. He employed only thirty people, but many of them had been with him since they'd left school. And his bread had now become an artisan product delivered to shops all over the west, along with cakes and pastries. Oh yes, Hughes the Baker was a major contributor to the obesity epidemic and no mistake.

He tried to smile at his own joke, but it faltered at the first twitch. He got up, toyed with the idea of putting on a hat, white coat, and wellies and strolling around the shop floor, but that idea foundered with one glance at the wall clock.

Almost ten-fifteen. A bit early for coffee. But his restlessness got the better of him. He grabbed his jacket, muttered a few words to the office staff as he walked through, and stepped out into the December air. He could have grabbed a coffee at The Warehouse a few yards away, but he was meeting up with Napier and so he set off in the other direction, towards the station and up the steps to the quiet residential streets of Clarendon, Alan, and Latimer Road, and a much-needed coffee at the top end of town.

He walked past the cars in the station car park. Only half a dozen today. He wondered if their owners had taken the early train north towards Shrewsbury and Crewe, or south to link up with the coastal line to Carmarthen for all points east. But then he remembered there was another strike today. These commuters would have been bussed to their destinations.

He, John Napier, and Roy Moyles had once taken the train from this station all the way to Edinburgh on a rugby weekend. TV programmes had been made about the heart of Wales line and the twenty odd stops between Llandeilo and Craven Arms in Shropshire. The scenery was stunning through the spa towns, over the Cynghordy Viaduct and passing the remote Sugar Loaf, but it didn't get you anywhere in a hurry. On the way to see an International at Murrayfield, and armed with some large cooler bags, there had been no hurry. And once you got to Shrewsbury or Crewe, the trains were plentiful, and a lot quicker. It had been a pleasant trip. Dan Hughes remembered it fondly as he got to the top of the steps and emerged at the bottom of Clarendon Road. As he did, a single magpie chattered its objection and took off from a nearby tree.

Hughes watched it fly off and silently cursed his wife.

———

HE WAS EARLY TODAY, the Baker. But, through luck, they'd been prepared, watching from across the railway tracks having arrived early. People took their dogs across the railway all the time to the swing bridge and the river. People who collected their dog's crap and bagged it up only to leave it on the path as if to say, 'Ooh, look how good we are, now clear it up.'

People could be arseholes.

Some people could be monsters.

Like Royston Moyles… and his friends. The Baker for one.

But today, seeing all the police around, buzzing in and out in their patrol cars, parked in the Co-op car park, had been a pain. A close call. But it changed nothing. They knew the Force was stretched.

The police could not be everywhere. And they only needed the right moment, one moment, to do what needed to be done.

At the end of the southbound platform, they'd found a spot where they could sit and wait and watch. The police wouldn't find them here. They'd dressed for the weather, or at least for what the weather might be in a part of the world where you could get four seasons in one day. But that added to the charm of this part of the world. There was CCTV in the station, but they'd avoided that. The crossing, to the north of the platforms, was simply some wooden planking laid to ensure no one tripped over proud rails. It still left gaps for the unwary paw or stiletto.

That didn't bother them. No stilettos. At least none that you wore on your feet.

They watched as the Baker walked to the steps that led up to the town. He'd be out for thirty minutes. That was his routine. Could be longer today. But it all offered an opportunity.

They knew how long it took to climb the stairs and how long – a little less – to climb down. They'd timed it half a dozen times. Now they waited an extra thirty seconds to be sure and went south along the paths to a place where the CCTV lost coverage. They took an under-pass beneath the railway and a lane that emerged onto Crescent Road. There they took off the ski mask but kept the hood and ambled back towards Latimer Road to keep watch.

It didn't matter how long the Baker might be. They had all the time in the world.

CHAPTER TWENTY-THREE

GIL HAD the Scooby camper van CCTV image from outside the school up on screen in front of him, as he held a phone to his ear. What had been planned as a simple stop and chat operation had turned into a farcical spectacle.

When Uniforms approached the van after the driver had returned to it following the delivery of a child to the school, a second person had gone to the Co-op. In hindsight, it would have been better to wait for the second person to return, but the Uniforms had not.

The result was a standoff between the van driver – who refused to open the van window to engage with the uniformed officer, claiming that he was under no obligation to do so – and the police.

That was when the second person, described to Gil by a bewildered Uniform as male, bearded, braided hair, and wearing baggy trousers and several layers of jumper under a striped woollen coat, walked out of the Co-op. He'd taken one glance at the police and the van and high-tailed it across the street towards Station Road carrying a carrier bag.

The reason for this sudden allergic response to the sight of Uniforms soon became apparent when a Co-op employee hurried out into the car park and shouted after the technicolour-coat man, 'Oy, you haven't paid for that!'

The camper van then tried to drive off and was prevented from doing so only by a Uniform standing in front of it. A second response vehicle was summoned, causing mayhem on the A483 running through town which, at that time in the morning, was stuffed with traffic carrying pupils to the secondary school on the other side of the river bridge. They eventually got the camper van driver out, and he was now in custody. He'd given his name as Lizard. The second man was nowhere to be seen.

Catrin, sitting just a few feet away from Gil and who'd enjoyed the theatre of the whole thing unfolding in front of her eyes, grimaced in sympathy.

'Any idea where this Gatch could be?' she asked.

'Last seen around the train station at nine-ish.'

'Could be in Birmingham by now.'

'Very funny. If he got on the train, we'd catch him. I can run faster than that bloody thing.'

Catrin let her eyebrows do the talking. They did cynical doubt really well.

'I've lost a bit of weight, I'll have you know.' Gil wanted to tell her how much but was stymied by his phone ringing again. Anticipating it to be something Gatch-related he answered it with a rather tetchy, 'Yes?'

'Sergeant Jones?'

'It is.'

'You were talking to one of my boys in the Salutation last night. He said you were asking about that twat Moyles?'

'I spoke to several people there. Who am I speaking to now?'

'Mike, it is. Mike Sedgely.'

'Morning, Mike. Thanks for getting back to me.' Gil had seen Sedgely Building and Maintenance vans around the town and its surrounding villages. Usually in proximity to some scaffolding or reversed into someone's drive. 'The boys said you wanted to know about Moyles when things went tits up with him.'

'Your company came up in conversation. Did he owe you a lot?'

'Enough. Give or take ten grand. We did the roof on one of his projects. But I wasn't the worst hit. D and B did the floors and extensions on two. They were hit for nearly seventy grand.'

'D and B?'

'Denby and Brewer.'

Gil sat up. 'Brewer?'

'Yeah. Crippled them that did. It was only the two of them and an apprentice.' Sedgely sighed. 'Jim Denby is still about. I use him now and again. But Sel wasn't young. He never got over it. Not long after that, he had the heart attack.'

'Sel as in Selwyn?'

'Yeah.'

'Any relation to Charlie Brewer?'

'His grandfather. They say that Moyles gave Charlie a job to make himself feel better about it all. I call bullshit on that. Sel Brewer's funeral was massive. He was well thought of. Salt of the earth. Moyles will be lucky to see a tenth of that number, unless all his debtors turn up to piss on the sod's grave. Then it'll be around the block.'

Gil pushed the imagery this brought to mind away and thanked Sedgely for his call. When it ended, he scribbled on a Post-it note and got up to stick it on the Job Centre board. Catrin waited until he'd sat down again before standing up and peering at the note.

'What's this? We already know who Charlie Brewer is.'

'Ah, but do we, though?' Gil restrained himself from humming the theme tune to the *Twilight Zone* for all of twenty seconds.

———

CATRIN SAT DOWN AGAIN with her list of numbers for the rescued motorists at the hotel. Not too many left, but as expected, none of them had seen anything untoward going on. They'd all been too busy worrying about their abandoned vehicles and getting in from the cold. She could eliminate people from where they'd been stranded. In effect, she only needed to talk to those who were on the road leading up to the crime scene area. Lucky for her, the lay-by where Roger Hunt had pulled in was. Sort of. The right side of town, anyway.

She rang the number and, this time, he answered on the second ring.

'Mr Hunt, this is Sergeant Catrin Richards, Dyfed Powys Police.'

'What can I do for you, sergeant?' He sounded as if he was moving outdoors, slightly out of breath.

She quickly outlined the reason for her call. Hunt explained he'd been in town doing a bit of shopping when the rain started. By the time he set off back up to his rental property in Gwynfe, the road had become a death trap. After he'd seen a lorry go into the hedges, he pulled in and waited it out. He always carried a blanket in the car. In his line of work, it wasn't unusual to get caught in the odd storm, and had some supplies from the shopping, so he'd been prepared to spend the night if necessary. But then the police turned up and instead of his Mazda, he'd found a seat at the Cawdor Hotel.

'And you saw nothing noteworthy while you were in the car?'

'I saw lots of things, people sliding into ditches, the lorry almost overturning. But nothing that I can think of that would help you.'

'No. We're ticking boxes, as you can imagine.'

'I heard on the news.'

'Yes, well, thanks for your cooperation. By the way, I hope you don't mind, but I have a small favour to ask.'

The line hummed quietly.

'My partner is a big TV nature fan. I bought him one of your books for Christmas.'

The line stayed quiet.

'It's the spin off one from the TV programme, *Wildscene.'*

All that came over the ether was a deep exhalation.

'Hello?' Catrin asked.

'I'm sorry, but I'm trying… I'm trying my best to forget that period in my life. I went through a rough time then. The book just brings back too many sour memories.'

'Oh, okay. Sorry I brought it up.'

'Not your fault, but I've made it a rule to distance myself from it and everything to do with it.'

He sounded upset. Catrin squeezed her eyes shut.

'I'd rather not. Sign it, I mean. I'm sorry.'

'No, no. You're alright. No big deal. I thought… never mind what I thought. He'll love the book, anyway.'

'Good. What I went through then… even thinking about it now…'

Don't cry. Please don't bloody cry.

'It's fine, Mr Hunt. Sorry to have brought it up.'

Wind crackled over the phone's mouthpiece. Catrin latched on to that in order to change the subject. 'You're out and about, Mr Hunt?'

'Yeah. It relaxes me. It's the one place I feel at ease with myself. With nature.'

'Well, you take care.' She signed off and sat there, staring at the phone, transfixed.

'Not going to sign it, then, is he?' Gil asked. His turn to comment on the half-overheard conversation.

She turned to look at him; her face stricken. 'Know when you regret saying something as soon as you open your mouth?'

'You must be mistaking me with Rhys Harries.'

'Apparently, the book and *Wildscene* hold bad memories for him. Crikey. Whatever happened to the season of goodwill?'

'That lost its fight with austerity and inflation months ago. Two knock downs and a submission.'

Jess came out of the SIO room.

'Gil, your friend is here. How about you two have a chat with the man who calls himself Lizard?'

'That'll take my mind off the wildlife,' Catrin said.

Gil got up and looked down at her. 'I wouldn't be so sure of that.'

CHAPTER TWENTY-FOUR

HAVING SENT Rhys off early on his expedition to check on Moyles's other properties, which the DC had got excited enough about to hum the theme tune to *Mission Impossible* all the way to the meetup with the tech in Llandeilo, Warlow revisited Moyles's burglarised office. And though Povey was still finishing things off at *Cân-y-barcud*, the tech in charge, Jo Tannard, was well known to the DCI. The first time he'd met her had been on a stretch of the Cardiganshire coastal path when a landslip exposed the hidden remains of two walkers, whose harrowing murder had brought Warlow back into the fold of Dyfed Powys Police from a poorly thought-out retirement.

'Ah, Mr Warlow, didn't expect to see you here today.' Tannard had an electronic tablet in her hand and a stylus in the other. A rangy woman with a calm smile that belied a thoroughness that working with Povey had engendered.

'I'm waiting for my DC to come back from playing Tom Cruise with one of your techs.'

'Ah, the camera scans?'

'That's it. Nothing like that here, I take it?'

'No, nothing like that.'

But then why should there be? The office had no bed. No possibility of some quiet-time-romping away from it all. Warlow cringed at the thought that the "all", thanks to Moyles's cameras, meant half the world via the internet.

'There is wi-fi. The solicitors downstairs have a router, but the town has a free network for visitors.'

'Right,' Warlow said, knowing none of it helped. Carmarthenshire had rolled out a digital connectivity initiative funded in part from European money for rural development in quite a few of its towns. But there were still black spots for mobile phone signals.

He stood just inside the door and, for the second time in as many days, surveyed the damage. Charlie Brewer had the all clear to return now that everything had been photographed and fingerprinted.

'What's that?' Warlow spied a wooden structure lying on its side. A smashed pot plant lay on the floor next to it.

'The plant or the stool?'

'Is it a stool?' Warlow walked over to it.

'Mr Brewer told us it sat against the wall and had a pot plant on the top shelf, a photo and some tissues on the lower level.'

'Okay if I pick it up now?'

Tannard shrugged. 'We're done with it.'

Warlow walked over and, already gloved, righted the stool. Except it wasn't a storage rack. Well, not strictly a storage rack. Once righted, it turned into a neat little multifunctional stool cum stepladder. In other words, whatever the hell you wanted it to be. The bottom two steps had a flip mechanism allowing them to be folded away inside the taller stool or brought out to act as steps up to a height of three feet. He stood back and considered it. 'Hmm, could do with one of these myself.' He fished out his phone and took a snap. 'So, anything jump out at you?' Warlow walked back to the door.

'Only one thing. That's the glass around the broken pane.'

'What about it?'

'What's left in the frame, the shards, mostly point inwards, but several point outwards.'

'Significance?'

'It could mean that the burglar caught something on the glass as he broke it from the outside and then yanked backwards as he withdrew.'

'Or she,' Warlow corrected her. 'I'd like to avoid stereotyping in the interest of inclusivity.'

Tannard grinned. 'I've missed that sense of humour, Mr Warlow. We've swabbed the glass shards but no sign of blood or fibres.'

'Shame.'

Warlow walked down the fire escape steps and stood in the little courtyard looking up at the park beyond. He stepped into the alleyway. Some small cottages lined the right side with stone walls arcing upwards at the end of the alley. At the rear of Napier's office, a low wall gave way to scruffy shrubs and not much else as the land rose towards the park. He wondered how agile you might need to be to scramble up there when his phone rang.

'Gil, what can I do for you?'

'How are your tracking skills?'

'I'd need the dog for that.'

'Aren't you part bloodhound?'

'Which part, and if it's the part I think you are referring to, those rumours are scandalous.'

'I can tell you've had your coffee this morning.'

'Only the three cups.'

'Right, well, have a Jaffa Cake with the next one. You're going to need it.' Gil explained the debacle over the camper van, Lizard, and the AWOL Gatch.

'So, you're saying he's gone into hiding in Llandeilo?'

'Last seen heading down Station Road.'

'Then I'd better get my skates on.'

'You don't know the town that well, do you?'

'Oh, ye of little faith. Didn't I tell you I once rented a house here whilst they were finishing renovations at my place in Nevern? A while ago, admittedly, but I used to walk a neighbour's dog for her. I know a few hidey-holes.'

'Then you've probably walked to the swing bridge. Gatch was last seen heading towards the river. He might be in Ammanford by now if he'd hitched a lift.'

'I'm already on it,' Warlow said. He took one last look at the rear of Napier's office, exited the alley, and set off.

———

RHYS CAUGHT a lift back to Llandeilo with the CSI tech. Of the three properties they'd looked at only one had triggered the IR sensor. Hardly surprising since two were long-term rentals. But the third was another NON property. A surprised couple, seeing four men at their rented doorstep, two of whom were in uniform, stood back while Rhys explained what they were looking for. The parents watched in horror, whereas the son, an eleven-year-old boy, and his twelve-year-old sister looked on with the indifference of youth, concerned only that their Mario Kart session had been disrupted. There were three bedrooms in the place and four cameras. Two in the main-bedroom light fitting and, much more disturbing, one in each of the other rooms. These were smaller rooms that would sleep children, as advertised. Though Rhys thought that perhaps tagging "family-friendly" into the description was now stretching things a bit.

The tech took many photos and tracked signals to another grill high on the ceiling, where he found another hub with the same capability for local storage but, as in *Cân-y-barcud*, again, with no USB drive attached.

Rhys briefed the Uniforms and left them to deal with the family and the much-appreciated reassurances and explanations. All avoiding any reference to Moyles at this stage. The story was that they were investigating reports of some rental properties having illegal surveillance. All of which was true. And if the parents sensed a more sinister agenda here, they twigged not to say anything in front of their kids. But since no drives were attached, the cameras would not have stored any footage. That, at least, gave both Rhys and the family some sense of reassurance.

And so, at around 10.30 on another grey December morning, Rhys stood in the portico outside the old post office in Llandeilo, now a bakery, once more enjoying the variety of goods on display through the window decorated with stuck-on snowflakes and spray-on snow applied around the edges, under the loops of tinsel and some fairy lights. He'd already been to Pitchfork and Provision for one of their signature sausage rolls, which he ate now, with the uneaten half still in its paper bag as ameans of holding it. In his other hand was another bag from the old post office containing a couple of lemon iced buns for later.

He'd texted Gina on the off chance she might be in the area. But she'd been co-opted into house-to-house calls in Bynea today after an attack on a man left him hospitalised. So, there was no chance of her nipping the twenty miles from there to Llandeilo for a quick coffee. Though the attraction of sitting in a café in a Christmas-bedecked Llandeilo compared with tramping the streets of the new estates on the edges of Llanelli invoked more than one choice comment from the officer in question.

These began politely enough.

Sorry, (groan) I wish I could.

before veering, in response to Rhys laying it on thick, into,

I hope you choke

when she got him to admit what he was eating and where he'd got the food. Having drawn a blank with his partner, Rhys decided he might as well check in.

He spoke to Catrin to find out how contacting the remaining waifs and strays – the motorists brought into the Cawdor on the night of the frozen rain – was going. She sounded a bit off when he mentioned the photographer, Hunt, so he'd offered to do the last one, the deputy head-teacher, since he was there on the spot.

However, Gil, overhearing where Rhys was, grabbed the phone and told him about Gatch and that he might well score significant numbers of brownie points were he to take the initiative and have a sniff around the town for said miscreant. Gil relayed Gatch's description.

After at first disbelieving him, the forwarded image of the aforementioned, via the wonders of 4G, triggered a classic Rhys response. 'Blimey, not many of those to the pound in Llandeilo.'

Gatch's most recent police photograph was a fair reflection of how he'd looked to the Uniforms who'd glimpsed him outside the Co-op before he'd run off. Like Lizard, he had his hair plaited and pulled back from his face in a kind of rattling ponytail. He didn't quite have as many piercings as Lizard, but the number came a close second. Add to that the full Gandalf beard and it was not a face you'd forget.

'Keep your eyes open and not on that sticky bun in your hand.'

Rhys, flummoxed, asked, 'How do you know—'

'Sixth sense. Or maybe something to do with the fact

you've been chewing all the way through this conversation. It's been like talking to a bloody horse.'

'Actually, sarge, it's a sausage roll. Haven't started on the bun yet.' Rhys's tone was smug.

Gil was having none of it. 'Since I know you can walk and eat at the same time, as it is your default mode, go see Mrs Roach, and then find DCI Warlow. He's also in the hunt over there, somewhere. Go on, clippity clop.'

Rhys put the phone away, munched the last mouthful of his sausage roll, scrunched up the packet and deposited it in a convenient bin. Like the good DC he was, he deferred further gratification by pocketing the iced buns for later and turned downhill towards the school.

Luck was always in short supply in cases of murder, but for once, Rhys ran into some at that moment. As he crossed the lane known as Bank Buildings and looked down the hill towards where the school and Mrs Roach were, he spotted someone running across the street at the crossroads, linking Crescent Road with New Road. No one in a multicoloured coat. But you could take coats off. What you couldn't do was shave off your Viking-style braided hair with bits of cloth woven into them, or your long beard.

The guy was only seventy yards away and had eyes only for where he was going. And he was going there in a hurry.

Rhys shelved all thoughts of Mrs Roach and ran across the road, stepped around someone dressed as Santa selling the Big Issue, and through the little tunnel between the butcher's and the pharmacy towards the town car park. If he put a sprint on, he reckoned he could intercept Gatch the Viking before he reached the Civic Hall.

CHAPTER TWENTY-FIVE

'RIGHT, MR… LIZARD.' Gil looked up at the man opposite him in the interview room and found it difficult to focus. Mainly because there was quite a lot going on, what with the piercings and the bat tattoo on his left cheek. 'That is how you want us to address you, right?'

'Changed my name by deed poll 2018,' Lizard said.

'As you do.' Gil smiled.

'From Lawrence Dixon,' Jess said, reading from the sheet on the desk in front of her. She looked up into Lizard's face and managed, unlike Gil, to retain eye contact. An action which unnerved Lizard.

'It's the way I feel inside,' he said.

'Like wanting to sun yourself on rocks?' Gil asked.

The duty solicitor, a tired-looking man called Paul Pilgrim, did not shift his gaze up from writing in his note-book. Though Gil thought he detected a muscle twitch somewhere at the corner of his mouth.

'Why am I even here?' Lizard demanded in a strident voice that, Gil had concluded already, was the only one he ever used.

'You're here because you were aiding a thief and

attempted to drive away from the scene of a robbery.' Jess kept her voice even.

'Bollocks,' Lizard said, or rather ejected, a bit like an over enthusiastic Jack-in-the-box. 'Gatch left the kitty box in the car. He was coming out to fetch it.'

'Very commendable,' Gil said with a slow nod. 'Only most people would've left the unpaid four items at the till and then fetched their forgotten kitty box, or wallet if they were over five years old, not bring the goods out of the shop with them.'

'Easily done, though,' Lizard said. He delivered the words animatedly. In fact, animated described his whole demeanour and posture. The man could not sit still. A twitcher, and not the type associated with watching birds.

'Easily done if you're a thief, I agree,' Gil said.

'What I want to know is why you lot were there. Why are you harassing me?'

'Asking you to answer questions pertinent to an enquiry is not harassment… Lizard,' Jess said.

Gil heard the tiny hesitation before Jess spoke the ludicrous name.

'Oh? And why is that, then? Is it because I don't choose to live like you lot? Tied down to a nine-to-five treadmill. Toeing the corporate line. Consuming resources we don't have. You need to wake up, like all the rest of the sheep. Capitalism is strangling the entire world. Just because I can see the truth…'

'There is that,' Gil said. 'Or we may be interested in you because a murdered man had threatened you by turning up toting guns and, on the day that his office was burgled, the camper van you were driving today was seen in the vicinity.'

Lizard floundered. 'What… burgled? The fuck you talking about?'

'Were you, or were you not, in Llandeilo on Monday afternoon, Mr Lizard?' Jess asked.

'It's not Mr Lizard, just Lizard. I know I... oh shit... yeah, we popped in. Dawnsong – that's Gatch's kid – she went to a birthday thing and we, me and Gatch, we came in to fetch her. But not to fucking burglarise anywhere.'

Neither Jess nor Gil could find it in them to comment on Dawnsong, though it had registered in that part of their brains that asked, why? Jess recovered first. 'Why did Gatch bolt when he saw the police, Lizard?'

Lizard guffawed exuberantly. 'Why do you think? Because he knows you lot will try to fit us up for anything. Like burglary.'

'Or theft,' Gil said as an airy suggestion. 'If by fitting up you mean catching someone with stolen goods in their possession running out of a shop?'

'I told you; honest mistake. Jesus.'

'Right.' Gil leaned forward. 'Monday afternoon, what time? When? And what did you do?'

Lizard looked at Pilgrim, who shrugged, clearly wishing he could be somewhere else. Lizard's leg bounced up and down as if attached to a piece of elastic on the ceiling. 'No effing comment.'

'Is that with one f or two?' Gil asked.

———

Rhys arrived at the Crescent Road entrance of the town car park after sprinting across it. But when he looked in the direction he expected Gatch the Viking to approach from, he saw no sign.

'Shit.' This meant that Gatch must've veered off somewhere. Rhys called up a map on his phone. The man must've taken the turning to Latimer Road that led to a small warren of streets all leading down to the station. The quickest way down was the steps leading to the station plat-form. However, the smart way would have been along the streets where you could duck behind a car or a van if you thought you were being followed.

Rhys chose the second option. As he hurried down Latimer Road, he called up DCI Warlow on the phone.

'Hello, sir. It's me.'

'I know. This is a video call, Rhys.'

'What?' Rhys looked at his phone. 'No, it isn't, sir.'

'Got you there. You're back from your day out, then?'

'I am, sir. Lots to tell you, but I am in hot pursuit of a wanted man called Gatch.'

'What?'

'Yes, sir. Sergeant Jones filled me in. I spotted him, Gatch, not Sergeant Jones, heading up Crescent Road. But he veered off course. My guess is he is heading down towards the railway and the river.'

'Good. I'm down in that neck of the woods in the same hunt.'

'I'll call if I see anything, sir.' Rhys cancelled the call and looked again at his little street map. Latimer Road led to Alan Road. But you could double back along Clarendon Road to Stepney Road.

'Shit,' Rhys muttered again, trying to work out the best option.

Once more, he trusted to instinct. Doubling back was what he would have done if someone had been pursuing him. As he joined the cut through to Stepney Road, he spotted a mane of braided hair turning back into Alan Road. But Gatch happened to glance back in Rhys's direction.

'Oy. Police,' Rhys yelled.

Too late. Gatch panicked. There could not have been more than thirty or forty yards between them, but the guy with the long hair had the advantage. By the time Rhys got to the top of the stairs leading down to the station, Gatch had disappeared.

'Shit,' Rhys said again on the empty steps.

His map told him that Clarendon Road ran down to Station Road. He took this, jogging down past a biggish building and getting to the end of a short drive that ended with a gate.

A gate? On a street?

He looked at his map again. Clarendon Road seemed to be split in two by properties and gardens.

'What the hell?' He turned and jogged back up to where the road became the entrance to the property. On his right was a slight uphill lane, unnamed on the street map. He jogged up an incline to see that it led to an alley backing on to the houses on both sides. Rhys ran, staring down to his right for a glimpse of anyone, but finding it all obscured by houses and gardens. He emerged on Blende Road and a ten-yard run to Station Road itself.

The rail unions, in their wisdom, had seen fit to call a strike for the three days before Christmas. Rhys was not a political person, but all he knew was that sympathy from people desperate to get home for the holidays was running low. Both for the unions and the government who, though not directly employers of striking workers in what was a privatised industry, had too much sway in fares and determining service levels in a rail monopoly, to pretend it had nothing to do with them.

But that meant the stations today would be empty of passengers. Therefore, someone looking like Gatch should be easy to spot on two open platforms, if indeed that was where he had gone. Ahead of Rhys as he walked towards the railway was a builder's merchant's storage yard. Beyond that, the eastern foothills of the Towy Valley rolled and dipped. If Gatch got over the river and headed in that direction, he might take days to find.

Rhys had a choice: left, back towards the town, passing the Jones brother's bus depot, or right towards the station and the bridge across the river.

And where the hell was Warlow when a decision needed to be made?

Rhys opted right and started jogging towards the station. Once he did, a figure emerged from behind a little joinery factory and sprinted towards the barriers leading to the open railway crossing. Some dog walkers, a mother and two kids with a brown Labradoodle, yelled in shock as Gatch sprinted past them.

Rhys turned on the afterburners, but Gatch was well over the railway line and heading towards the river by the time the DC got to the barrier and around it. He was halfway across when he heard the sharp crack of wood splintering, followed by a yelp of surprise and a deep groan. On the other side of the railway, a muddy path led to a kissing gate at the swing bridge over the River Towy. Twenty yards along the path, Rhys skidded to a halt when he came across Gatch spreadeagled on the floor and a satisfied-looking Warlow standing over him.

'Gatch has tripped, DC Harries. Better check him over. After you put some handcuffs on him, that is.'

'Right place, right time, sir?' Rhys said, stooping over the fallen man.

'You can't do this,' Gatch muttered.

'I think you'll find we can. You're nicked, sunshine,' Warlow said.

'For what?'

'Stealing for a start. I'm sure we'll find a few other things to tack on once we go through your pock—' Warlow never finished because a scream of horror cut him off. A woman's voice, full-throated and raw with anguish.

'What the hell is that?'

'Sounds like it's coming from the station, sir,' Rhys said.

'Okay, call it in, get him up on his feet and frogmarch him back to the Uniforms. I'm going over to see what the fuss is about.'

————

THE FUSS WAS COMING from the family with the Labradoodle. They were at the top of the steps and fifteen feet above the station platform, where it turned at right angles to become a cobbled path leading up to the bit of Clarendon Road where Rhys had got lost.

Warlow hurried. The woman with the dog had her arms around both children, staring down at Warlow, her face sheet-white with shock. The dog stood at her knees, reading the emotion, confused by the noises coming from the woman and children.

'You okay there?' Warlow asked.

'Someone's fallen. Someone's fallen on the platform.' The woman's voice was more a wail than a sentence.

'Where?'

'Down…' The woman hadn't moved. 'William looked over and… he's down on the other side of where we are.'

'Okay. Come back down and stay over where the cars are.' Warlow took out his wallet and showed his warrant card. 'I'm a police officer. Let me have a look and I'll come back to you, I promise.' Warlow waved for them to come down. The children were crying. The woman was shaking. He helped them along the low barrier and put them to stand where it was safe. Then he walked along the deserted platform, open to the elements, except for a small area no bigger than a bus shelter where people could shelter.

Freeze maybe, but at least covered by a canopy.

Just beyond the steps was a grey structure. A large rectangular box that contained something vital for the signals or the trains. But between it and the supporting wall of the steps was a narrow gap. And in that gap, unmoving, lay the body of a man.

Warlow hurried over. The man was unconscious and barely breathing. Blood had pooled around his head.

'Hello? Can you hear me?'

No response. Warlow felt for a pulse in the neck. There but thready. However, Warlow sensed something familiar about the round face, half obscured by the blood oozing from a cut on the forehead. He glanced up to the parapet where the woman and the children had been a moment before. Had this man fallen? It wasn't a great height, but it didn't need to be if you fell head-first. He wore a padded jacket and jeans. Not wanting to risk too much movement, Warlow felt for, and found, a wallet in the jeans' back pocket. He teased it out, using his coat sleeve as a makeshift glove. Inside were cash, cards, and, yes, a driving licence. He read the name. Hughes. Of course. He had met this man before in the Cawdor Hotel. But knowing who he was did not help in the slightest explaining what the hell he was doing poleaxed down here.

But then he remembered someone saying that there was a bakery down here somewhere.

Warlow said, not expecting an answer. 'Is that why you're down here, Mr Hughes the Baker? Were you on the way to work? Or was someone waiting for you on the stairs?'

CHAPTER TWENTY-SIX

ANOTHER CIRCUS, this time at the train station.

Once the paramedics had taken Hughes off to West Wales General Hospital, Tannard, as the nearest CSI, set up shop on the northbound platform. The rail network was offering a replacement bus service to all points north as far as Craven Arms, with a pickup point in the station car park. Warlow posted a Uniform at the far end of Station Road to intercept the buses and any likely passengers.

Uniforms took Gatch to HQ and Warlow phoned everything through to Jess to give her a heads up he was on his way.

'If he's anything like Lizard, he won't be saying much,' she said on hearing of his arrest.

'Well, I doubt he'll be singing Christmas carols, but neither will he be pulling crackers with his other SJW gang members unless he sings a song we all like hearing. He might have kids.'

'Kid. Dawnsong,' Jess said.

'I beg your pardon?'

'That's his kid's name,' Jess explained.

After a moment's silence while he contemplated this,

Warlow mumbled, 'Well, kids are excellent leverage at this time of year.'

'True. Gil and I will have a chat. What about you and Rhys?'

'Rhys has gone over to talk to Hughes's staff at the bakery. I'll hang about until Tannard has screened the scene since this is where the action is. I'll keep in touch.'

'You do remember it's CID's Christmas bash tonight. At The Black Swan in town.'

'Oh, God. I'd forgotten.'

'You won't get away with that excuse. Not now I've reminded you. I'm calling in after work. If I don't, Lily from downstairs will have my guts for garters. She's already reminded me at least half a dozen times. And made me promise to remind you and the others. I'm only showing my face for half an hour.'

Warlow sighed. Lily was a superintendent's secretary of long-standing and a self-appointed social secretary for all things bash-related. 'I suppose it's a necessary evil. What time?'

'From 5.30. I expect the karaoke will be in full swing by the time I get there. What's your go-to tune again?'

'Hmm, maybe something from the 80s. Whatever I choose usually goes down like a lead balloon. Or 99 of them.'

'OMG, as Mol would say.'

'It's the Gil effect. Don't ask him about karaoke, for God's sake.'

'I already have. His answer, of course, was that he prefers to sing in a group and usually REM songs. He then pretended to show me a photo from last year of five people sat at a table and said, "That's me in the corner". I should have known.'

Warlow chortled quietly. 'I'm a bit like you. Not my cup of tea, but if I don't appear, my name is mud.'

Jess rang off. Rhys returned, and they walked across to join Tannard on the steps leading up from the platform.

'No witnesses?' Warlow asked the DC as they crossed the car park.

'No, sir. No trains running today. Apart from dog walkers, this place is deserted.'

'Did you speak to the staff at the bakery?'

Rhys flipped up on the page of his notebook. 'Umm, according to them, Hughes seemed a bit hyper this morning. At least that's what the secretary thought. He left earlier than usual to get coffee.'

'What time?'

'No one saw him in either coffee shop and he left the office at just around 10.15.'

'Then this took place between 10.15 and 10.45. Not long before you rang me and Gatch came haring around the corner when you flushed him out.' Warlow pointed up.

'You don't think that he did this, sir?'

'He was in the area.'

'But I saw him come from the other direction.'

'Maybe this was opportunistic. Maybe he saw Hughes, lost it, went for him and then realised what he'd done and buggered off back into town in panic.'

Rhys nodded. But with little conviction.

'Let's see what Gil and Jess get out of him.' Warlow joined Tannard at the steps. She beckoned them up to the point where the woman and her son had peeped over the parapet.

'Anything?' Warlow asked.

'We're gathering evidence. There isn't much, but there are some blue threads here at the edge of the wall. Have a look.' She had a camera in her hand. A big one with a digital display screen. The image it showed was of the weathered coping stone she stood next to. Tannard enlarged the image to show Warlow a group of small blue threads caught on an outcrop on the stone.

'We'll need to check if it matches Hughes's jacket.'

'If it does?' Rhys asked.

'If it does, then it looks as if this was a push,' Tannard said. 'Not a long way to fall, but then it doesn't have to be if you land head-first.'

'Christ.' Warlow spoke for them all.

———

JESS SUGGESTED that Catrin sit in with her for the Gatch interview. All three of the team still at HQ stood in the observation room watching the suspect toy with a plastic cup of water while he waited.

'I didn't realise they came in twos,' Jess said. 'It must be a vibe.'

'Scruffy Viking eco-warrior,' Catrin muttered.

'What's his actual name?' Jess asked.

'Andrew Gachot.'

'French?'

'Father,' Gil explained. 'Andrew is from Guildford.'

'Right.' Jess gathered herself. 'Let's see what he has to say for himself.'

She and Catrin walked the few yards to the interview room and opened the door. A different solicitor sat in with Gatch. But she had the same wish-I-was-somewhere-else expression on her face as Pilgrim had in the other interview room.

Catrin took the lead and made the introductions, repeating all the right words as required by PACE. When all that was done, Jess began with a gentle opener.

'Andrew, or would you prefer Gatch?'

'Andrew is fine,' he said. 'Only Liz calls me Gatch. He likes the company.'

'Okay, Andrew. Did you, or did you not have any contact with Daniel Hughes today?'

'Who?'

Jess decided to be direct to assess how he'd respond to Hughes's name.

'Do you know Daniel Hughes, Andrew?'

'Hughes? Who is he?'

Jess sat back, happy that the name had been firmly planted in Andrew Gachot's head.

'What were you doing in Llandeilo this morning, Andrew?' Catrin asked.

'Right, yeah, I need to explain all that. Me and Liz came in to bring Dawny to school. It's Christmas, so I thought we'd surprise the girls with some wine. Be good on Christmas Day to have a drop of wine.'

Jess waited. Already she'd worked out that Andrew was a very different specimen from Lizard. They'd called up his records. No history of theft or threatening behaviour, but a conviction for aggravated trespass over an HS2 protest site in Buckinghamshire and criminal damage for painting a sign on a bridge. Andrew Gachot, unlike Lizard, grew up in a middle-class family and attended a private school.

'So, why did you steal three bottles?' Catrin asked.

'I didn't steal them. I left my cash in the van. I only had a tenner, so I gave him that and said I'd get the rest in like two minutes. I swear it was just a mistake.'

'So, why did you run?' Catrin asked.

'You lot were with Liz, man. I knew you'd been up at the site. We thought you'd try to split us up. Take the van. Starve us out.'

Jess wasn't having it. 'What, like a siege? This isn't the Middle Ages, for God's sake.'

'I wouldn't put it past you. When I was at HS2, up in Leekston Woods, they infiltrated the camp. Sent in a woman as a mole. Eight months she was with us. You lot are capable of anything.'

'So, where are the bottles of wine now?' Catrin asked.

'I stashed them. I can get them back to the shop anytime. And I will. I was on the way to do that when two of your lot attacked me.'

'You mean caught a thief who was running away?'

'I'm not a thief!'

'But you were down near the train station in Llandelio?'

Andrew looked confused. 'That's where I hid the bottles. I'd been back into town to do a recce. Still lots of your lot around. What's going on? Is it because of Moyles?'

'What do you know about Royston Moyles?'

'That he was an arsehole that liked to scare people.'

'Let's get back to Daniel Hughes.'

Andrew frowned. 'I know the name.'

'He owns the bakery,' Catrin said.

Andrew's eyes lit up. 'Right. Hughes Bakery. Yeah, that's the place down on Station Road. I've seen him about. A bit too fond of his own apple turnovers if you ask me. But we've bought his bread. Not bad. Why?'

'Mr Hughes was found on the station platform this morning. We think he may have been attacked. At about the same time as you were in the area.'

Andrew blinked several times at this. 'No, wait. This is crazy. I'm sorry about the wine, okay? I can get the bottles. We have the money. You can ask Liz. I didn't attack anyone. I don't know this bloke, Hughes.'

'But you knew Moyles?'

'Moyles? What this got to do with...' Andrew froze as his mind clued in to what Catrin had said. 'Moyles is definitely dead then?'

'Mr Moyles was found dead on Monday, yes. But we are treating his death as suspicious.'

Andrew sat forward. He looked on the verge of passing out. 'Wha... why am I... Jesus... you believe I have something to do with... oh Jesus. I'm going to be sick.'

To be fair to Andrew, he was as good as his word. He half turned, thankfully away from the dry solicitor, and deposited, in a spattering retch, whatever it was he'd had for breakfast that morning – oats by the look of it – over the laminate flooring.

Both Jess and Catrin pushed back with a scrape of chairs in a reflex movement.

'Shit... shit.' Andrew gasped in a trembling voice, hunched over in his chair.

'Stay where you are, Andrew,' Catrin ordered. 'We'll get someone to take you back to your cell.'

Pale and sweaty, with dribbles of vomit over his chin and running out of one nostril, Andrew looked up, breathing through his mouth. 'I haven't done anything to anyone. It's not my way. I don't do violence...' He shook his head before letting it drop low between his knees.

Jess led the way out, the duty solicitor almost falling over herself as she followed. 'I hate the smell of vomit,' she said, looking pale herself and rushing for the loo.

Gil said from the end of the corridor. 'It's like an episode of *The Last of Us*.'

'Can you get someone to clean that up?'

'Yeah, the sick squad is on the way.' Gil held two thumbs up. 'One way of getting out of answering questions.'

'Seemed pretty genuine to me.' Catrin pursed her lips.

'Not the same animal as old Lizard, that's for sure,' Jess said.

CHAPTER TWENTY-SEVEN

JOHN NAPIER'S SECRETARY, Caroline, took the call from his wife at five minutes to five that Thursday afternoon. No, Caroline hadn't seen him since he'd left that morning. He'd picked up a letter and she'd assumed he'd gone for one of his extended coffee breaks. He'd mentioned something about Dan Hughes wanting to meet. But no, she doubted they'd have gone to the pub that early, nor stayed there all afternoon. But yes, she was happy to call in the café and The Farmer's snug on her way home just to check.

Caroline put the phone down and paused. Bad enough having the police upstairs all yesterday and today, tramping about up and down the fire escape, taking photographs and with their vans and cars parked right outside the door.

It was unnerving, to say the least. And the very last thing she wanted to do tonight was call in a pub. Lots of people were taking the Friday off, or taking half days, which meant that the pubs would fill up early with people finishing work. But Olwen Napier had been insistent. Her sister was over from Australia and they had a big night planned. John had promised to be home mid-afternoon but both his secretary and his wife knew that sometimes work, or the booze, especially at Christmas time, could distract him and he would lose track of time.

Caroline had planned on coming in tomorrow for a half day, clocking off promptly at midday to get things sorted out at home. She was expecting her son and his wife down from Cardiff and wanted to get things right.

Napier had no clients booked, but paperwork needed to be sorted before the beginning of the next working week. At ten to five, she locked up and walked along King Street toward the brightly lit Rhosmaen Street, past the lit-up town Christmas tree next to the cemetery.

Most of the shops had made an effort for the holidays, so it was quite a cheery little stroll with more people than usual trying to find last-minute presents in the galleries or stocking fillers from Peppercorn or Toast. The Café Braz stayed open until five-thirty. But when she called and asked, no one had seen John Napier that day. Not even for coffee at midmorning.

That was odd. Her boss was very much a creature of habit. He had his little ways, especially with the local landowners and businesspeople, many of whom were his clients. He always bought them something for Christmas. A bottle of whisky for the men, some perfume, or toiletries for the women. He was a man who liked to keep everyone's cap straight, as he so often said. She understood that. But Caroline didn't like the way he sometimes made fun of these people once they'd left the office, after he'd chatted them up and oozed false bonhomie face to face. He seemed happy enough to take their money for revisiting their wills, at a hefty fee, or sorting out trust funds for their kids, at an even heftier one. She found it rude and disdainful. And she felt equally uncomfortable when he always suggested himself an executor, just to make sure all went smoothly for those left behind.

Of course, none of that would be done for free.

The Farmer's Arms was, as expected, busy. This was not a pub that Caroline frequented. In fact, she hadn't been in here for years. And it didn't look like much had changed since she'd been there last. But she knew about the snug. And this afternoon, it contained four people, not one of whom was John Napier.

'And he hasn't been in lunchtime for a quick one, either?' Caroline asked the landlady.

'No, *cariad*. Not today. To be honest, I wasn't expecting him, not after what's happened.'

Caroline paused. 'Why? What's happened?'

'Surely, you've heard about Dan Hughes. Awful, it is. They say he fell off the steps down by the station. The ones on Clarendon Road.'

Caroline knew the steps, of course she did. But she could not quite envisage someone falling off them. 'Was it icy? Is that what's happened?'

'No one knows, but there are loads of police down there. Someone said he might have been attacked.'

'Attacked?'

'Hard to believe, isn't it? Especially after what happened to Royston Moyles. Don't know what the bloody place is coming to. Not safe to step outside your door.'

That shook Caroline. First Moyles. Now Daniel Hughes. Outside the pub, she drew her coat about her and looked up at the thinning crowds. The shops would all shut soon. Then there would be a change. A shift in the town's atmosphere. A switch from the sleepy little town where people came to wander around and eat ice cream and buy artisan chocolate and pottery and paintings, to a nighttime venue for people to come and drink and eat. And at this time of year, drinking overtook the eating by a long chalk.

The town could become rowdy, especially around closing time.

But it was also an old town. One with dark spaces and

alleys. Old stables and hostelries where drovers once lodged. Little cut-throughs that hardly anyone walked along, even in daylight. Cul-de-sacs that even Caroline had to research when an address came across her desk. She didn't fancy walking along one of those much later than six pm.

Outside the pub, night had thrown its cloak over the town. Traffic was easing. The cold, damp air sucked the heat from her hands. She'd ring Mrs Napier when she got home.

But not now.

Not yet.

First, she wanted to get in from the dark. Especially after what she'd heard from the landlady of The Farmer's.

———

WARLOW GOT to The Black Swan at 6.30. Or, as Gil would no doubt have said, just after half past merry and a quarter to silly. But there was still a good couple of hours to go till carnage. If he was asked to put money on it, the table in the corner, the one playing drinking games already, would be the first to descend into the depths.

He found Jess and Catrin sitting in an opposite corner at a table with Rhys and Gina.

'Welcome to the madhouse,' Jess said as a roar erupted from the drinking corner and a female officer that Warlow recognised from traffic stood up and promptly downed half a pint of amber liquid without it touching the sides.

'Gil not here?' Warlow flicked his gaze around, searching for the big sergeant.

'Been and gone, sir,' Rhys said. 'Schools aren't breaking up until tomorrow. Very late this year, he said. Last school concert of the season.'

'Another one?' Warlow asked. 'He should become a newspaper critic.'

'He's that already, sir,' Catrin muttered in a low voice. 'A critic anyway.'

Another roar from the drinkers brought a wry smile to Warlow's lips. 'Looks like things are warming up.'

'That's one way of putting it,' Jess said.

'How's the baker, sir?' Catrin asked.

Warlow glowered. 'Bad. In a coma and on his way to Morriston Hospital, if he isn't there already.'

The team looked suitably shocked. 'So, not much chance of an interview, then, sir?' Rhys asked.

Warlow clamped his lips shut by way of an answer.

Catrin stood up. 'Can I get you a drink, sir?'

Warlow waved her down. 'I'm on my feet. Can I refill anyone?' He glanced at the table. Everyone, bar Rhys, had clear liquid in their glasses and he surmised from that they were all on soft drinks. All except Rhys, who had a bottle of Corona in front of him.

'Maximum of three, sir,' Rhys said by way of an unnecessary explanation. 'Gina's driving.'

'As usual,' Gina said, pretending to complain. Rhys took the bait.

'I did offer,' he said.

The party had taken over a function-room in the pub. A room with its own bar that was way too small to accommodate the alcohol requirements of the group of Dyfed Powys's finest there that evening. Warlow took ten minutes to get his half of lager and spoke to a dozen people in so doing. By the time he got back to the others, music had started up and the brave, or foolhardy, first karaoke artist of the evening had chosen an old favourite to start things off as he launched into *Sweet Caroline*. Rhys was swaying in his chair in time to the song. Gina, with an indulgent smile, shook her head.

'I love this one, sir.' Rhys grinned.

'Not only you, by the look of things.'

The drinking games table had all responded to the call and piled into the space in front of the singer, waiting for the chorus, ready to wave their arms and join in to what had become a bit of an anthem. And when it came, chaos struck. One officer, who was almost as tall as Rhys, threw an arm up and struck a dangling Santa attached to the ceiling via a string of lights which promptly clattered to the floor.

Someone shouted for the music to stop. In a different corner, a group began a loud version of a police siren and half a dozen others followed.

From behind the bar, a man in a Black Swan polo shirt emerged and reached for a stool. He scooped up the Santa and the lights, placed the stool under where they'd fallen and then folded out some steps from within the stool, clambered up them and reattached the decorations. He stepped down, folded back the steps and, to huge applause, took a bow before going back behind the bar.

'Not much of a stripper was he,' Catrin said as *Sweet Caroline* started up for the second time.

Jess stood up and picked up her drink. 'Right, I'm going to mingle so that my face is seen and then I'm off home. What about you, Evan?'

'Right,' Warlow said. Or rather muttered with his eyes fixed firmly on the repositioned, dangling Santa.

'Evan?' Jess said, following his gaze. 'I know that look. What is it?'

'That stool the barman used. There's one just like it in Moyles's office. Charlie Brewer said they used it as a storage rack.'

'Looks more like a stepladder to me,' Jess said.

'Exactly,' Warlow whispered and glanced at his watch. 'I could be in Llandelio in fifteen minutes. Rhys, see if you can get hold of Tannard. She might still be there at the train station. She was when I left. Ask her to meet me in Moyles's office. And see if Gil wants an escape from the concert. He can meet me there, too.'

Rhys stood up and reached for his phone. 'Want me to come, sir?'

'No,' Warlow said, looking at each of the team. 'You lot stay here and… have a good time.' The glint in his eye as he emphasised "good time" twinkled brighter than the fairy lights on the tree in the corner.

'Evan?' Jess asked, as if she was addressing a naughty ten-year-old.

'Something or nothing. Certainly not worth dragging you lot away from… this.'

'I wouldn't mind,' Catrin muttered.

'No, I'm going.' The DCI took one sip of his drink and put it down on the table. 'I need to scratch an itch. Otherwise, I won't sleep. I don't need to tell you I'd like to be wheels up by eight tomorrow.' He took one last, slow look around, smiled and said, 'Otherwise, you lot enjoy!'

As he walked away, and still smiling to himself, he heard Rhys ask, 'I think he's secretly glad he got an itch.'

'You better believe it,' Jess said.

And though he didn't turn around to confirm it, he could guess that Jess had delivered that last sentence with her eyes narrowed in suspicion.

CHAPTER TWENTY-EIGHT

TANNARD STOOD OUTSIDE Napier's office in her puffer jacket as Warlow walked up from where he'd parked outside the church.

'Don't say it,' Warlow said as she watched him approach. 'And I'm apologising already if this all proves to be a waste of time. Especially to you, as I'm sure you've got a home to go to.'

'I do. But you rarely get a chance to work on a case like this. Good for the CV.'

'You're not leaving us, are you?'

'No. But never say never.'

'Christ, what it is to be young. I read somewhere that people these days move jobs every five years.'

Tannard had a hat on against the cold and the furry bobble on the top wobbled as she turned to accompany Warlow in through the alleyway to the fire escape at the back of the building.

'I'm afraid I'm more of a dinosaur,' Warlow said. 'Here for the duration and probably well past my sell-by date and heading for extinction.'

'I doubt that,' Tannard said. 'Oh, and I've been up and

unlocked the door.'

She walked on, her feet clanking on the metal treads as she climbed. Warlow followed, pushing aside a wafting piece of the police tape no one had bothered to remove from a balustrade, until he stood once again on the threshold of the room which looked a great deal tidier.

'Brewer been cleaning up, I see.'

'Yes, well, we thought we'd finished here.' Tannard's tone was dry, bordering on Saharan.

She flicked on a light. Everything was back in its place, or at least Warlow assumed it was since he'd never seen this room before the burglary. But his focus zeroed in on the stool, now upright with the "steps" pulled out as shelves holding a fresh pot plant to replace the broken one, an air freshener, and on the stool seat, some books that looked like they might not be a permanent fixture. He walked across to the stool and then peered at the ceiling. Plain except for a central light fixture that looked too modern and slim to house anything other than the electrics.

'Damn,' he said.

Tannard followed his gaze. 'Are you looking for a ceiling space?'

'I was. But there's nothing here.'

Warlow walked around the room. There was nothing suggesting the need for a step up. No tall shelves or cupboards that might need a ladder to access.

'Ah well,' he said.

A shadow appeared in the doorway. Tannard looked up to see Gil, a little out of breath, standing there.

'That sounded like a sigh of defeat.' Gil wheezed out the words. 'Does that mean I missed all the fun?'

'You've missed bugger all. I had a brainwave but…'

'The DCI wondered why they had a stool with stepladder capabilities,' Tannard explained.

'I thought maybe there'd be an attic or a roof space in here,' Warlow added.

'But there isn't,' Tannard said.

'No,' Gil agreed. 'But there is on the landing that goes down to Napier's office.'

Warlow's head shot up. 'What?'

'Yes. Outside the door that leads down. They use the landing for storage. Files, spare copy paper, but there's a small square space above a grey caretaker's cabinet full of cleaning materials.'

'Show us,' Warlow said.

Gil crossed the room to the door that led down to Napier's office. Warlow had stuck his head in but never been through it. Just as Gil had described, a small landing of forty-square foot led to the stairs. But on the left of the door, the wall space was occupied by the grey cupboard and stacked reams of paper and office materials. And there, above the grey metal cupboard, was a small recess in the ceiling framed in white-painted wood. Impossible to reach because of the cupboard, even if you were tall enough.

Gil came through carrying the stool. He unfurled the steps and placed it next to the cupboard. Tannard supplied a torch and Warlow stood on the steps. He had to get to the very top to lean forward enough over the top of the cupboard to reach the ceiling access. He pushed up, and the panel lifted. Shifting it to one side, he put his head through. Cursed, pulled his head out, and then fiddled with his phone to get the torch working. There was not much room. He would struggle to get a shoulder through. But as he scanned the tiny little roof space, he realised he wouldn't need to. Not to reach the black box that sat next to a plastic yoghurt carton within easy reach. He took three quick snaps before looking down at the other two.

'Something there, isn't there?' Gil asked.

By then Warlow was clambering down, hardly believing how difficult it was to keep his balance. It was a bloody awkward spot.

But, he mused, that was probably deliberate.

'What did you see?' Tannard asked.

'Not sure. But I took some photos.' He swiped over the phone's screen and found the last image and enlarged it with his fingers so that she and Gil could see.

From Gil's mouth, came a whispered, 'Oh, Christ.'

Warlow didn't have time to ask him what he meant by it because Tannard was already speaking. 'That looks like a portable hard drive. Yes, I can just see a name on it, World-mem. See it?'

But Warlow's eyes were on the yoghurt pot. Light from the camera flash had reflected off its surface, but it didn't matter because lying on the sheet of hardwood that was being used as a base for both pot and box was a single black USB stick.

'Looks like we found where Moyles kept his trophies,' Gil said.

'It does,' Warlow agreed.

He looked up at Tannard, who shrugged. 'Well, better tonight than tomorrow night, that's all I can say.'

CHAPTER TWENTY-NINE

On Friday as Warlow walked into the Incident Room with a loud and cheery, 'Merry Christmas,' he looked up at the assembled officers and secretaries and noted at least half a dozen people wincing. They'd be the ones who had not had the sense to leave The Black Swan before five past carnage and who were now paying the piper.

He saw no wincing on the faces of his team. And he expected nothing less. He didn't even bother sitting down. The team were up to speed on what had been found at Moyles's office last night. But it would do no harm to have a quick recap.

'Gil, what news on the hard drive?'

'Tannard is cloning it as we speak. It will take longer to go through all the individual thumb drives, but once they've copied everything from the hard drive, they'll let us have a look at it. I'm expecting her within the hour.'

'All thanks to a fallen Santa,' Jess said with a grin.

'You take your wins where you can in this game,' Warlow said. 'Charlie Brewer in yet?'

Rhys answered, 'Uniforms have picked him up, sir, so he should be here shortly.'

'Good. So, it'll be you and me doing the honours with Mr Brewer,' Warlow said. 'Meantime, someone have a comb through his social media. You never know. That just leaves our two eco-warriors.'

Catrin glanced at Jess, who nodded for her to respond. 'We had a long chat with them yesterday, sir. Andrew Gachot, Gatch, threw up on hearing what he was here for.'

'I take it neither of you think he's likely for the killing?'

Jess wrinkled her nose.

'What about Lizard?'

'He's full of piss and vinegar.' Jess's mouth sagged in disapproval. 'Plus, he has an alibi for the time that Moyles was killed.'

'From his fellow protesters?' Warlow asked.

'Yup,' Jess said.

Catrin stood up. 'There's also a witness, a dog walker, who says he saw someone at the bottom of the steps at the station at around the time Daniel Hughes fell or was pushed. Someone dressed in black. Bobble hat, ski mask, the works.'

'At the time of the incident?' Warlow asked. 'I don't remember seeing anyone like that.'

'Weren't you across the swing bridge?'

'Come to think of it, yes.'

'I don't remember anyone either,' Rhys said with a frown.

'It had already happened by the time you got to the top of the steps,' Warlow said. 'Plus, you would not have been able to see Hughes on the station from where you were.'

'A man in black,' Gil muttered.

Warlow considered the new images of the station steps

that were now pinned to the Gallery. 'OK. Our eco-warrior is not a prime suspect in the Hughes attack and unlikely for Moyles, then. It doesn't make much sense that Gatch would be heading back towards where he'd just thrown someone off some steps. What about the break in at the office?'

'They do not deny being in Llandeilo, sir,' Catrin said. 'But apart from simply causing a nuisance, what would be their reason for ransacking Moyles's office?'

'Didn't Brewer say they took a computer? Easily sold, sir,' Rhys said.

'They are,' Warlow agreed, but with little conviction. 'Lizard and Gatch may be many things, but they do not strike me as junkies.'

'What about this story about the theft of wine?' Gil looked from Jess to Catrin. 'Is that believable?'

'Daft as it sounds, these two live by their own code. I suspect they would have paid up,' Jess said.

'There is also the fact that we have effectively removed all forms of transport for the protesters,' Catrin said.

'And there are kids up at that site. It is Christmas…' Gil dangled the observation.

'Right, I get the message. I'm no Scrooge. We need written statements from both, but then they can go with a warning that we may need to question them further, and if we do, I do not want to be chasing them all over the town. And tell them to stop off at the Co-op and pay what they owe. Warn the manager and make sure the Vikings understand I will personally check with them later.'

Gil put on a winsome face. 'Tidy. And, God bless us, everyone.'

Warlow jutted out his lower jaw. 'Someone less likely to get a part playing Tiny Tim in *A Christmas Carol* would be hard to find, Sergeant Jones.'

'Oh please.' Gil affected a look of great dudgeon. 'As a young boy, I could play a wonderful Victorian orphan.'

'What, stuck halfway up a chimney?' Jess said.

'You may well mock. But at one point I was considering a career on the stage.'

Everyone waited for what was to follow. When nothing did, Gil said, 'What?'

'Just tell us,' Catrin said.

'No, I don't want to make a scene.'

'Oh my God,' Catrin said, seeing Gil's smirk. 'I think I'm going to be sick.'

'We always watch the *Muppet Christmas Carol* on the day,' Rhys said, easing in a non sequitur. 'It's my cousin Cai's favourite.'

'Don't use Cai as an excuse. It's yours, too,' Catrin said.

'It's a brilliant film. Michael Caine as Scrooge—'

Gil interrupted with a terrible impression of said actor, 'You were only supposed to blow the bloody baubles off.'

It earned a smile from Jess and Warlow, but blank responses from Catrin and Rhys, who were clearly waiting for a punchline to drop.

'Wasting my time here,' Gil muttered and got up. 'Right, I'll get things moving on the Gatch and Lizard front.'

'That's not a statement you hear every day, Sarge,' Rhys said. He was saved the ignominy of scathing looks by his phone ringing. He listened for twenty seconds and then said, 'Charlie Brewer is in, sir. Interview room three.'

'Then let's go.' Warlow made for the door.

Jess followed with a word to Catrin. 'You and I can observe. Bring one of those mince pies, if you like.'

Rhys turned with a look of abject horror. 'That's actual mental cruelty, that is.'

'Don't be such a fuss-arse,' Gil said. 'You can have one with your tea later.'

———

CHARLIE BREWER WAS happy to answer Warlow's questions. He'd been cooperative throughout and that showed no sign of changing. His was a voluntary interview, though Warlow made sure he was cautioned and understood that everything would be recorded. When asked whether he wanted a solicitor present, he answered with a firm 'No'. Even after Warlow doubled down and asked if he was sure. That caused the tiniest of furrows in the young man's forehead, but no change in his decision.

'What is it I can help with, Chief Inspector?'

'How long had that little shelving unit that doubled as a stool been in the office?'

'The stool?' Charlie repeated the question with his eyebrows raised. 'It's been there forever. As long as I've been in the office.'

'Do you remember it being moved?'

'Moved? What, like as furniture rearranged.'

'Yes. Moved so that it was not in its usual position.'

Charlie looked away in thought before looking back at Warlow. 'No.'

'You never moved it?'

'No.'

'Did Royston Moyles?'

'No. Not as far as I could remember. It had a plant pot on it that someone had given him. It broke in the burglary.'

Warlow wrote something down. A signal for Rhys to step in. 'Your grandfather did some work for Royston Moyles, didn't he?'

'He did. More than once. But yes, he did a project not long before he passed.'

'Were you close, you and your grandfather?'

Charlie didn't flinch. 'Close enough. I mean, he lived

out of town, but not too far away. He was a practical man. Taught me how to use a saw and a hammer.'

'When Moyles went bankrupt, he owed your grandfather a sum of money, didn't he?'

Charlie's mouth flickered with an uncertain smile. 'Is that what this is about? Royston Moyles owing my grandad money?'

'You knew about it?'

'I did. But he'd done work for him before and been paid. The bankruptcy affected not only my granddad.'

'Was he angry?'

Charlie tutted and then sighed. 'He didn't exactly dance around the table. He called Royston a few names.'

'What about you?' Warlow leaned in to ask the question. 'Were you angry for what it did to your granddad?'

Charlie sat back. 'If this is about his heart attack... I know what the rumours are. But my grandfather didn't die because Royston Moyles owned him eleven thousand pounds. He died because of the twenty cigarettes he'd smoked every day since he was fourteen. The bankruptcy was genuine. Royston wasn't brilliant with some business decisions. But afterwards, he didn't run for the hills. He started again and employed me to help.'

'Out of pity?'

Charlie looked miffed at that. 'I'd like to think because of my qualifications. But I have thought about that and okay, perhaps Royston felt he was paying back a little.'

Rhys picked up on something already said. 'When you say started again, you mean with the rental properties?'

Charlie nodded.

'How could he do that, though? If he owed money, surely—'

'The rentals and the land are all in his wife's name. He was effectively employed by her.'

Rhys shook his head. 'But seeing him do that… all brazen like, must have left a bad taste?'

'In my family or the town?' Charlie asked.

'Both,' Warlow said.

'My granddad was my mother's dad. She wasn't happy to start with. Didn't want me going anywhere near. But work isn't easy to come by here. Not this kind of work.'

'And you never felt the urge to get back at him for what he'd done? Moyles, I mean?' It wasn't a subtle question, but then that was exactly why Warlow had brought Rhys in.

Charlie frowned. 'Hang on. What are you trying to say?'

'I'm asking if you were angry about what happened to your grandad. It's a simple question,' Rhys continued.

'I didn't feel the urge to get back at him. My grandad was not a well man before Royston went bankrupt.'

Warlow sensed the truth in Charlie's words. He'd heard a different version from Gil whose conversations in the pubs of the town had brought out a skewed take on things as they were wont to do. There had been a simmering anger, of that there was no doubt. But Charlie knew his grandad better than any builder. And he came across as an even-tempered sort of bloke.

But Warlow had been caught out by that before.

'Mind looking at some photographs, Charlie?'

Another agreeing shrug followed.

Warlow glanced at Rhys, who slid out a photograph of the grey janitor's cupboard from the landing outside Moyles's office. 'Recognise this?'

Charlie peered at the image with a perplexed frown. 'It's the cupboard outside the office.'

'Any idea what's in there?'

'A mop, cleaning sprays, a hoover, bleach for the toilets. The cleaners use it.'

Rhys slid over another image. 'Do you know what that is?'

Charlie frowned. 'I don't. I presume it's an access way to a roof space. We don't have an attic in the office.'

Rhys moved the image to one side and slid out another. This one taken on Warlow's phone showing the contents of the roof space.

'What is that?' Charlie asked, gazing. 'A black box and a yoghurt pot and is that a thumb drive next to it?'

'Have you ever seen any of these before, Charlie?' Warlow asked.

'No.'

'Does it surprise you to hear they were found in the roof space above the janitors' cupboard outside your office?'

Charlie's expression showed no panic. 'Yes, it surprises me. I've never been up there. I've seen that little spot in the ceiling, but it's awkward to get to. You'd need a step lad—' He stopped there and looked up, his expression suddenly stony. 'Has this got anything to do with Royston?'

'You tell us.'

Charlie looked genuinely hurt. He glanced from Warlow to Rhys and back again. 'I think I would like to speak to a solicitor, after all.'

CHAPTER THIRTY

As soon as they were out of the interview room, Catrin
met Warlow and Rhys in the corridor.

'What do you think, sarge?' Rhys posed the question
before Catrin could speak.

'Brewer? He seems genuine, but then most narcissistic
psychopaths are. They believe their own crap, don't they?
That's what makes them so dangerous.'

'Do you think he's one of them, sarge?'

'Who knows? But the story of his grandad being done
over, and then him winding up working for the man that
caused all the misery, it's a bit odd.'

'Perhaps the man did have a conscience of sorts. That's
why he employed Charlie boy,' Rhys said.

'Moyles has been painted as a total bastard by those
that he's employed. Yet, Hughes and Napier stuck with
him, didn't they?' Warlow made a good point.

Catrin grimaced. 'Funny you should mention Napier,
sir. When you were with Brewer, DI Allanby took a call
from Napier's secretary. His wife has been on the phone to
her, sounding hysterical. He didn't go home last night.'

'What?' Warlow didn't try to hide his surprise.

'DI Allanby's on the way to Napier's office now.' Catrin glanced at her watch. 'In fact, she's probably there by now.'

'Christ. Moyles, Hughes, and now Napier?' Warlow's left hand came up to rub against the back of his neck.

'Do you think something's happened to him, sir?' Rhys asked.

'I hope to God not, Rhys. But they were the three bloody Musketeers, were they not?'

'There could be a simple explanation, sir. He could have crashed on somebody's couch,' Catrin suggested.

'He's a sixty-something-year-old man. Not a teenager. I smell fish.' Warlow began walking down the corridor, issuing orders as he walked. 'Rhys, get the kettle on. Where is Gil?'

'Fetching the Human Tissue For Transplant Box, sir.'

'Good.'

'Mince pies?' Rhys asked, hopefully.

'Exactly.' Catrin tilted her head. 'They're not going to eat themselves, as Gil said.'

'Fine, but we hold off on them until Jess gets back.'

Rhys stopped walking.

Warlow prepared a look of disapproval but then gave in. 'Alright. But just the one.'

'I bloody love Christmas,' Rhys said and hurried off towards the kitchen.

———

JESS PUSHED OPEN the door to Napier's office on George Hill. For once, there were no response vehicles or CSI vans parked nearby. Napier's secretary, Caroline, glanced up as Jess walked in and sighed with relief.

'Thanks for coming. I didn't know who else to call.'

'You were right to. Best we're kept informed.'

'Tea? I've put the kettle on.'

'Never say no to a cup of tea.'

The secretary disappeared through a door at the back of the office.

'Caroline, are we alone?' Jess asked.

'We are.'

'Then if you don't mind, I'm going to record this. Saves taking notes.' Jess found the app on her phone, pressed a button on the screen, and put the phone down on a desk.

'I've only come in for a couple of hours.' Caroline's disembodied voice came through the open door. 'As soon as I sat down, Mrs Napier rang. She sounded… stressed. Five minutes after that, I rang you.' She stuck her head back into the room. 'Sugar and milk?'

'Just milk.'

Caroline emerged a few seconds later with two mugs.

'It's not been twenty-four hours yet, I realise…' Caroline said.

'You don't have to wait twenty-four hours. Common misconception. If the circumstances are out of context or out of character, that's enough to warrant suspicion. And given what's happened, you did the right thing. When did you last see him?' Jess continued.

'Yesterday morning. He said he was going to go for coffee early. He'd go to the café unless we were very busy.' She gave Jess a wry smile and dropped her voice. 'Little secret. We never are. He goes to meet Dan Hughes for a chat.' She paused and then added in that same hushed voice. 'Such horrible news about him. I mean, falling off steps? How can that happen?'

Jess steered the conversation back to why she was there.

'So yesterday, John Napier left early, you say. What time?'

'Tennish.'

In her head, Jess heard Gil's voice asking, *Isn't that Sean Connery's favourite sport?* She managed to quash it and at the same time realised that he was like some kind of dad-humour parasite in her head. 'And you didn't see him after that?' She dragged her thoughts back into focus.

'No, he didn't come back after lunch. But it was two days before Christmas. I mean, we wind down. Everything was on hold until next week. Mostly until January. Solicitors are traditional in that way. Here, they are, at least.'

'No calls or texts from him, either?'

'Nothing. But again, it's Christmas. Business gets talked about in pubs. Very generous that way, is Mr Napier. Buys clients drinks. Meets them for a swift half.' Caroline rolled her eyes up at that.

'So, you weren't that surprised not to hear from him?'

'No, not two days before Christmas.'

Jess changed tack. 'Did anything unusual happen yesterday?'

'No. Same old. Letters to type, post to answer, files put away and retrieve. Unless…' Caroline paused as a memory kicked in and she squinted to recall it. 'There was a handwritten letter addressed "private and confidential" to Mr Napier on the mat when I got in yesterday morning. Way before the post arrived. Delivered by hand, I assumed.'

'What was in it?'

'It was marked FYEO John Napier.'

'Did he read it?'

'He did.'

'Did you?'

'No. He kept it.'

'Is that normal?'

Caroline made eyes to the ceiling again. 'Sometimes people pay in kind. They'll provide a turkey or half a lamb in season as top up for the bill. It's still very rural around here. Little notes like that are not too uncommon.' Caroline seemed apologetic.

'Did you see him leave?'

'He was at his desk. I saw him pick up the letter after dealing with some other stuff. He read it, pocketed the letter, put his coat on, and walked out of the door. He said he'd see me later.'

'And you can see the street. He walked down towards the town?'

'No. He turned right.'

'Is that where the café is?'

'No, the café's to the left. Right takes you past the churchyard and the road out of town.'

'So–'

Caroline interrupted, 'He may have been going to meet someone. Or he fancied a stroll back into town along the scenic route of Crescent Road. Sometimes he did that if the weather was good.'

'Yesterday wasn't that special, if I recall.'

'No, it wasn't.'

Jess took a big swallow of tea. 'Can I ask you about the janitor's cupboard on the landing outside Royston Moyles's office?'

'The one full of cleaning materials?'

'You use it to store copy paper?'

'We did. But the cleaning materials have taken over. The copy paper and letter-headed paper and envelopes are stacked next to it.'

'Did everyone in the office use it?'

Caroline expelled a little puff of derision. 'The cupboard. No. Well, Mr Napier never cleaned, so he didn't go up there. And I was the one who replenished the stationery.'

'Have you ever needed to go into the roof space above the cupboard?'

'Is there a roof space? There's a little hatchway, but I've never been up there. Probably full of mice.' Caroline shuddered. 'This building is old.'

Jess finished her tea. 'What I'm going to need from you, Caroline, is a list of people who contacted Mr Napier going back a couple of days. Who phoned him, who called in, that sort of thing, okay?'

Caroline nodded. 'I had started to do that.'

Jess smiled. A secretary with initiative. She liked that. Napier didn't know how lucky he was. 'Just one more thing. Can you show me how you would access the landing from here?'

'Of course. Through that door.' She pointed towards a door in the right-hand corner of the room.

'Do you mind?'

Caroline led the way and opened the panelled, many-times painted door in dark blue that caught a little on the carpet as she pulled on it. Beyond it, a stair led upwards and, in a carbon copy of the landing above, boxes of stationery had been piled up for ease of access.

Jess took the stairs, two longish flights with a little winder in the middle to switch directions. Eighteen steps later, she stood in front of a police tape stretched across in front of the cupboard.

Caroline stood on the winder.

'So, you wouldn't come up here much?'

'Only to replenish the stuff we have at the bottom. That landing was a kind of spill-over storage space.'

Jess turned, smiled, and said, 'Thank you, Caroline. You've been really helpful. If you hear from Mr Napier, please let us know, though you'll only be here for another couple of hours, right?'

'If that.'

Jess said her goodbyes and walked out into the mid-morning normality of the busy town. The holidays were fast approaching for those whose lives followed the normal, untroubled existence that was still, unlike many other places in the world, the norm in this town and this country. Some people appreciated that it remained that way thanks to people like Jess Allanby. Not that she was expecting any applause or even the odd thank you. But a clue as to just exactly what the hell had happened to John Napier would not go amiss.

Turning right out of Napier's office brought her to a junction. Straight ahead to King Street and the café and shops or right again to Bank Terrace, which ran downhill in a curve, skirting the cemetery that Warlow and Rhys had crossed when they first visited the burglary site. Except this time, Jess did not stop at the gate that cut through. She continued downhill on the road. Which, much like Clarendon Road, became a traffic-free street halfway down, marked by a red-topped T sign indicating no through road for vehicles. The buildings here were all Georgian townhouses, of three or four storeys. And at the very bottom stood the old coaching inn, The King's Head, bastardised by a twentieth century, mock-Tudor cladding. Beyond that ran the busy road that cut through the town and led to all points north and south.

Jess had a thought. She walked back up to the terrace and once more entered Napier's office.

'His car? Where does he normally park?'

Caroline put her hand over her mouth. 'I should have told you. He has a permit for outside on the terrace. I checked, and it's still there. It's the blue Jaguar.'

'The blue one?'

'Yes.'

Jess thanked her again. She'd passed the car on the way down and on the way up. So, Napier had driven nowhere. Was it too early to ask questions of residents? Too presumptuous to knock on doors? Probably. But her gut was telling her otherwise. She said that to Warlow when she phoned him a minute later.

'Would do no harm to get some Uniforms calling in to his usual haunts,' Jess said.

'Once we do, the press will get wind.'

'Do we have any choice? They're already here, sniffing around like lost dogs.'

'Okay, I'll get Gil to get things organised. You come back here and we'll have a catch up.'

'It's almost Christmas, Evan.'

'Don't. I've already caught Rhys humming Jingle Bloody Bells. Plus, I've saved you a mince pie.'

CHAPTER THIRTY-ONE

WHILE HE WAITED for Jess to return, Warlow retired to the SIO room. The crime scene reports in his inbox showed that the surveillance equipment find from the second property were identical in all respects.

His eyes strayed around the tiny space. He'd received a few Christmas cards from colleagues. Easier to dole them out at work than post them. Given the number of strikes—'like being in a bloody baseball game, *myndiawli,*' as Gil said—using internal mail seemed like a smart idea. Warlow had received one from everyone in the team, including Sion Buchannan. The notable exception was Two-Shoes. That he'd been struck off her Christmas card list came as no surprise and carried not a jot of regret.

For a lot of people, late morning of the Friday before Christmas Eve signalled the start of the holidays. Except that, over the years, Warlow had spent at least a dozen neck deep in some case or other. He'd always tried to be around for when the boys woke up on Christmas morning, though sometimes, his Christmas only lasted until midday.

Bodies had no bloody respect for the festivities.

He pondered that thought for a while. Let it rotate like

a spitting rotisserie cone in the window of the Kebabitstan restaurant and take-away which he'd been able to smell from his digs when he was with the Met all those years ago. Of course, all crime should've been banned for Christmas. That was a given. And if police officers ever offered up a prayer, it would be one that contained that plea. That it never worked out that way spoke volumes. Criminals could not give a thieving, murdering toss. Yet somehow, crimes, especially serious crimes, committed over Christmas carried an extra dollop of tragedy. Unless, of course, they had been planned to coincide. If they had, then that dollop of tragedy was topped off by a drizzle, heavy or otherwise, of maliciousness.

Warlow sat back, his eyes on the Christmassy scenes on the cards he'd set up on a filing cabinet. Reindeers with red noses, stars in the east, wise men with funny hats. But he saw none of them. Instead, his brain busy wondering about twisting the knife, sticking the boot in, and wanting those left behind after a death, to suffer at a time of supposed rejoicing.

What was it they were missing here?

Motive?

If this case did indeed have that drizzle of maliciousness and vindictive terror, then it meant someone had planned this very, very carefully. Someone who knew Moyles's habits. Understood his foibles, even. Knew he might call at *Cân-y-barcud* to ready his tawdry little peeping Tom setup that very day. He was still examining these thoughts when the door opened and a large figure filled the gap.

'It was open,' Sion Buchannan said.

'Cogitating,' Warlow answered.

'I'm all for that. Should be taught in college.'

'Agreed.'

Buchannan stepped into the room. The small space

immediately became tiny. 'No point me asking how it's going, then, is there?'

'You can ask, but you'll be disappointed with the answer. And as of this morning, we seem to have a misper added to the mix.'

'Who?'

'John Napier.'

Buchannan adopted a pained expression. 'The solicitor?'

'The same. Disappeared as of yesterday's morning. And, like Hughes, a pal of Moyles.'

'Shit.'

'Indeed, Superintendent. Couldn't put it better myself.'

Buchannan remained standing. 'I'm here to kill two birds with one stone. Or since you're sensitive, and the sensitivity consultant who gave a talk I was forced to attend yesterday said we should seriously consider our word choices in an effort at evolving from violent language, I should probably have said that I'm here to feed two birds with one scone.'

'Really?'

'Really.'

Warlow could only shut his eyes and count to ten, hoping for the rising red mist to fade quickly.

'Anyway,' Buchannan continued. 'As said, I'm here to kill two birds with one stone.'

Warlow grinned. 'Good for you, sir.'

'The first stone was to catch up. Now I'm sorry I asked. The second was to ask where to drop off a tenner for the cause.'

'What cause?'

'Your two sergeants put out a shout for some kids up at Llanfynydd. Something about them being short of funds over Christmas.'

'You don't mean the protesters?'

'I don't know the details. I only heard kids and presents.'

Warlow's grin returned. Gil and Catrin. The old, and the young. A pair of softies if there ever were one.

'Can I leave it with you?' Buchannan handed over a tenner.

'You can indeed. Maybe there is something to this goodwill lark after all. Even in the middle of all this mess.'

'Hold that thought, Evan. Hold that thought.'

———

IT TOOK Jess twenty-five minutes to get back to the Incident Room. It was now approximately 11.30. Still as good as his word, Warlow insisted on another round of teas and mince pies.

'I do not want to be eating these next week,' he muttered as he bit into his second of the morning. But his irascibility had less to do with sweetmeats and more to do with the case that seemed to have more twists than Chubby Checker. Something he mentioned to Gil that earned a nod from him and Jess, but a blank stare from Rhys. However, Warlow was in no mood to explain the 60s to the DC. Again.

'Rhys, tell me what you have.'

'We contacted everyone who stayed in both *Cân-y-barcud* and the second property Moyles had cameras in over the last six months. Everyone we talked to was completely shocked, but they also had sound alibis for the day of the killing. Every one of them also said they had no idea they had been filmed. As you might expect, many of them are very upset.'

'Someone will need to provide counselling, I don't doubt.' Warlow narrowed his eyes. This was going to take a while to untangle. 'Gil, what about that portable hard drive from the roof space?'

'And the thumb drives,' Rhys said.

'Tannard got a bit held up, sir,' Gil said. 'Some of the stuff she's found is of underage kids. As you might expect on family holidays. Images of them changing clothes. Nothing overtly pornographic. But they have to treat that stuff carefully.'

No one spoke. Everyone in that room knew that, coming from Gil, there was no argument. He was a veteran of Operation Alice before joining Warlow's team.

'Jess, Napier?'

'He'll be the third victim, if indeed it turns out he is a victim. I've told the Uniforms to be as subtle as possible in their door-to-door.'

It was a mark of how serious all this was that no one even said good luck with that.

Shows how bloody befuddled they all are, thought Warlow. *Like me.*

'What do you make of it, Jess?' he asked.

Jess blew out her cheeks. 'He's walked off into the sodding sunset. That's what I make of it. He gets a hand-written letter, or at least a hand-addressed envelope. Reads the note inside the office and then leaves.'

'This is before Hughes is attacked?' Gil asked.

'Yes,' Jess answered.

They all glanced at the snaking timeline that now had added Post-it notes in a different colour for Napier.

'Disappearances. People attacked in train stations. Told you we'd end up in a bloody Agatha Christie novel,' Gil muttered.

Rhys looked very perplexed. Warlow picked up on it. 'Come on, spit it out. What's bothering you?'

'I don't understand the handwritten letter bit, sir. Why not a text?'

'Letters can be burned, Rhys,' Catrin explained. 'Texts leave a trail.'

'Do you think it could've been Brewer who wrote it?' Jess asked.

Warlow had no answer.

'We could always ask him?' Rhys suggested. He'd already demolished two mince pies, but was eyeing the last one in the box.

'Go on.' Gill tipped a wink towards the box. 'As Mr Warlow says, it's considered bad luck to carry on eating mince pies into January.'

Rhys frowned. 'I wouldn't know. They tend not to last much past Boxing Day in our house.'

'Why does that not surprise me?' Catrin said.

The DC grinned. Thankfully, not showing too much of the mouthful of pastry and minced fruit he was devouring in the process.

'Just make sure there are no crumbs on your trousers when we go back in,' Warlow said. 'Let's pretend to be professional, at least. How long until his solicitor arrives?' Warlow might as well have been tapping his foot, even if all he was doing was standing in front of the Gallery staring at the photographs of Moyles, Hughes, and now Napier.

'He's getting someone from the Napier practice,' Catrin said. 'Shouldn't be long.'

Warlow growled. He turned and zeroed in on Gil, who was searching through Hughes's phone records.

'Anything?'

'No. Texts from suppliers, his wife, the rugby club secretary about a Boxing Day match, oh, and from his son who was arriving today from Birmingham. All in the last twenty-four hours before the incident.'

Warlow tried not to think of how much the Hughes' Christmas had been ruined. But if there was one consolation about their victims all being of a certain age, it was that their use of texts and other forms of social media were minuscule compared to the average millennial. Warlow took some notes from his pocket and put them on Gil's desk. 'For the whip round.'

Gil glanced up at the DCI.

'Sion Buchannan,' Warlow said.

'There's forty quid here. That's not all the superintendent.'

'I said I'd match his donation,' Warlow said.

Gil brought up a wry smile.

'Why them, though?' Warlow asked. 'The eco-warriors?'

'Sergeant Richards?' Gil turned to Catrin at the next desk.

'We got talking to Andrew, that's Gatch, after he'd written his statement. It turned out that the reason they were in town was to get the van fixed.'

'Ignition coil and distributor on the blink.' Gil pursed his lips. 'That's why they went for the wine. The cheap wine. Soften the blow with the others.'

'They were also on the way to the toy shop,' Catrin said.

'How many kids?' Warlow asked.

'Two. There's Dawnsong and the other couple has one as well.'

'Bottom line,' Gil said. 'The van repairs will eat up their Christmas.'

'But fraternising with the enemy, I mean—'

Gil cut him off. 'Mr Buchannan texted me to say he'd left a tenner with you.' He smiled at Warlow and held up the two twenties. 'Somehow, that ten has turned into forty. It's a Christmas miracle.'

Catrin's smile blew all Warlow's credibility out of the water. 'Thank you, sir.'

'Yes, well, it is Christmas. Now, where the hell is that solicitor?'

The door to the Incident Room opened and in walked Jo Tannard, smart in a dark suit and carrying a messenger bag. She stood on the threshold and held up the case.

'I come bearing gifts,' she said.

'Where's your Santa hat?' Gil asked.

'Believe me, when you see what's in here, you might be asking for a refund from *his* grotto.'

CHAPTER THIRTY-TWO

THEY GAVE Tannard some space as she took out a laptop, a small black oblong box and a USB cable. 'We cloned the hard drive. That's what this little black thing is. Sleeker than the five terabyte box we found at the office.' The laptop screen came to life and Tannard plugged in the cable and clicked an orange "S1 portable" icon.

'The files were date labelled on the hard drive. It looks like the thumb drives were transferred over for storage on an ad hoc basis. Not every month has an entry. Either those months were not collected or they were scrutinised later and removed.'

'How far back?' Catrin asked.

'Four years.'

Catrin sat up. 'That coincides with Moyles taking over the rental business, after his bankruptcy.'

The screen filled with little yellow boxes – date stamped. Tannard pointed to them. 'Monthly data.' She clicked on one. 'As you will see, they're split into two. CYB and MH.'

'That would be *Cân-y-barcud* and *Maes Haf*, the other place,' Rhys said.

'We've begun to go through them. It will take a while. But there is another file here labelled GS for "Good Stuff".' Tannard sounded almost apologetic.

Warlow felt a knot tighten somewhere behind his belt.

'And, as you might expect, these are collated files in date order. They contain video images of people doing what people do when they're in bed, on holiday, assuming, naturally, they are alone and not being observed.'

Jess was tight-lipped, her arms folded. 'Good God.'

Tannard clicked the GS label. Another list of files opened. 'There is more, or worse, depending on how you look at it. There's a file labelled COC XXX clips. The acronym might not be what you might assume. It stands for "caught on camera XXX". And how do I know? Because there is a website where genuine hidden camera clips – or at least we think they are genuine and not actors – can be accessed via pay-per-view. These clips have been sent out into the world via the site. In fact, we have proof because we found at least half a dozen matches on the PPV site. There are fifty-two of them in this file. For ease of access, we've put these on thumb drives so that more than one of you can access at a time.' Tannard put four of the little drives on the desk.

'I hate to ask but there's nothing involving kids here, is there?' Gil asked.

'No. Nothing overt. There are some images of kids getting undressed for bed in their bedrooms. But it doesn't appear that they've been clipped. Having said that, there is one file labelled "Chicken". That one only has kids with an age range between ten to seventeen. There are only half a dozen. And nothing unpleasant. Candid images only.'

Gil looked relieved.

'This is great work, Jo,' Warlow said.

'It was you who found the hiding place,' Tannard pointed out.

'I'm a suspicious bugger by nature,' Warlow said.

A Uniform appeared in the doorway behind them. 'Brewer's solicitor is here, sir.'

Warlow gave him a thumbs up. 'Right, Gil, Rhys, your turn to take a shot at Brewer. I'll help Jess and Catrin with these… files.'

'Necessary evil.' Jess turned to Tannard. 'You suggest we start with what's on your thumb drives?'

'I do. They're the short clips Moyles, or someone, collated. It means you'll get through them quicker.'

'What are we looking for, ma'am?' Catrin asked Jess.

The DI pursed her lips. 'Evidence of a crime that Moyles was involved in. Let's start from that angle.'

'So, we're fishing,' Catrin said.

'In a dark and muddy pool,' Gil said. 'Anybody want popcorn?'

Neither of the women answered him.

————

THE SOLICITOR who sat with Charlie Brewer was a young woman. And not that much older than he was. Gil had come across most of the duty solicitors in the area, but this one he had not met. She introduced herself as Enid Morris, pronouncing the E as the E in exit, the Welsh way. Smart, and from the way she kept glancing at Charlie, as if wanting to reassure him all the time, Gil guessed she might have the hots for the bloke.

Rhys picked the baton up from where they left it. He showed Charlie the image of the janitor's cupboard and the access door to the roof space again.

'I've never been up there,' Charlie said after a quick glance at Enid.

'You were not aware that in that roof space was a hard drive and several thumb drives?'

'No. I had no idea until you showed me.'

Rhys slid the photo back into the folder.

'Are you any good with computers, Charlie?' Gil asked.

'About average.'

'No IT training?'

'No.'

'How about Royston Moyles?'

Charlie shrugged. 'Roy could use a computer. I doubt he had any training, though.'

'Did you ever see these portable drives that we found in the ceiling space in his possession?'

'No.'

Gil sat back, allowing Charlie to feel that he had passed that test.

'Ever been to *Cân-y-barcud* or *Maes Haf*?' Rhys asked.

'Both, once or twice, yes. We had an issue with a leaking chimney in *Maes Haf*. I met with a builder last spring to get it sorted out.'

'And you were never asked to visit either property to collect surveillance materials?'

'What does that mean?'

'We found cameras in both properties, and recording facilities.'

Charlie looked nonplussed.

'Are you telling us you didn't know about the cameras?' Gil asked.

'We didn't have cameras. These properties are isolated enough not to need security. No one would ever find them without a map. And if there were cameras there, we would need to inform the clients. It's a legal requirement.'

'And yet, that is what we found. At both properties. Subtly positioned, too.'

Enid spoke. 'My client has already answered your question.'

Gil decided to attack from the flank. 'He has. Let's move on. When was the last time you saw John Napier?'

Enid's eyes, focused on the notes she was taking, shot up. She looked confused. 'What relevance does that have to this interview?'

Rhys answered, 'We've had a report that he didn't return home last night. His wife is concerned for him. We're trying to establish his movements and whereabouts. And since both he and Daniel Hughes, who's been transferred to the neurosurgical ward at the University Hospital in Cardiff, were associates of Mr Moyles, we think it's highly relevant.'

'I haven't seen him for a couple of days. I've been working from home,' Charlie said.

'And you didn't leave him a message yesterday?'

'No.' Charlie made a show of thinking. 'No messages.' He paused before asking, 'What's on the drives?'

'Don't you know?'

'How could I know?'' He pleaded. 'I've never seen them before.'

'Right,' Gil said. 'You did. The thing is, Charlie, we've had a root around in your social media history. I say root around. Most of it is out there if you care to look. Four years ago, when Royston Moyles declared bankruptcy, he had the nerve to announce it via his Facebook company page, RM Enterprise. Pretty callous if you ask me. But then some would argue the quickest and best way to get a message across to lots of people. However you feel about that as a means of breaking up, there was an outpouring of vitriol from those people that he left in the lurch.'

Charlie Brewer's expression resembled that of Gatch's before he threw up.

'Now, we know you don't have a Facebook account these days, very wise if you ask me. Far too easy to post something that you might regret. Royston Moyles shut down his account, but not before he'd complained to us because of some of the quite nasty things that people wrote at the time. And we couldn't help but notice one comment from a certain C Brewer.' Gil pulled out a sheet of paper and read from it. 'Some people deserve to go to hell. Some people deserve to rot there. If there is anything I can do to help you on your way RM Enterprise, just give me a bell. I'll bring my own rat poison.'

Charlie dropped his head. 'I was angry. My granddad was angry. My mother was angry. So were a lot of other people. I was just a kid, still in college. I didn't mean any of that. I didn't understand business then.' He glanced up. 'I told Royston that was me. He laughed it off. He said I was at the back of a bloody long queue.'

'Sounds like he had a thick skin.'

'He did. And I regret writing those words. It was spur-of-the-moment stuff.'

Gil grinned. 'That is the beauty, and the beast, that is social media, though. No filters. No convenient three-hour delay while people sober up and have time to think things through. It's there in black and white.'

'I can't deny it. But that was four years ago. I've… I've grown up a lot since then.'

Gil saw Enid's right-hand slip down under the table. He suspected it was now giving Charlie's a squeeze. And somewhere in the back of Gil's mind wriggled the fact that a girlfriend had been mentioned along the way. And her name had not been Enid.

Charlie, it seemed, was a player.

'But you can see our problem with all of this. We have motive, we have opportunity, we have proximity to the victim,' Gil said.

'I didn't kill Royston. He gave me a job. I helped him with marketing. He wanted to pivot towards young families and couples on their honeymoon. That sort of thing.'

I bet he did, thought Gil.

Enid's hand came back up. She looked at Charlie and made a zipping motion with an index finger and thumb across her lips.

Charlie, whose hands had stayed firmly in his lap, nodded miserably.

'Did you meet Royston Moyles at *Cân-y-barcud*, Charlie?' Gil asked.

'No comment.'

'Did you attack Daniel Hughes at the station in Llandelio?' Rhys asked.

'No comment.'

'Did you—' Gil got no further with a third, Napier-related question, as the door opened to reveal DS Richards with a kind of desperate urgency writ large on her face.

'We need a quick word,' she said.

Gil smiled at Enid. 'Why don't we take a break? Have a word with your client. We'll be back in fifteen minutes, okay? I'll get someone to bring you refreshments.'

Charlie, who had gone very pale, did not look up. Gil added a last word of advice. 'Deep breaths, Charlie. I'd put my head down between my knees if I were you. Don't want you fainting. *Esgyrn Dafydd*, in this room I'd stay off the floor if I were you at all costs.'

CHAPTER THIRTY-THREE

'APOLOGIES FOR DRAGGING YOU OUT,' Warlow said once Gil and Rhys had joined the team in the Incident Room. 'Looked like you might be on to something, but then we struck lucky with Napier.'

Gil did a sad clown impression with his eyebrows.

Catrin leant over her desk and jiggled the mouse. A clear picture of the A483 also known as Bridge Street, appeared on screen. It showed a line of pastel-painted houses behind the iron fence guarding pedestrians from the two-foot drop onto the road below. Another click of the mouse set the video rolling. A man appeared from the right and walked through the shot, heading down the hill.

'Napier,' Gil said.

'Yep. This as seen from the wholesalers on the eastern side of the street. It's a stockroom as well behind the shutters. Hence the security cameras.'

'What time is this?'

'10.17am yesterday.'

Napier walked out of shot on screen. 'Where does he go from there?' Gil asked.

'Ah,' Catrin said. 'That's where it gets interesting.

There's a scrap metal merchant a couple of hundred yards past the bridge. I need hardly tell you catalytic converters are full of precious metals. They've had half a dozen attempted burglaries in the last two years and they have cameras front and back. We've watched the street view from 10.15 to midday and no sign of Napier passing.'

'So, where did he go?' Warlow asked and turned to Gil. 'You're the local expert. Options?'

Gil walked to the Gallery and to the map they'd pinned up following Hughes's attack. Not that there was any evidence of an attack, but Warlow opted for that as a working premise. It remained the best explanation for anyone taking a head-first dive over a four-foot wall twenty feet up.

But now they were talking about Napier. Gil used his finger to trace the journey from the wholesaler on Bridge Street down to the bridge over the River Towy. 'Okay, once he's over the bridge there's a walkway down to the river-bank, but then only fenced-off fields until the scrap merchants. But just before the bridge, Bridge Street continues until it peters out into an unpaved lane around Castle Woods, back into Dinefwr Park. No houses. Just open fields, and the castle, of course.'

'Dinefwr Park, that's a National Trust property, isn't it?' Jess asked.

'Seventeenth-century manor house with newish turrets. Very popular,' Gil said. 'But it's open country. Even that close to the town. In ten minutes, you're in the middle of the valley in fields. You could even walk out a couple of miles downriver.'

'But why would he go there?' Warlow asked.

'Great castle, sir,' Rhys said. 'I've been with school and with Gina. It's amazing. You get high up. And looking down from the ramparts it isn't hard to see yourself repelling attacks and that.'

'Oh God, he's gone full Robin Hood on us,' Catrin said.

'I'm just saying,' Rhys said. 'And this time of year, it wouldn't be busy.'

'Agreed,' Warlow said, much to Rhys's surprise and delight. 'The most likely scenario is a clandestine meeting at a quiet spot. But I have no reason to pull the trigger on a full-blown search of a huge National Trust property for a misper. Not on the day before the holiday weekend.'

'Course, there is a possibility he was picked up by car between the two surveillance cameras,' Jess said.

'Good point. Let's check ANPR data for that time. Between 10.15 and midday. Check for known number plates. Brewer's, the camper van, anyone who springs to mind. In the meantime, Gil and Rhys, keep plugging away at Mr Brewer.'

'He's not happy,' Rhys said.

'No, but that doesn't mean he's guilty,' Jess said.

'*Esgyrn dafydd*, this case…'

Jess elevated an eyebrow. That's a new one on me.'

Gil grinned. 'A much politer way of saying foxtrot, foxtrot, sierra, ma'am. Literal translation, Dafydd's bones. Most common equivalent, goodness gracious, or heavens above.'

'Mild for you,' Catrin commented.

'I wanted to leave him with a softly, softly vibe. Before I go back in and poke him with a sharp stick.'

'It would be useful to find something else we could poke him with,' Jess added with a rueful smile.

'Talking of poking, how are the XXX files going?' Gil kept his face straight while he looked at Catrin.

Her puckered expression said it all. 'Not funny. I mean, to think this stuff has been posted online. How anyone can find any of it remotely titillating is beyond me. There's a lot of middle-aged writhing and a bit of moaning. Let's just say it isn't Love Island.'

'More like Love Handles,' Jess said.

That earned an appreciative nod from Gil. 'Top notch segue there, ma'am. I might even use that myself. Right, young Robin.' He threw Rhys a nod. 'Let's get back to it.'

'Chance of a quick pee first, sarge?' Rhys asked.

'Yep. But use the small one.'

'The small one?' Rhys asked, confused.

'Toilet. As in Little John.'

'Oh, God.' Catrin groaned.

Gil, pleased by the reaction his Robin Hood-themed joke induced, egged the pudding. He smiled, said, 'Tidy.' And walked out whistling the *William Tell Overture*.

'That's not—' Catrin began.

'Don't,' Warlow said. 'You'll only make it worse.'

———

WHILE GIL and Rhys went back to the interview room, Catrin opened the COCXXX file from Tannard's thumb drive once more. The clips were anything from thirty seconds to three minutes long. She'd watched a dozen already. A dozen more than she ever wanted to see. Gil had joked, but there was a genuine sense of dread as she clicked open the little media player that ran the video clips. There was a soundtrack, too. But she'd turned that way down. Bad enough to spy on these people, let alone have the soundtrack of their private lives and intimate whispers worm their way into her head.

She'd asked Jess and Warlow what they were looking for. And Warlow answered only with a vague, 'You'll know it when you see it.'

The trouble was there no unseeing it.

So far, Catrin had watched two dozen people have sex

over an age range of between thirty and sixty-five. Sometimes the acts were passionate, at other times, more mechanical. Once, memorably, like two dogs howling. Literally. And naturally, her thoughts turned to her and Craig and not because of the howling. They'd been together almost six years, and by now, knew which buttons to press to please each other. She preferred please to pleasure each other. Somehow, the verb to pleasure made it all sound a little tacky.

But now that they were in the middle of IVF, some, if not all, of the spontaneity had gone. Craig, of course, would not complain. When the time was right, ovulating wise, it meant an increase in frequency. And Craig was a bloke. All he ever needed to get him hot under the collar was a lascivious wink. In fact, sometimes when her contact lenses were playing up, Catrin fended him off with a giggled, 'No, that was not a lascivious wink,' comment. It became their little joke.

Catrin sighed, the mouse's arrow hovering over play on the media player. She wasn't sure she wanted to tell Craig about what she was doing now. Pornography, this may well be, but she'd have preferred a newer, made-up term. Intrusography. Because that was what this was. A lurid imposition on these people's lives when they were at their most vulnerable. They weren't to know that the intimate secrets of what they did and what they said had been recorded and shared with the world. None of these people gave their permission. So long as the server wasn't in some third world back street somewhere, they might even get the clips taken down.

At that moment in time, she loathed Moyles for what he'd done.

Gritting her teeth, Catrin clicked the mouse and pressed play.

Absolute darkness.

And yet, even though no light penetrated the space, he could tell it was small. No current of air moved over him. No suggestion of height above. The bonds that held his arms to his sides meant he could barely move, but his elbow rubbed against a wall.

On both sides.

His legs were rigid from the tape that ran from thigh to ankle. And he was too stiff and inflexible to wriggle much thanks to an allergy to any proper exercise developed by constant exposure to beer. The surface he was lying on was hard and gritty. If he moved his head an inch off the floor and let it fall, it resonated with a dull thud and a flash of pain, suggesting a very hard surface.

Stone.

Perhaps granite.

And the tape wound around his mouth and his eyes left only his nostrils uncovered; a gap through which he breathed with a desperate hope that nothing would block those small passages, but which also meant that the smell of the space was all pervading.

A dead space.

Dank. Decaying. The stench of the crypt.

Of course, he'd tried making noises. Pathetic attempts at shouting out. But the tape wound tight blunted everything.

He'd been a fool to accept the letter at face value. And he'd read into it what he'd wanted to believe. That was his downfall.

Dan Hughes had been right to be wary.

Guilt by omission, was that what he'd called it?

He'd tried searching Moyles's office to see if he could find anything incriminating. But the computer he'd stolen had nothing on it except the man's business. And he was more than familiar with all of that, regardless.

He'd gone along with the letter because whoever had written it knew Moyles's secrets.

'I know where he keeps the videos.'

That sentence had been the key. He hadn't recognised the handwriting, but in this age of emails, who the hell wrote to anyone? Of course, he still received handwritten letters from his clients, many of whom did not possess computers because of their age, or because some farmers didn't see the need. He'd assumed the boy, Brewer, wrote it. He knew Moyles's office, after all. And perhaps Moyles had even recruited him to be a part of his sordid little games. Not wanting to discuss any of this where there was a risk of being overheard and where the police were near made sense when he'd read the letter. And who would begrudge him a walk to clear his head to a quiet spot of contemplation?

But he'd been wrong.

In every way.

He hadn't met with Brewer.

Instead, he'd met someone dressed in black with a ski mask and a gun in his hand. If he moved his tongue inside his mouth, he could still feel the bruise where the barrel of that gun struck him. Three times. He'd had no choice but to comply.

The enormity of his situation lay like a ton weight on his chest. With tape over his eyes and a gun in his back, he'd been made to stumble along a path, then made to sit. He'd expected a bullet, felt a pathetic surge of relief when all that happened was an order to step down, or rather fall, into a space. Then the tape over his legs, then pushed onto his back, then the scrape of something heavy being positioned over him.

He'd screamed. But the noise through the tape emerged as a high-pitched growl.

He had no idea how long he'd been there.

He had no idea if he'd ever get out.

In the absolute darkness, in a space that smelled of his own urine and abandonment, John Napier screamed again.

CHAPTER THIRTY-FOUR

Rhys went into a cubicle in the men's. He shut the door and took out his phone.

The thing had vibrated in his pocket in the Incident Room in the middle of the disclosure and discussion about Napier. Of course, he'd ignored it. But knowing there was a message there waiting for him was a siren call that had to be answered. He wasn't as bad as some when it came to phones. He knew people who couldn't go two minutes without looking at theirs. And one of his modes of relaxation was to sit with a sandwich, or a pie, or some kind of food and scroll through a gazillion reels. In its own way, it was entertainment.

Vacuous, his mother called it.

She was probably right, too.

And he didn't need to be sitting here to do what he needed to do. Evacuating the male bladder could be done standing up. But Rhys had worked out that the inconvenience of sitting depended on how you looked at it. Yes, if you were a woman, you needed a cubicle to sit. But it left your hands free to answer your phone while you did it.

Genius.

The ultimate in multi-tasking. Letting the autonomic system do its thing while you called an Uber, checked your bank statement, or answered your messages.

Which is exactly what he did now.

His message was from Gina and said:

Sorted.

Sorted what?

Totally Sam has Covid.

Totally Sam was everyone's nickname for Gina's sister's partner. A name earned from an affectation of his. In a deliberate effort at avoiding using filler words such as like and you know, Sam thought it smarter to use "totally" instead of "yes".

'Coming to the pub, Sam?'

'Totally.'

Sometimes he abbreviated it to "totes". Rhys texted back:

Shit. We were with him on the weekend.

I've tested. Neg. You need to test too.

Will do.

We forget going out. Now my mum wants to do tomorrow night instead of Christmas Day since we're all neg, except Sam. That means we can go to your mum's Christmas Day.

Brilliant.

The thought of his mother's red cabbage and pigs in

blankets evinced a small moan of anticipation. He hoped no one was listening in the next cubicle. He texted back:

> Can't wait to wake up Sunday morning with you and check out my stocking.

> Thought I'd wear mind

Sitting on the loo, Rhys grinned.

> Now I deffo can't wait.

He signed off, dressed, and pocketed his phone. He was grinning as he met with Gil outside the interview room door.

'Good one, was it, whatever it might have been?'

'Got a text from Gina, sarge. Her sister's boyfriend has Covid.'

'Glad to see that's cheered you up.'

Rhys's smile slipped. 'I'm not... it's not that. I'm not happy that he has Covid. It's... just Gina, sarge.'

'Right. Thanks for that clarification. Obviously, I'm not going to ask for details. Get your game face on and let's see what other little surprises Charlie Brewer might have in store. Capiche?'

'No, thanks, sarge, I'm trying to give them up.' The grin returned.

'This might be a very long Christmas.' Gil opened the door and walked in.

————

JESS WAS SAVED from a deep dive into the mire of Royston Moyles's prurient video collection by her phone buzzing. She stood up from her desk and walked to the "stairwell of conversation", as Rhys called it, where you would often find people fielding personal calls away from the buzz of police activity. Especially when the weather did not invite a stroll outside. And on this 23rd of December, as lunchtime approached, the grey winter day looked cold and miserable enough to merit an inside chat.

'Hi, Mum.' Molly's voice chirped over the speaker in Jess's ear.

'Hi, Mol. How's the last-minute shopping going?'

'Oh, I'm all done. It's Bryn who is completely useless.'

'I heard that.' Bryn, Molly's boyfriend, voiced his objection a little distance away from the phone's mic.

'Where are you two?' Jess asked.

'On the way to Carmarthen. M&S to be specific. To find something for his mum. Honestly, he's been in London for months. John Lewis, that massive M&S at Marble Arch. He says he didn't know what she liked. I mean, they practically shove ideas into your hand as soon as you walk through the door in these places.'

Jess felt a smile blossom. Molly, who'd been to London all of three times in the last two months, was now a veteran of Oxford Street and, her new favourite place, Marylebone High Street.

'What are you doing for lunch?' Jess asked.

'Could be KFC, could be Greggs.'

'Or you could buy some fruit in M&S.'

'Stop being so motherly, Mother,' Molly ordered. 'But since I am going to be there, anything you need M&S wise?'

'I'll have a think and text you. Mostly, we're good. Chocs and wine. What else is there?'

'What about Cadi? Did you get her anything?'

'She's a dog. She'll eat whatever we leave behind and think it's a lottery win. But no. Were you thinking…

squeaky toy?' Jess almost said, '*Another squeaky toy*' but held back on it.

'She can't eat chocolate, you know that. So, a squeaky toy might be a good idea. I'll call in to Pets R Us.'

'I think it's Pets at Home.'

'Whatever. Oh, and by the way, I got a card from Dad.'

'Lucky you,' Jess said.

'I'm going to have to show it to you. I don't understand half of it. But he said it's unlikely he'll call over Christmas.'

The initial thought that sought to form the words in Jess's mouth was, *So, what's new*? But she said, 'That's a shame.' Ricky, Molly's father, was working undercover in Manchester. Convenient as an excuse for lack of communication.

'Yeah. We'll have to make do with Evan and Cadi. It's a no brainer,' Molly said.

Jess sighed. But there was a resigned smile on the end of it. However, her thoughts snagged on the card from Tricky Ricky like a mental hangnail.

'What's so weird about your dad's card?'

'What isn't? It's like this festive bat hanging upside down.'

'Maybe he had a limited choice.'

'And it doesn't even look like his handwriting. It could be he's trying to disguise it, of course.'

Something cold rolled over in Jess's chest. 'What?'

'Yeah. So weird. I mean, he left a number for me to text—'

'Tell me you didn't?' Jess barked out the question.

'What? No, I didn't. Like I say, the card is weird.'

'Molly, is that card at home?'

'No. I have it. I was going to—'

'Take a photo and send it to me. Of the card and what's written inside,' Jess said.

'Why, Mum? You can see it later.'

'Please, Mol.'

'Fine. I'll do it when we get to Carmarthen. I can't reach my bag 'cos it's in the back seat.'

'As long as you won't forget. I'd like to see.'

'My God, Mum, you've gone into full cop mode. You're frightening my boyfriend.'

'Good. He should be scared. Terrified in fact.'

'And *Nadolig Llawen* to you, too, Mrs A,' Bryn sang out.

Molly giggled. 'What time are you home?'

'Good question. Stay with Bryn until I text you, okay?'

'Why are you saying it like that?'

'Because. Now, go get that squeaky toy.'

Jess stood, letting the dark thoughts that had gathered in her head roil after she'd ended the call. A card from Tricky Ricky was one thing, but written in a different hand and with a contact number? That was way off kilter. She checked her phone for texts. Nothing from Molly yet. She couldn't wait.

With a resigned plod, Jess went back to her desk and opened Royston Moyles's files.

───────

CATRIN WAS on file number twenty-three.

Number twenty-one had been distressing enough.

Number twenty-two had caused her to swallow back a little plug of vomit that had appeared at the back of her throat.

Had Gil had counselling after he'd been made to watch stuff like this for Operation Alice? He probably had. But then he'd had to watch things that were exponentially worse. So, what she was having to do, he would describe as a walk in the park and nothing more than one would expect to see after the watershed on TV.

Especially on Channel 4.

This clip was graphic enough, the woman on the bed, the man above her. The beast with two backs the consequence. The woman's face was attractive, but half in shadow because of the bedside lamp that was on. She had dark hair, looked after herself from what Catrin could see, and had a small mole on her left cheek. For some reason, Catrin zeroed in on it because her mother had one. The consultant she'd seen when she was worried about it had called it a malar melanocytic naevus, malar being the anatomically correct term for where it was positioned.

Her mother's dermatologist had taken photographs and measurements and asked if it had changed at all. It had not over a period of thirty years, and a common mole had been diagnosed. That her mother had always embraced it did not deter Catrin from insisting she had it looked at when it appeared to be getting a little darker. By then her mother had done a bit more gardening and the dermatologist had warned her to make sure to use factor block everything when she was outside. Something Catrin did even on a cloudy day.

And so, the detective sergeant watched as the woman moved and the man changed position and flopped onto his back while she budged over to make room. Both had a flushed, post coital look about them.

But it was only then that the man moved his arm so that his face came fully into view. A view that triggered a whispered, 'What?' of surprise from Catrin as she reached for the mouse and froze the frame before turning up the volume.

'Okay? That was so good. Thank you.' She knew the voice. There was no mistake.

On screen, the man leaned over and kissed the woman gently on her lips and stayed up on his elbow to look at her closely. That put him in profile for the camera. A profile that Catrin, and many more people, knew only too well.

She paused the frame again, blinked, and looked around at Jess, who wasn't taking any notice at all as she was too busy frowning at her own screen and the anatomical unpleasantness displayed on it.

'Um, ma'am,' Catrin said.

'Hmmm?' Jess looked over distractedly.

'I think you'd better look at this.'

'Do I have to?' Jess came back with a mock protestation.

'Yes, ma'am, you definitely need to see this.'

Jess gave Catrin her full attention. 'Why?'

'Because remember DCI Warlow saying you'll know it when you see it? I think I've found the "it".'

'Should we get DCI Warlow from the SIO room?'

'I think so. I definitely think so."

CHAPTER THIRTY-FIVE

'ROGER HUNT?' Warlow asked, for the third time. 'The bloke off the telly that you were trying to sweet talk into signing Craig's Christmas present?'

'It is, sir,' Catrin said. 'I'd swear on it.' Catrin's cheeks were flushed with excitement.

Warlow stared at the frozen image on the screen, trying to dredge up a memory of the morning he and Gil had been at the Cawdor and Hunt's name had come up. 'A bit like you, Charlie Brewer was in awe of this bloke. In fact, he boasted Hunt had stayed at Moyles's properties more than once.'

'That's corroboration,' Jess said.

'Moyles would have known it was him.' Catrin voiced the thought that had already occurred to Warlow. Suddenly, a whole vista of opportunity and motive opened up in front of them.

'You're thinking blackmail thoughts, Catrin,' Jess said.

'The more we find out about Moyles, the more I think he's capable of just about anything.'

'I'm with you there,' Warlow muttered. 'We need to have a chat with Mr Hunt.'

Catrin stood up. 'I still have his number, sir. I'll try him again; pretend I'm angling for him to sign Craig's book. Pretty please.'

'Worth a try, I suppose. See if you can get him to tell us where he's staying.'

Catrin left the room and headed for the stairwell of conversation.

Warlow stood with Jess, whose frown of concentration had shifted not at all since Catrin had showed them the image.

'Hang on, didn't Brewer say he was giving Hunt a lift that morning at the hotel?'

Warlow grinned at her. 'Jess, you're a bloody marvel.' Warlow took out his phone. 'I'll text Rhys and tell him to ask Brewer about that lift. See if Hunt told him exactly where he was staying in Gwynfe.'

'It also puts them together as possible co-conspirators, though,' Jess added.

Warlow sent Rhys the message and got a couple of blue ticks in response. Catrin came back into the Incident Room a minute later looking disappointed. 'Not answering, sir.'

'Never mind. We've got Moyles's records for the rental property. Let's see if we can find out where and when Hunt stayed.'

Jess moved back to her desk with purpose.

'Do we know who the woman is?'

Catrin opened a new window and googled Hunt.

Then she opened another window and searched for Roger Hunt's wife. A few clicks later, an image of Hunt next to a woman at an awards ceremony appeared on screen. Hunt in a dinner jacket, the woman in a cocktail dress. Thin with toned arms and long, fair hair.

'Got a picture of Hunt's wife, sir. She is not the woman in the bed with him,' Catrin said, her eyes on the screen.

Warlow's phone buzzed. A message from Rhys. Warlow read it, his expression a very long way from enthralled.

No luck with an address for Hunt

'*Scheisse*,' was Warlow's muttered reply.

He had nothing against Gwynfe, but he had been there. The village was tiny; a habitation on the western slopes of the Brecon Beacons National Park. To say that Hunt was staying in Gwynfe might mean anywhere within acres of sparsely populated land and lanes where grass grew down the middle.

'Why don't I give his wife a ring, sir? See if she has an actual address?' Catrin asked.

'Good idea.'

'How should I play it?'

'Be honest. Tell her we've found something of his and are trying to trace him.'

'What if she asks what it is?'

'Tell her it's come up as part of an investigation into something else and we need to find out if it is his, but that we are not at liberty, etcetera.'

Catrin nodded. All of that was true.

It didn't take long to find Hunt's address in the Cotswolds and a listed phone number. A landline that Catrin tried and got an answer to on the fifth ring. The woman who answered listened but said very little by reply. Catrin came back to the desk where Warlow was sitting.

'Something's up, sir. She didn't want to speak on the home phone. But she gave me her mobile number. I suggested a video call so you could be a part of it.'

They retired to the SIO room and set up the phone on the desk. The woman who answered was in a small room with a door shut behind her. Lydia Hunt looked gaunt, her cheeks drawn in and her teeth a little too large for her face.

'Sorry. The kids are home. I didn't want to speak in front of them. For some reason, I still want to keep as much of this as private as I can. Spare them the pain. More fool me, I say.'

It was a strange conversation opener. Catrin introduced Warlow. He stood a little behind the sergeant after insisting she sat in his chair. That way, they would both be in shot.

'We'll be brief, Mrs Hunt,' Catrin said. 'We're trying to trace your husband, and we think he's in this part of the world. This part being Carmarthenshire. Someone has mentioned the village of Gwynfe. Are you able to help us?'

A smile flickered and died on Lydia Hunt's lips. 'No, I'm afraid I can't help.'

Warlow frowned. 'When was the last time you spoke to Mr Hunt?'

'Seven weeks ago,' Lydia Hunt said. 'Scarlet, that's our daughter, had a thing in college. I couldn't go, so he went.'

'The—' Catrin was saved from asking by Mrs Hunt interjecting.

'Has he done something stupid again?'

'What do you mean "again"?' Warlow asked.

Lydia Hunt frowned. 'I forget that not everyone follows Twitter. When Roger left *Wildscene*, it lit up like a house on fire. All conjecture. An illness. His politics. Bullying. All horse crap. I played my part, but I suppose it was only a matter of time before the idiot did something equally self-destructive.'

'Mrs Hunt, are we to assume Roger Hunt doesn't live with you anymore?'

'It's not an assumption.' Lydia Hunt's response was as bitter as ashes. 'You're in Wales, yes?'

'Yes.'

'That's where it happened, so I assume there's a link.'

'Mrs Hunt,' Warlow said. Whatever had triggered her

venom could be important. 'Can you tell us what happened between you and your husband?'

'God, what time is it?' She glanced at her watch. 'Still too early for a bloody drink?' She sighed, and Warlow read the simmering anger behind her eyes. 'Roger Hunt, the darling of the wildlife watchers. What we, that means me and his adoring fans, weren't to know was how much Roger liked to put it about. If you think about it, and I have, believe me, the opportunity was there once he got the job. Weeks away in out of the way places. Off down to Wales, to the back of beyond. Cornwall. The Highlands of Scotland. It still makes me feel sick.'

'What does?' Catrin urged her on.

Lydia Hunt took a deep breath before explaining. 'Fourteen months ago, I got an email from an old friend. A flatmate of mine. Someone I lived with as a student in a house share. We had a pre-Roger fling. It didn't last more than a term, but it meant more to him than it did me. He's kept in touch. Though he's been married and divorced twice. But he always sends me cards on my birthday. I suspect he still carries a torch. The email was… apologetic. But good old Miles said he couldn't tell me in person. I still don't know whether to thank him or hate his guts for what he sent in that email.'

'What did he send?'

'A clip of my husband romping in bed with another woman.'

Warlow sensed his pulse tick up. 'How did he get it?'

'Miles was highly sexed. He admitted he watched porn, and this popped up. An unfortunate phrase that he used, not me, though, knowing Miles, I suspect it was deliberate. He's that kind of bloke. But of course, I watched it. Thirty seconds of film that ended twenty-five years of marriage. I lost it. I told Roger his sodding career was over. I told him to piss off and get out.' A momentary intake of breath tinged with regret caught her and she steadied herself. 'I was angry. I still am. I wanted revenge. We had enough money, but I wanted to see him suffer. I told him that if he didn't give up his TV work, I'd tell the world. That was fourteen months ago. He hasn't been back in this house since. The kids don't actually *hate* me for chucking him out, but they've changed towards me as well. Fucking Roger.'

'Do you still have a copy of the clip?' Catrin asked.

'I do.'

'I'll text you my email address. Can you send it to me, please?'

'What?' Lydia Hunt let out some derisory air. She looked taken aback. 'Why?'

'Because it may apply to a case we're investigating.'

The ire that had been driving Lydia Hunt slowly leaked away to be replaced by a kind of horrified suspicion. 'Shit. What has... oh God, have I said too much here?'

'No. You haven't. But we would like to see that clip, Mrs Hunt,' Warlow insisted. 'And if you hear from your husband—'

'Ex-husband.' Her correction was automatic.

'—Please let us know.'

'Bloody Roger. I can see it's going to be another merry sodding Christmas, thanks to him.' She paused and then added in a quieter, softer voice, 'He's alright, is he?'

'As far as we know. But we'd like to get in touch with him as soon as possible.'

'I mean, he was a good father. I'll give him that. Just a shitty husband.'

Warlow heard the words and felt them thud home like arrows in a target. The same could probably be said about him. His career had meant long hours, which had left his two boys with his wife, Jeez Denise, for long periods while he was out putting bad people away. But he'd made the effort whenever he'd been home. Made every minute count.

They'd come through it. Not as a family, because that ended when he and Denise split up, though they'd stuck it out until the boys had left home. Just how they'd stuck it out – the bickering, the silences, the pointed fingers, the vodka (in Denise's case) – were dark memories that Warlow kept in a locked mental drawer he hardly ever, ever opened. But now and again, he was forced to examine its contents. And often at the strangest of times.

Chatting with Lydia Hunt had been one of those times. He listened while Catrin took more details and forwarded her email address, but he'd disengaged.

'Sir?' Catrin's voice brought him back. 'Are you okay?'

The sound of a slammed drawer echoed in his head. 'No. I don't like rogue players like this. Hunt is in the wind and I think we need to find him.'

Jess joined them. Warlow filled her in. Jess listened and then told them what her search results had thrown up. 'I have Hunt booked in on at least three occasions at *Cân-y-barcud* in the last two years.'

'That seals it, then,' Warlow said grimly. 'Catrin, get some CID bods looking up all the rental properties in and around Gwynfe.'

'Wow,' Jess said, 'How many will that be?'

'I'm hoping it won't be that many. In fact, I'm *sure* it won't be that many, but in the meantime, Catrin and Rhys can get out there. At least they'll be on the spot if we find an address for him.'

It hadn't escaped Warlow's notice that Sengupta had mentioned in her report that some of the injuries to Moyles's face could have been made by the barrel of a gun.

'You are not to approach him if he's found,' Warlow

warned Catrin. 'We'll call in the cavalry for that. Now, I will relieve Rhys his duty in the interview room. You two will have to deal with his enthusiastic puppy mode once he learns he's off on a mission.'

CHAPTER THIRTY-SIX

'THE THING IS, CHARLIE,' Gil said, 'the thing I'm having most difficulty with swallowing, is you not knowing anything about Royston Moyles's surveillance activities, when you were supposed to be his right-hand man.'

Warlow watched the young man on the other side of the table. He looked a little scared, and a little bored, but not terrified. Enid, the solicitor, looked equally bored. And perhaps that should not have been a surprise. Since Warlow had let Catrin and Rhys off the leash, he and Gil had been at it with Charlie for a good twenty minutes. It was now well after 1 pm. Everyone was tired. Everyone was hungry. But those little bodily distractions were useful in catching people off guard. Warlow milked them, waiting for the one little slip that would let the officers in. Dyfed Powys Police HQ wasn't Guantanamo Bay, but experience had taught him what little physiological and psychological tricks worked.

Charlie sighed. 'I can't help it if he'd hidden stuff in the roof space. I went nowhere near it. He must have gone there late at night or early in the morning.'

'And you never noticed that little step stool out of place.'

Charlie looked genuinely confused.

Warlow decided on one last pre-lunch attack. 'How well did you know Roger Hunt?'

Charlie frowned. 'I don't *know* him. I recognised him the other day, but then so did lots of other people. My dealings with him had all been online through the booking network.'

'Why would you have had dealings?' Warlow asked. 'Isn't that system automated?'

'It is. But he had certain requests. He wanted to be sure to be left alone. Didn't want the cleaners turning up or me or Royston. He said he was setting a camera up in the garden to film nightlife. Foxes and rabbits. He didn't want his equipment disturbed, is what he said.'

'No,' muttered Gil. 'Someone else was disturbing his equipment.'

Enid gave Gil a disapproving glare.

Charlie picked up on it, though. 'What do you mean?'

But Warlow was not about to be distracted. 'And he always booked under his own name?'

'Of course. Who else?'

'Why all the questions about Roger Hunt, whoever he is?' Enid asked.

Again, Warlow ignored the question. 'When you gave him a lift from the hotel the other morning, did he mention where he was staying?'

'No. I mean, it was in Gwynfe. He'd mentioned that. I made a joke about it. Him not staying in one of ours. But no, he gave no address like a house name or anything.'

'Did you chat to him in the car?'

'Not really. He was subdued. But then he didn't get much sleep in the hotel lounge.'

Or he was contemplating wreaking revenge on his enemies.

Charlie seized the opportunity to deny everything once more. 'I don't know Roger Hunt any more than anyone else who's seen him on TV. I didn't know Royston had anything in his roof space, either. And I had nothing to do with what happened to him.'

Warlow nodded. 'Okay. Let's hope we find nothing else that might scupper those answers.'

'Else?' Charlie asked, looking unhappy.

But Warlow had already scraped back his chair to stand. Gil followed suit, and they exited, leaving Charlie and Enid to talk amongst themselves.

———

Jess had brought her own lunch. Gil had done the same, only he had enough sandwiches for half the Incident Room and so Warlow availed himself of one of the Lady Anwen's ham and tomato with lots of black pepper and a smear of mustard between bread thick enough to buffer a train.

'Want to see the Hunt clip?' Jess asked Gil.

'No, but I will. Though I'd better eat first. From what I've heard, I might not have much appetite afterwards.' Gil bit into an egg and cress.

Jess had an opened foil pack on the desk and the remnants of her hummus and crackers had formed a little layer of detritus on the bottom. She scrunched the whole thing up and reached for her tea. 'What about Brewer? He still a likely candidate?'

Gil twitched his nose. 'I think he's a good lad caught in the middle of a *storom gachu.*'

Warlow donned Catrin's translator mantle and mouthed "shitstorm" by way of explanation.

'He has motive and opportunity, but everything else we have is circumstantial,' Gil said.

'There is a lot of it, though.' Jess looked at the board. 'Access, contact with Hunt, intimate knowledge of Moyles's business.'

Gil turned to Warlow. 'Is he still your number one person of interest?'

'For now, yes,' Warlow said, though he had to admit he could have been a little more convincing in that confirmation.

The three officers sat for a moment to refuel, weighing up what evidence they had. Gil finished his sandwich, rubbed the crumbs off his hands in a lets-get-back-to-work kind of way and said, 'Right, the XXX files. Where do I start?'

Jess indicated a desk. 'Use Catrin's. She still has the thumb drive attached.'

Gil didn't bother getting up. With a thrust of both legs, he sent his chair across the six yards to Catrin's desk, grabbed hold to stop from overshooting, and positioned himself with his hand on the mouse. 'How come even her desk smells nice?' he asked, not expecting any sort of answer.

'Any news from Cardiff about Hughes?' Jess asked Warlow.

'Stable,' he muttered.

A dimple appeared at the corner of Jess's mouth. 'Not your favourite word, I know.'

'Better than deteriorating, I suppose.'

'What number file was it, ma'am?' Gil called over.

'Number twenty-three.'

Gil clicked and clicked again, then narrowed his eyes to watch.

Warlow finished the last bite of his sandwich. But his enjoyment was interrupted by Gil's astonished voice.

'*Mam Fach,*' Gil said.

'Christ, I hope not.' Warlow wheeled around.

Jess sent him a quizzical look.

'"Oh, mother" comes closest,' Warlow explained. 'Or maybe mama mia? Except here it's little mother—'

'I know her,' Gil cut short the mother discussion.

'Who?' Jess sat up.

'The woman with Hunt. That's Megan Roach. She's the deputy head at my granddaughter's school.'

Warlow got up and joined Gil at the desk. 'You mean the woman who was at the Cawdor the other morning? Looks nothing like her.'

'With all due respect, DCI Warlow,' Gil added the mock formality for effect, 'she is now blonde and was wearing a mask. But I've seen her dozens of times over the last couple of years at the school. Even before we moved down here. Don't forget, I've been to more Christmas concerts than you've had sardines on toast.'

'The supper of kings,' Warlow muttered.

Jess joined them. 'She's had a makeover since this?'

'I suppose so,' Gil said.

'And why was she wearing a mask the other day?'

'She was still wearing it when I went to the school to look at their CCTV to check on the Viking's camper van.' Gil turned in his chair to dress the DI. 'Said she had a cold and didn't want to transmit it to the kids.'

They all felt it then. The sensation that this was important in a way yet to be determined. But the ball was rolling towards the skittles here.

'When does school break up?' Warlow asked Gil.

'Today at half three.'

'Then we've got time. I think Jess and I need to have a word with Mrs Roach, don't you?'

Gil dredged up a knowing smile. 'The kids will be like wound-up toys with two days to go to Christmas. I'd take riot gear if I were you.'

They took the Jeep.

'When was it the shortest day again?' Jess asked, looking up at the grey December sky.

'That was Wednesday. Things are looking up now, as I am sure you've noticed. We've gained an extra minute of daylight since then already.'

'You can really tell,' Jess said.

Warlow snorted. 'You're not one of these people who get S.A.D. Are you? You know, Seasonal Affective Down in the dumps.'

'I won't deny it gets to you when the weather is so rubbish you can't even go outside on a weekend. But I haven't got time to be depressed.'

'No. And Cadi won't let me sit inside regardless of the weather.'

'But it would be nice at this time of year to go somewhere dry and warm where there is plenty of light.' Jess added a dreamy lilt to the sentence, ladling on the longing.

'Alright, alright. I can't help it that my son lives on the west coast of Australia where it is twenty-five degrees tonight with no rain in sight for the foreseeable.'

'You lucky sod, Evan. You must be looking forward to it now?'

'I am.' He sighed. 'But this bloody case has been a distraction I could have done without.'

'Hmmm,' Jess mumbled. 'Do you think we're going to find Napier trussed up like a Christmas turkey somewhere?'

'If he isn't already dead, then I suspect he might well be soon. Whoever killed Moyles and attacked Hughes is a planner. I doubt he's got sherry and mince pies on the agenda for John Napier.'

Jess stared out of the window as the Jeep ate up the miles on the south side of the river, heading east towards Llandeilo.

'How's Molly?' Warlow asked.

'Fine. Full of it. She's a real Christmas bird, is that one. She's got a couple of parties to go to with Bryn, but Christmas Day is always the same. Of course, not quite the same without her dad, but that's where you step in.'

'Me?'

'I hope you have your Christmas jumper ready.'

'Yeah, about that.'

'Only kidding. No, Molly has Christmas on a clip-board. We get up. She opens her stocking. She's eighteen, but on December 25th she's eight again. Then we have scrambled eggs and smoked salmon. Shower and change for the day. We'll swap presents while I have a sherry and listen to Christmas music while lunch is prepared.'

'You do?'

'Oh yeah, but good stuff, some classics. Vince Guaraldi does a jazzy Charlie Brown Christmas album. And of course, this year we will have guests for breakfast. You and Cadi. We'll expect you at about ten just in time for the smoked salmon.'

'Sounds like fun. I'm looking forward to it.' Warlow grinned.

'It's for them, isn't it? Christmas. It's for the kids. Vicarious pleasure for us oldies seeing how much they enjoy. Not forgetting the religious bit, which we do.'

'You're not a midnight mass kind of person?'

'As a kid, my mum took me. There is something special about it, too. Something that makes you think different thoughts. But then you come home and there's a reality TV programme on about how stupid people look naked.'

'Interesting options for emphasis in that sentence, aren't there? How *stupid* people look naked, or how stupid people look *naked*. Ah yes. Certain channels, between 3 and 6, always succeed in showing us how far we've come as a civilisation. Oh, and thanks for the card, by the way.'

'Crap, that reminds me. Molly got a card from someone. Supposedly her dad, but written not in his hand, or his hand but badly disguised. It has a contact number to text. I wanted to ask you what I should do about it?'

Warlow glanced across. Jess was still smiling, trying to make light of it. As if doing so might make it less significant.

'Hang on, isn't he under cover?'

'Yes. But mind you, it's just the stupid kind of thing he'd do.'

'At the risk of offending her dad, if it was him, I would not respond.'

Jess persisted, 'My feeling, too. But she's going to ask why.'

'You know why. This could be a fishing expedition by someone who isn't Rick.'

Jess winced. 'That's what I thought. Right, that card goes in the bin. Thank you, Evan.'

'It's tough for her, isn't it?'

'It is. Despite all the bluster, she's still a kid and still hurting.'

'Ah well. Let's see what a bit of Cadi therapy can do to ease the pain.'

Jess brightened at that. 'She's looking forward to it. And so am I.'

'Me too. But tell me Molly's not cooking the bird?'

'She's pigs in blankets only.'

'Thank God. A bit of charred pork did no one any harm.'

Jess grinned. 'I'll be sure to tell her that.'

CHAPTER THIRTY-SEVEN

CATRIN SAT in the passenger seat of the job car Audi which Rhys was driving. That meant she could be active on her phone, liaising with the CID officer who'd been tasked with finding which B and B Roger Hunt was renting. She'd been waiting for a message for fifteen minutes. The pressure was on because if she didn't get an answer soon, it would mean they'd need to pull over until she did because there was little chance of a good signal the further up the Bethlehem Road they travelled.

'Funny, us on the way to Bethlehem two days before Christmas, isn't it?' Rhys said, enjoying the joke.

'Fancy yourself as a carpenter, then, do you?'

'No, I meant, Joseph and Mary.'

'So did I?'

'Oh, right, because he was a carpenter.'

Catrin bit back a carping retort. 'But we're not going all the way to Bethlehem, are we?'

'No. The Gwynfe turn off is about a mile ahead.' Rhys glanced at her phone. 'Better hurry with that thing, sarge. I doubt there's much signal up ahead.'

Catrin gave him one of her very best thanks-for-mansplaining looks.

They'd just come through the lights at Ffairfach and under the railway bridge, taking a right up past the old school, when her phone chirped.

She took the call and spoke for a minute. Her phone chirped again, a different tone, this time a text.

'Right,' Catrin said. 'I have an address. That was Donat on the phone. It took her a while to find the address because he hadn't booked it under his own name. And it has been taken off sites because of renovation. But whoever booked it said they wanted it, regardless.'

'How do you know it's Hunt?'

'It's unfinished, this property, and Hunt, or whoever he was pretending to be, said it didn't matter. He just needed one room to store equipment. He explained that he'd be watching wildlife and he didn't mind camping. It's our best bet, anyway.'

The road, appropriately enough called the Gwynfe Road on the map, climbed steadily up from the river valley. Narrow lanes with neatly topped hedges ran east. Sometimes the view on either side was obscured by the naked branches of trees. Beyond them, the bare slopes of the eastern edge of the Black Mountains. A black on white sign at a junction told them they were now three miles from Gwynfe itself, where the chapel and the hamlet were, and eight from Brynamman at the top of a different valley.

Catrin followed the pin she had on the map, downloaded and now working offline because they had no signal.

'Go right,' she ordered. 'Head for Trap. It's south from here and it should be on the right.'

Rhys glanced out of his driver's side window. All he could see was a bank of low trees. 'It's a woodman's cottage, is it?'

'*Ty Coed*. As it says on the tin.'

The turning was a dirt pull-in twenty yards down the road marked by a closed metal gate and no sign. Catrin opened the gate, and the Audi bumped along, brushing up against foliage thankfully stunted from winter die-back. Already this car had done its fair share of off-roading, most of it with Rhys at the wheel. But this lane was short and curved down in a semicircle to where the property sat surrounded by trees. It appeared to be little more than a hut with a new door and windows, but with tarpaulin draped over one half of an unfinished roof. Next to the finished half of the property sat a modern-looking, black, one-man tent. The kind that took ten seconds to erect and half a minute to put away.

Rhys got out and called out, 'Hello? It's the police. Anyone here?'

No answer.

Catrin pushed her door open. Though they were only forty yards from the road above, the place had a silent, brooding feel to it. In summer, all the deciduous trees would be leafy. Now they were bare-limbed and stark.

'Nice spot,' Rhys muttered.

'Depends on what you're after. If your vibe is scary witch house in the forest, this fits the bill.'

Rhys walked over to the tent. Everything was zipped up. Rhys called out again, 'Hello? It's the police.'

Silence.

Squatting, Rhys pulled the zip open to reveal an interior with a folded sleeping bag, lamp, and a small bag of clothes. Nothing here had any label.

'Could be anybody's,' Rhys said, standing up.

Catrin stood behind him. It felt gloomy and oppressive in this hidden, silent place. The sort of place where bad things could happen and no one would know for weeks or months. She turned and faced the hut. 'Okay, nothing for it, is there?'

'I'll get some torches from the car,' Rhys said.

'Got anything made of iron?' Catrin asked.

Rhys paused in his walk. 'Iron? No.'

'Pity. They say iron is good against witches,' Catrin said.

'I've got a metal drinks bottle,' Rhys said.

'That'll do. How's your aim?'

'Played a bit of cricket,' Rhys said with the boot of the Audi open. 'If there is a witch, I can bowl my googlie at her.'

'Don't be so disgusting and hurry up with that torch.'

———

Jess unbuckled her seat belt and was about to get out of the Jeep when she heard Warlow mutter, 'Would you call me a sneaky old sod?'

'Wouldn't dream of it, Detective Chief Inspector.'

'Right. Well, I am. So, you go in and meet Mrs Roach. I'll stay here cogitating for a minute or two.'

'Sure?'

'I am. I'll follow you in.'

Jess exited, pulling her coat tight around her. She walked down through the Co-op car park towards the busy road that bisected the town. There'd be a lollipop lady watching over the kids in an hour. But for now, traffic moved as normal. She took a right and walked up the hill parallel to the school's stone wall. Iron gates opened on to a tarmac school yard. The reception comprised another wire gate and an intercom system.

Jess approved. No such thing as too much security. Not in this day and age. She pressed the button. It took two goes, but then a voice answered. Jess explained herself, and the door into the school opened. The secretary, wearing an apologetic expression, came out and opened the gate to Jess, who showed her warrant card in response. From inside the school came the sound of a piano and the mechanical singing small children often produced. It was all in Welsh, but Jess guessed the theme might have been Christmas related.

'Did you say it was Mrs Roach you wanted?' The secretary had the low, earnest voice you associated with church deacons and undertakers.

'I did.'

The secretary showed her teeth in a rictus grin. 'Such bad luck. A minute before you rang, Mrs Roach left.'

'Where to?'

'Family emergency, she said, she didn't say where exactly. I am so sorry.'

'Not your fault. Did she say she was going home?'

'I assume so. But an emergency can happen anywhere, I suppose. All I know is that she was in a hurry. She looked very distracted. Just a minute before you rang the bell.'

'Is that right? Then where is she parked?'

'Most people use the shop car park—'

'And that is where I was lucky enough to bump into Mrs Roach.' Warlow's voice came from behind the secretary. She turned in time to see Mrs Roach walk through the door with Warlow in attendance.

'Lucky I stayed with the car, otherwise it looks like we would have missed one another.' Warlow grinned.

Mrs Roach still wore a mask, so it was only her eyes that betrayed her when she said, 'Yes, that was lucky.'

Jess exchanged a glance with Warlow. No words were spoken, but they were implied in that look and said, *You sneaky old sod.*

'Mrs Roach has agreed to have a word with us here as

opposed to the station,' Warlow said, heavy on the affability.

Roach glared at the secretary. 'I'll be in my office.'

———

THE DOOR to the finished half of the hut was locked. But the other half, with a weighted-down tarpaulin roof, was accessible, thanks to an MDF sheet held in place by breeze blocks and some four-by-twos that Rhys removed easily. Inside, dry walling had been completed, but pipes running out of the walls suggested a bathroom was yet to be fitted.

'I hope the other half of this place is better,' Catrin said.

The doorway leading into that finished half was sealed off by another MDF sheet, this one hung as a door. But when Rhys tried the handle, the lock rattled, and the door stayed shut.

'Loose,' he said. 'There may be a way…'

'Are you sure?' Catrin looked doubtful.

'Wait a minute.' Rhys disappeared and came back with a little tool kit and a screwdriver. He bent to inspect the handle again. 'This looks like an old, recycled rim lock with loose handles and no metal keep, just this gouged-out space in the wood to hold the latch bolt.' Rhys threw Catrin a glance.

She stood off to one side, her arms folded. 'You lost me at rim lock. Not because it's complicated, but because it's nuts and bolts. I get enough of that at home with Craig.'

'I didn't know he was a DIY guy?'

'Craig can turn his hand at anything.'

Rhys doubled down on his grin and earned a warning chin down glare from Catrin.

'It's bloody dark in here. Any chance you can hold the torch, sarge?'

Catrin obliged, and Rhys got to his knees to unscrew the surface mount of the black lock. Three minutes later, the lock came away from the door with a rattle, now only held in place by the loose screws holding the handle to wood on the other side. From the toolbox, Rhys produced a small prise bar and began levering away at the lock. After a few minutes of yanking hard, something tore, and the lock fell to the floor, spindle included, leaving a sizeable circular hole in the MDF doorway.

'You've broken that,' Catrin said.

'Nah. It was rattling because the screws were loose on the other side. It's all good.'

'Doesn't look good.'

'I think the Wolf would approve.'

'You're probably right.' Catrin went to push the door, but it remained stuck.

'The MDF is swollen. Maybe a bit of elbow grease would help.'

'Let me try.' Catrin put her shoulder to the door and pushed. It didn't budge.

'Want me to…' Rhys offered

But Catrin was nothing but determined. She shoved harder. 'It's a bit st—' The sound of wood groaning ended that sentence before it developed legs. The door swung in a few inches. Rhys peered through. 'Ah, they've hung a drape up to stop the drafts.' He put his arm through and swept the material back before pushing the door open to reveal the dark interior beyond.

CHAPTER THIRTY-EIGHT

MEGAN ROACH SAT on her side of the desk. There were three stacked plastic chairs of the sort you might find in an assembly hall set against the wall. Warlow pulled two down and he and Jess sat at slight angles to each other, waiting.

The deputy head still had her mask on. During Covid, Warlow had interviewed while wearing masks and he'd always found it challenging. It meant you only had the eyes to read. A difficult skill. But Jess had become very good at it.

'I've been expecting you,' Megan Roach said. She looked calm. She kept her voice even. What gave her away was the way she had to hold on to the wrist of her right hand with her left to stop it shaking. 'I thought when Sergeant Jones came, that...' Her words dried up as the last vestiges of desperate doubt kicked in.

But Jess was not for letting her off the hook now that the bait had been set. 'Why did you think we'd come, Mrs Roach?'

'Roger,' she whispered.

Jess glanced at Warlow and the tiniest of nods from

him said he wanted her to take the lead here. 'Where is John Napier, Megan?'

The eyes above the mask narrowed. 'John Napier? Why?'

'Because he's been missing since yesterday morning.'

The eyes squeezed shut and a barely perceptible, 'Oh, God,' came through the mask.

'He's been missing for over twenty-four hours now and we believe he might be in harm's way. If you have any knowledge, now would be a good time to tell us, Megan.'

Little nods from the deputy head. 'How much do you know?'

Warlow answered this time. 'We know that Royston Moyles filmed people who stayed at his properties. Filmed them and then uploaded videos of a sexual nature.'

Megan moved her head up and down slowly.

'We've seen clips of you with Roger Hunt some time ago.'

Another nod. 'Fourteen months ago. That's when those… that's when it happened.'

'You and Hunt were having an affair?'

'He came to the school to talk to the children. He loved coming down here to this part of the world. Red squirrels were his thing. We still have some up near Llyn Brianne, and Roger had sighted some further south. But he would never broadcast that. Telling people isn't always in an animal's best interest. There are sick people in this world.' She looked into the officers' eyes. Neither of them disagreed with that sentiment.

Warlow waited. A little part of his brain wanted to agree with her, but he stayed quiet and watched Megan put her shaky hands under the desk.

'You don't plan these things. I'm married, but it isn't what you might call a happy arrangement. I don't blame my husband, but we don't have children. Though of course, I have dozens of children here.' A hand came up in a vague wave and her eyes softened. 'Roger is charming. I only wish we'd met years ago.' She fixed Jess with her dark eyes. 'Have you seen the clips?'

'We've seen one,' Jess explained. 'Sergeant Jones recognised you.'

She exhaled a resigned wheeze. 'He would. He has the police officer's eye, I suppose. We had no idea, of course, Roger and I. But Royston Moyles put the clips on the internet.' She shook her head. 'Why would anyone do such a horrible thing?'

'Moyles has a lot to answer for,' Warlow said.

'Someone saw the clip and told Roger's wife. She is not a forgiving person. Not that I would expect her to... I mean, I have never met her. I'm not sure what kind of person she is.'

A woman scorned. Fury and rage were always a nasty mix.

'But so far, this clip has not reached the press. Roger's wife asked whoever told her not to broadcast it. She wouldn't tell Roger how she knew, either. Not for a long time. But I am "that woman with the mole on her cheek". I couldn't deny it.'

'That's why Roger left *Wildscene*?' Jess asked.

'It is. He couldn't risk the mess. He didn't want it all coming out. And his wife didn't either. She set the terms. For the sake of their children, Roger had to leave and take the blame. Roger is an honourable man. He didn't want to besmirch the programme. It's too important to him. They know nothing of the videos. Instead, he pretended to have a mini breakdown. They're in fashion these days, aren't they? Everyone seems to have a label. He said he wanted to concentrate on publishing books. Very believable because he is a fantastic photographer. But he was more concerned about me than anything.'

'You?'

'Roger's fans are not the people who pay to watch amateur peeping Tom clips for entertainment. We only found out about the clip, saw it I mean, and understood where it came from, six months ago. His wife's solicitor sent his solicitor a copy as part of the messy divorce he's going through. As soon as we realised where it had come from, Roger approached Moyles. Offered to pay him money to remove the clip from the site and warned him to stop doing it. But they were empty threats. What could he do? If he exposed Moyles, he'd expose himself and us. Moyles denied everything. The clip is still there. Besides, someone might have recorded the clip already. The only alternative would be for Roger to claim it was deep fake if it ever got out into the wide world. You're familiar with that, I expect?'

The digital superimposition of media celebrities into pornography was nothing new. But for it to succeed, you required a great deal of digital information as source material. That meant most individuals were relatively safe. Whereas Hunt, with hours of TV footage, would be a prime target. He could well get away with the double bluff.

Megan Roach shook her head. 'These days they can make people look like whichever celebrity they want, can't they? It's horrible and frightening. But who would want to go to the trouble of deep-faking me?'

'What do you mean?'

'You've seen the clip? I have certain very recognisable features.'

Warlow recalled the mole on her cheek.

'I've been terrified about that. If it came out, I wouldn't be able to stay in this job. It wouldn't be fair to the school or the children. All that horrible publicity. My marriage isn't… that doesn't matter so much. But when I told Roger about altering my appearance, he became furious. He understood, but something altered in him then. I dyed my hair, paid for a little Botox. Some fillers. My husband, and just about everyone else, thinks I'm mad. But people do this all the time, don't they? And the ultimate thing was to have the mole removed.'

Megan pulled down the mask. She was an attractive woman, with subtle makeup. But nothing hid the large red mark on the right side of her face over the cheekbone. 'I paid a lot of money. Not a botched job either. But the surgeon says I've reacted to something, and it's become hypertrophic.' She let out a bitter laugh. 'It's almost twice as big now. I thought that if I got rid of it, then it would make me far less recognisable. Now I may need more surgery at some point. It's all taken months to do. Roger had gone to Patagonia for a while but when he came back last week and saw me…' Megan sounded wistful. 'I'd never seen him like that. He got very quiet. Really quiet. All he'd say was that something needed to be done.' Megan looked up at the ceiling and shut her eyes. 'At the hotel, when he saw the junior manager taking photographs of the motorists having coffee and rolls, he pushed me. I caused the tray of food to fall, but Roger orchestrated that.'

'Why?' Warlow asked.

'I don't think he wanted anyone to see him there. People had, but the photographs were the last straw. He must have hated being exposed in the hotel like that. But you must believe me. I had no idea he'd do anything…' Her voice caught on a sob.

'Do you know where he's staying?' Jess asked.

'Somewhere up in Gwynfe. A place he's camped in before. The owner is trying to do it up as a rental property, but they have no money.'

'Did he tell you he planned to do something to Moyles?'

Megan's face crumpled in misery. 'No. I would have

stopped him if I'd known…' She paused, regret and wistfulness straining her voice. 'But he's changed. He's become so bitter.'

Warlow recalled the first time he'd seen this woman at the hotel. 'Last Monday, you were in the hotel with Hunt.'

Megan sighed. 'We'd met. I was in town for the church group and we arranged to chat in the lay-by. We were there when the black rain came. We didn't think twice about a bit of rain, but then both our cars got stuck.' She let go a mirthless laugh. 'It happened in minutes. The rain turned to ice and you know the rest. We weren't there to do anything but chat. We aren't teenagers, and to be honest, I've already accepted that it's over between us. Moyles poisoned all that. But Roger wanted to see me. Said he had a way of sorting things out.'

'What way?'

'He wouldn't say. He came to say goodbye. Told me he'd be going away. This time for a long while.'

'Think hard on that, Mrs Roach. I need you to tell us how that conversation went. Can you do that?'

Wiping away a tear, Megan Roach nodded.

————

WHAT LIGHT there was in the room came from the doorway they'd come through. Rhys went over to the windows front and back and drew the curtains. Daylight, tempered by the filtering trees all around, oozed in and showed a kitchen of sorts. A sink, worktop, Formica table, and wooden chairs. But it was the wall between this room and the unfinished one that drew the officers' eyes. Catrin saw it first as she stepped in and pivoted.

'Look at this,' she said.

The wall, unpainted but plastered, had become a Gallery arranged in three distinct blocks. At the top of each array was a candid photo of a man. On the left, Royston Moyles standing outside *Cân-y-barcud* next to his Land Rover, staring toward whoever was photographing him, but with no recognition. Not seeing anything but the vista that was to die for. Beneath that, photos of Moyles outside Napier's office. Moyles on the street in Llandeilo. Moyles with two other men outside The Farmer's. These last few were flat. The type everyone could do with a camera phone, whereas those of Moyles up at the rental property had depth and looked as if a long lens had been used.

The second group had a different man at the top. A man outside a small building under a bakery sign.

'That's Daniel Hughes,' Rhys said.

Beneath were more candid shots of Hughes walking along near-empty streets. Photos of the little station at Llandeilo and the steps leading up to the town.

'He's planned it all out,' Catrin whispered.

But she didn't dwell on either Hughes or Moyles. Her eyes flicked to the third group. John Napier, outside his office, unaware that he was being photographed.

'That one looks like it might have been taken from the churchyard,' Rhys said. 'I recognise that bit of wall.'

More images of Napier. At a house neither of them recognised, outside The Farmer's, and another location. This one without Napier. That it was a church was obvious, but which church was a different question. There were views taken from several angles. Above, looking down, from a churchyard with old stones, and from a distance. In every case, the setting and the composition were remarkable. Hunt had an eye. There was no doubting that.

'Is this Llandeilo Church? Looks small,' Catrin asked. The images were stunning. The building looked like it had been dropped into a setting right out of an Edgar Allan Poe poem. Catrin had done the Raven and The Haunted

Palace in school and they'd both stuck in her head and gone some way to stoke the fires of her dislike of anything too spooky. And as she looked at these photos, she half expected to hear distant bells, bells, bells. One image drew her eye. Taken from below with oddly angled gravestones in the foreground and a path winding up to the left. The ivy-covered building was unusual in that it appeared to have two roofs. Behind, tall trees and greenery made up the timeless backdrop.

'Is there another church in the town?' Catrin asked.

'I don't know,' Rhys said. 'Could be. I'm not a religious architecture expert. But those images of Napier outside his office, that's from the churchyard in town.'

'The same churchyard as in these other photos?'

'Hard to say.'

They ruminated, looking around. There was tea, coffee, and milk on the table, but nothing else. 'He's been here all this time, scheming,' Rhys said.

Catrin took photos of everything and began to text. 'Crap. No signal. Let's get out of here. When was the last time we got a signal? Can you remember?'

'About a mile back.'

'Right. You drive. If anyone can recognise these photos, Gil can.'

CHAPTER THIRTY-NINE

'AND THAT'S IT?' Jess asked.

Megan Roach held the DI's gaze. 'I don't know what else to tell you. Before we were picked up by your lot in a Land Rover and taken to the Cawdor because the road got too dangerous to drive on, Roger kept apologising, We met in the lay-by and I could see he wasn't himself. He kept saying how sorry he was that he'd put me through all of this and how it turned out. When I asked him what he meant, he said it was better that I didn't know.'

'What did you take that to mean?' Warlow asked.

'He was upset about my scar. Had been for days. We hadn't seen each other for months and in that time… as I say, we both realised that whatever we had, it had gone. Soured by Moyles.'

'How did you feel about that?' Jess asked.

'I've asked myself that many times. I've accepted that we were breaking the rules in what we'd done.'

'Rules?' Jess asked.

'Matrimony. Faithfulness. Vows we'd both made to other people.'

Warlow hardly ever heard these terms being used these days. 'Would you call yourself a religious woman, Megan?'

'I believe there's something, if that's what you're asking. And I suppose I've come to terms with the fact that what happened to us was a kind of punishment. Those commandments may not be laws, but they are a way to live. Something to believe in. We can't say that to children anymore, of course. But I am not a child. I think I may have strayed too far from the path and paid the price.'

Not quite the postmodernist viewpoint he was used to hearing from the criminals he normally dealt with. Not that Megan here was criminal. There was no evidence of that. Not yet at least.

Warlow's phone buzzed. Gil's name appeared in the caller window. The DCI raised a hand in apology and stepped out of the room.

'Gil. Any news?'

'The kids hit the jackpot. They found Hunt's place. Photographs of everything. Hunt has become the hunter it seems.'

'What about Napier?'

'There is a possibility. I'm sending you an image from the wall Hunt has plastered with photos. You'll know it. I'm sending some Uniforms as we speak, too.'

Warlow watched the image come through, blurry with a little arrow and a circle that gradually filled in as it downloaded.

'Shit,' he said when he saw it.

Back in the deputy head's room, Jess was still quizzing Roach about Daniel Hughes.

'But he fell, didn't he?' She sounded shocked.

'Fell or was pushed,' Jess said.

The look of horror on Roach's unmasked face spoke volumes.

'We need to go,' Warlow told Jess. He turned to Megan

Roach. 'And there's nothing else you can think of to tell us?'

She shook her head.

'Where are we going?' Jess asked as she got up.

'Gil thinks he knows where Napier might be. There's a church not far from the castle—'

'Llandyfeisant?' Megan Roach's question came out high and urgent.

Warlow and Jess pivoted to look at her.

'What do you know about—'

'I… I didn't think it was… I d-didn't…' Roach stuttered out the words.

'What?' Warlow barked.

'Monday night. That was one of the reasons I was in Llandeilo. The church group meeting. It was about Llandyfeisant. The remedial works. Roger asked me last week to borrow a key. He wanted to document it all for a book. I didn't see the harm. He was going to give me the key back but he asked if he could hang on to it for a bit longer.'

'Don't go anywhere except home,' Warlow said, and something in his voice made Megan Roach start like a frightened animal.

———

THERE WOULD BE NO SNOW. The weather remained too mild for that. In fact, the forecast had rain for Christmas Eve. But the lowering clouds gave this mid-winter afternoon a palpable prescience as Warlow drove quickly towards the town and branched right at the crossroads to take New Road towards the parks.

'I thought Napier was seen heading towards the river?' Jess asked.

'He was. On foot,' Warlow explained. 'Did I ever tell

you that I stayed in this town after Denise and I split? I used to walk the neighbour's dog. His name was Taran, the dog, I mean. Pre Cadi.'

'So, you know your way around. I'm impressed.'

'Not as well as Gil. But we can drive into the park and drop down through Castle Woods to the church. We'll be there in five.'

'There's a church in the park?'

Warlow hissed. 'We're in Wales. You can't turn without tripping over something ancient. And I don't just mean Gil. This church is old. Funny name, too. *Llan* means church, I daresay you've worked that out by now since every other place name is a *Llan* something. *Dyfeisant*, means Saint Tyfi. Another martyr from the twelfth century. But like a lot of these places, there's another story. Old walls under the graves that were probably Roman, or older. Places of worship tend to be sticky like that. There was a Roman fort on the ridge above us.'

Warlow was as good as his word. He drove through the park entrance on Carmarthen Road and five hundred yards later, pulled in. The park closed at four and they'd seen no traffic. On their right a huge open meadow obscured a view of the Grade II listed Newton House and on their left a lane guarded by a wooden five-bar gate led down into Castle Woods and the valley floor, invisible behind the trees. They dropped down on foot through the gate and the lane became a steep descent to a kissing gate and damp steps, slippery with moss, winding down. At a turning, Warlow heard Jess gasp behind him. Her first glimpse of the graveyard and the church roof below her, hidden in this hollow, and surrounded by a horseshoe of overgrown woodland. Except to the west, where the tumps of the old circular churchyard sloped away to the valley floor beyond.

'It's a while since I've been here,' Warlow said.

'Are there services, still?' Jess asked as she followed Warlow.

'Not since the sixties. You heard Roach. There's a preservation society. If I remember rightly, the whole thing was rebuilt in the late nineteenth century.'

A rough blue plastic sheet shelter had been constructed over part of the sloping graveyard. Scaffolding clung to the south wall of the church itself, too. Warlow walked across to look inside the tarpaulins. Uprooted gravestones had been set against a larger one that still stood. A collection of wood, branches, and broken pallets were piled up on a flat topped, full length grave marker that had, through time, lost all its letters.

Whoever was restoring all this had been working hard. He had no idea what the regulations were for moving graves or gravestones, but such things must happen. The earth, and those buried within it, could move and shift with time.

Warlow led the way down and around along the path to the north corner of the church where the wall stood only a few feet away from the bank of the hill and the little stream that gushed there. A stream that Taran often stopped to drink from.

It was a storybook setting. A hidden gem in a town full of pleasing little corners. Hardly anyone knew of this place now, though at one time Warlow had read that it had reinvented itself as a tourist information centre in the last century. No longer. Now lichen and moss crept over the stones and Roach's group had their work cut out to restore this place.

He took Jess to the church's door and the view, somehow more evocative than ever in the impending gloom, out over the valley floor to the left leading to the river and, directly ahead the imposing castle on its hill, a dark silhouette in the distance.

'Bloody hell. All that's missing are some cawing ravens and the creak of a coffin lid. How come you never told me about this place?' Jess said.

'The church looks spectacular coming at it from the castle. Which is the way I walked the dog. But the view isn't why we're here.' He turned to the door.

'Should we wait for Uniforms?' Jess asked.

'It'll be fully dark by the time they get here. It's getting dimmer by the minute as it is.'

Jess glanced up at the sky with a frown.

The iron gate guarding entry to the porch was ajar. Warlow tried the door and it opened with a magnificent and prolonged creak. 'That should go directly to the BBC sound effects archives,' Jess commented in a whisper.

Inside, the stained-glass window at the eastern gable just about let in enough light to see. On their left, a wooden scaffold was set up against the inner wall and underneath it, tins and sacks of materials sat.

'Nothing much here,' Warlow said.

But Jess's eyes were on the pots and an incongruous looking plastic green jerrycan. She walked across and picked it up. 'Petrol,' she muttered. 'I don't see a generator, do you?'

'So, why petrol?' Warlow asked. 'Is it used as a diluent?'

'Not as far as I—'

The whump of noise that suddenly filled the air answered their question in a sudden flare of light from somewhere outside. Warlow hurried back to the door and stepped out. The graveyard was lit up by the tarpaulin shelter merrily ablaze.

'Look,' Jess pointed up. Warlow followed her finger to the dark figure running up the steep steps above them.

'Police,' Warlow yelled. 'Stay where you are.'

The figure took no notice. Warlow began running up

through the path in the graveyard. The smell of petrol was strong here.

He'd gone ten yards when he skidded to a halt.

Petrol.

'Shit,' Warlow said and turned back towards the shelter. Its closed end was what had been set alight, the sheets melting and dripping gobbets of molten plastic. The open front end was of course still intact. But flames were already licking at the roof. A roof that would also drip molten red-hot plastic into whatever was beneath. Including the little arrangement of wood on that granite slab.

'Shit,' Warlow repeated.

If that was Hunt they'd seen running away, he'd set fire to this shelter for a reason.

And that reason, up to now, had been revenge, pure and simple.

Warlow ran towards the bonfire.

'Evan?' Jess screamed.

'We need to tip this thing over.' He was at the side of it now, desperately sizing it up. It wasn't a complicated arrangement, three two-by-two batons made the bottom frame, a mirrored arrangement above and uprights at the front and back and at the middle of the longest length with the thick plastic stapled to the wood at intervals.

'Jess, we can grab the base and lift it. You get to the front end.'

Warlow reached for the two-by-two, the heat from the fire hot on his face. Jess did the same. 'On three,' he yelled. 'One, two, three.'

They both grunted as they lifted, but it came up easily enough and then Warlow shoved with all his might and pushed the thing over on its side. He ran to the little stack of wood and immediately he could tell it, too, had been doused in petrol. He threw the branches and bits of wood away from where the shelter was burning a few feet adjacent. Jess helped him. They were both aware that the petrol-soaked fuel was only feet away from the flames. But in two minutes, they'd cleared the slab. Warlow picked up the one remaining branch and struck the stone three times.

Nothing.

He struck it again and waited.

From underneath, they both heard a weak and muffled groan.

Napier.

Still alive.

'Any point us going after Hunt?' Jess's hair was stuck to her forehead and her face had a sheen of sweat.

'Bugger that. Let him run, he won't get far.'

Warlow was right about Napier. Right about him being alive. But he was wrong about Hunt not getting very far. But that truth remained, like a shadow on the horizon, yet to be discovered.

CHAPTER FORTY

NAPIER ENDED up in hospital with severe dehydration and exposure.

'Better that than being bloody barbecued,' Gil commented. No one had dared gainsay him on that score.

The solicitor recovered enough to give a brief statement about the handwritten letter and the proposed meeting at the church. He'd been worried enough by Moyles's death to go along with it. He swore that although he'd known about Moyles's hobby, he'd had no part in it. But Hunt had met him with a gun. That put an end to any resistance Napier thought about putting up. Hunt wanted justice. At least, a kind of justice. He wanted Napier, Hughes, and Moyles to pay. He had not been prepared to listen to any mitigation. In Napier's opinion, the man was beyond reasoning with. In fact, beyond reason. The words Napier used were that Hunt had gone mad, accusing him, as well as Moyles and Hughes, of ruining his life.

'Think he really has a gun, sarge?' Rhys had asked on Saturday – Christmas Eve –morning.

'Maybe. Whether it's real or not is a different matter.'

They'd come in for the debrief, all of them, but

Warlow was calling a halt to proceedings at midday and insisting everything stayed on hold until Wednesday. After the team enjoyed the two bank holidays. They did as much as they could that morning, but the focus had already shifted to catching Hunt.

Warlow couldn't wait for the headlines. Roger HUNT.

At lunchtime, with everyone gone to festivity preparations except Warlow, Buchannan put his head around the SIO room door.

'Déjà vu,' Warlow said. 'Is it only a week ago we last did this?'

'No sign of our man?'

'He's gone to ground. He knows this part of the world better than most. He could be *cwtched* up with a red squirrel as we speak. Have stashes of nuts dotted everywhere for the winter.'

'Or he could be on a ferry to France,' Buchannan said.

'He won't be too happy that we scuppered his plans. I hope you have a burly PC guarding Napier's bed?'

'We do. But I wanted to congratulate the team. Looks like I missed them.'

'Ah, I let them all go. They've worked their arses off, as per.'

'You're still here, though?' Buchannan came up with a lopsided grin.

'Another half an hour should see me right. I want to clear my desk before I go.'

'Ah yes, the trip. When are you off again?'

'Couple of weeks.'

'Lucky bugger. Make the most of it. You deserve it.'

Warlow grunted. 'It's a team effort, you know that.'

'I do. Still, we'll miss you when you're gone.'

'It's only a month. And please, promise me you will not let Two-Shoes anywhere near my lot.'

'You have my word. Merry Christmas.'

'To all who sail in her.' Warlow lifted an imaginary glass.

'You don't mean Two-Shoes, do you?' Buchannan asked.

'Please. It's a saying, that's all. A toast that's a change from Merry sodding Christmas.'

Buchannan smiled. 'You really need that holiday, don't you?'

CHAPTER FORTY-ONE

ON CHRISTMAS MORNING, Catrin Richards held up the last of her presents from Craig. Probably the smallest, too. A light oblong box that she'd almost missed at the bottom of the swag bag. As she picked it up, Craig got up.

'More coffee?' he asked as he hurried to the kitchen.

'Okay,' she said with the slightest of frowns. She peeled off the wrapping paper. Inside was a two-pack, quick-result, pregnancy testing kit.

'What's this for?' she asked, wondering why she felt both annoyed and touched at the same time.

Craig, coffee-less, was standing in the doorway.

'Don't take it the wrong way. I just wanted you to know that I believe in us, Cat. These are for when it happens. Because it will. This time next year it'll be all teddies and rattles.'

Catrin got up and walked over to him, reached up and put her arms around his neck, wanting the feel of his arms around her.

The detective sergeant didn't cry easily, but this morning she let the tears come and hoped the ghosts of

Christmas past, and especially of Christmases yet to come, were both watching.

'You've made me cry, Craig Peters,' she said.

'It's a gift,' Craig said and held her close.

———

RHYS BROUGHT GINA a cup of tea in bed at a little after 7.45am. They'd woken up early, and she'd moaned a yes when he'd suggested tea. But when he got back to the bedroom armed with two mugs, the bed was empty. He heard the toilet flush and then Gina appeared dressed, not in stockings, but in cold weather gear.

'This is… different,' Rhys said. 'Where are you off to? Aren't we going to exchange… stuff?'

'We are. But I got chatting with Betty, the FLO coordinator, yesterday. I asked her how she spent Christmas and she said that every Christmas morning she goes down to the homeless shelter and makes people tea and toast for an hour. It really got to me. I mean, we're so lucky to have us and this…' Gina looked around at the recently decorated bedroom. 'I want to give something back to the Gods of luck. So, I said I'd go to the shelter for an hour, too.'

'You?'

'Yes, me.' She cocked her head. 'Does it surprise you that much?'

'It doesn't surprise me one bit,' Rhys said. 'It was the "I'd go" that surprised me. Why not "we'd go"?'

Gina's smile was brighter than the Christmas lights in Trafalgar Square. She walked over, stood on tiptoes, and kissed him on the cheek.

'You're a good bloke, Rhys Harries.' Then she took the cup and sipped the tea and nodded over the rim to a chair. 'I put your clothes out ready.'

'You know me too well, Gina Mellings. Give me two

minutes.' He headed for the loo but put his head back around the door. 'Besides, I'm an expert at making toast. Didn't you know that?'

'I knew you were world-class at eating it.'

'Hah,' Rhys said and lifted the toilet seat with his big toe like the gentleman that he was.

───────

BY 11.30 CHRISTMAS MORNING, Gil Jones was a man marooned. The only Y chromosome in a house full of Xs hidden in a wife, two daughters, and three granddaughters whose fathers had gone to the pub for pre-lunch drinks. Two pre-lunch drinks maximum on pain of death from the Jones girls. Gil cried off, using a heavier than usual Saturday night wine session with the Lady Anwen as his excuse. Even though he'd hardly drunk anything the previous evening.

No, Gil's reticence was work-related.

At Buchannan's request, after Warlow and the team left, he'd returned to the Incident Room to sift through the file marked "Chicken" on Moyles's hard drive. Doing it brought back memories of Operation Alice that he'd hoped to have forgotten. Thankfully, what he'd seen in "Chicken" had been nothing close to the things he'd come across in Operation Alice.

But there'd been something.

He'd seen a young kid. Nothing salacious, dressed in pyjamas. But that face rang a distant bell. From where; he had not yet sussed. But he would.

He'd immediately requested access to some misper files that had been a part of Op Alice. Thankfully, they'd take a few days to come because access to such files needed approval. Which meant putting a game face on for Christmas. Not enough of a game face to cope with the pub banter his sons-in-law would be enjoying, but enough to make sure everyone else enjoyed a good time.

And he'd have a drink with the food. And he'd try to forget that face he'd seen.

After all, he might be wrong.

Then again…

'*Tadcu, dere.*'

Eleri, one of the three fairy queens dressed for the part – including wand – that ruled the roost on Christmas Day, grabbed his hand and dragged him into the living room. 'The Snowman,' she announced.

'Fantastic,' Gil said and settled down to watch a film he'd already seen a dozen times.

Because that was what grandfathers did if the fairy queens requested it of him. Two minutes later, he had all three of them sprawled over him in the chair.

His daughter, Melody, walked in, took one look and giggled. 'Bet you wish you'd gone to the pub now?'

'Never in Europe,' was Gil's reply.

———

THE LUNCH WAS TERRIFIC. Even the pigs in blankets came out grade A and Warlow drank, not excessively, but too much to go home. Not that he'd expected anything else, and the sofa beckoned tonight, when everyone eventually crashed. The Bluetooth speaker had delighted Jess, and after examining the trackers and a pithy, 'Are you trying to tell me something?' tease from Molly, she'd spent half an hour examining her never-lose-anything-ever-again trackers and whispering, 'Brilliant,' under her breath.

By return, Warlow had received a snazzy tracker he could wear on his wrist and link up to his phone. It registered texts and told him how far he'd walked and did a dozen other things. He'd been toying with the idea of getting one for ages.

'How did you know I wanted one of these?' he asked Jess.

All she did was glance at the dog and tap the side of her nose.

'Don't say that.' Warlow frowned. 'Cadi knows all my secrets.'

But it was still early and Molly and Bryn disappeared upstairs to choose some more after-dinner games to play. They'd already played the yes/no game with Post-it notes stuck on their heads. And Molly asked everyone to supply two music tracks of their choice, which she played to the others. Everyone took a guess as to whose choice it was. The person who'd chosen then had to explain their choices. A kind of Dessert Island Discs. A pun perpetrated because they'd played it over pudding and Molly insisted on being the games master in a Bjork accent.

Jess chose a Motown track as her go-to dance choice and then a song that reminded her most of taking Molly to school. *Dancing Queen* was the track they both used to sing along to. Warlow took the nostalgia route and chose *Believe in Life* from Clapton's *Reptile* album. It reminded him of a road trip he'd done with the boys and Denise in 2001. His second was Free's, *On My Way*. From the band he discovered in his teens. It took him back to discos in a workingman's club, drinking pints of cheap lager with hair that was an arrestable offence.

Bryn's choices were of things Warlow had never heard of that sounded repetitive and trance-like. But Molly chose something from The 1975, the band and, once again and for the same reasons, *Dancing Queen*. A choice that brought laughing tears to both her and her mother's eyes.

And now they were going to play some drawing games, according to the youngsters.

'They're taking a long time to find those games,' Warlow said.

'I wonder why?' Jess replied with a couple of exaggerated blinks.

'By the way, I ran the phone number on Ricky's card. It's not registered. Burner, definitely.'

'So, someone was fishing?'

'Could be. May have nothing to do with Ricky, though.'

'Are you thinking the Menzies?'

'Could be,' Warlow said. The Menzies were a local family with two members in jail on drugs charges thanks to Warlow and Jess. Their attempt at recruiting Molly had backfired spectacularly. But there were other people behind the Menzies who had been stung, who were still at large. Vigilance was the name of the game. 'She did the right thing in not ringing it.'

They were both silent for a moment, Warlow aware that Jess was regarding him with an appraising look in her eye. 'How are you holding up, Evan?'

'Hey. This is great, honestly.'

'Molly can be a bit full-on at Christmas.'

'She's a tonic, that's for sure.'

'I'll tell her that.'

'And thanks for the invite.' Warlow twirled his glass of Passimento. 'Me and Cadi were heading for ham and chips.'

'Sounds bloody marvellous.' Jess dropped her voice. 'And a lot less washing up.'

Warlow smiled. 'I am having a lovely time. And Cadi is too. Though if she's upstairs with those two, she might get an education.'

'They're young.'

'They are. All that energy. But as for today… when I'm

back from Oz, I ought to take you out for a meal. To repay you for this.'

'Wow, what's brought this on?'

'I appreciate this… normality.'

'I don't expect payment, Evan.'

'I know you don't. But I'd like to. Somewhere nice.'

'You mean an actual date?'

'They're just words, aren't they?' Warlow said airily.

Jess threw a balled-up paper napkin at him just as Molly walked in. 'Hey, no fighting. Not until after we play Speedy Doodle.'

'That's what it's called?' Warlow asked with a pained expression.

'It is.' Molly started unpacking the game.

Cadi came over to Warlow and nuzzled his hand. *'Dim arall i ti, miss.'*

Jess tilted her head.

'Sorry,' Warlow held up a hand. 'I'm telling her there is no more. She's had so many treats already today.'

'But it's Christmas,' Molly said and flicked the dog half an inch of gravy bone from an opened treat box she'd given the dog for Christmas. 'Don't worry, when you're away and she's my dog, she'll be fitter than ever.'

'As long as you don't make her wear those bloody Christmas antlers anymore.'

'But she's so cute in them,' Molly sang. 'I've got a ton of photos. There'll be a ton more when she's here with me.'

'About that,' Warlow said. 'Have you asked your mother if it's okay? I'm away for a good while.'

'It was her idea,' Molly interjected.

'It's all arranged,' Jess said. 'I've spoken to your sitters, the Dawes. I'll drop Cadi off with them when we're tied up.'

Warlow looked at the dog. 'See, holidays are fun.'

Cadi tilted her head, picking up on Warlow's softened tone.

'And if anything happens to me, you'll be fine here,' he added, ruffling her head.

'But would we be?' Molly delivered the words in a candid, throwaway remark, while she arranged cards from the game on the table.

Warlow, not for the first time in the Allanby's house, was lost for words. Luckily, they had Bryn to pierce the emotional balloon. 'Right then, shall I deal out the cards?'

'Good thinking, Bryn,' Jess said, with a glance at Warlow that clearly told him he'd just received a compliment from her daughter. And they both understood what a rare and wonderful thing *that* was.

CHAPTER FORTY-TWO

DURING THE COLD WAR, the Royal Observer Corps built 1563 blast proof underground, radiation resistant monitoring posts throughout the country. As observation posts in case the bomb dropped. It meant that two lucky people could be locked deep inside to wait it out until the dust settled. Difficult to know if anyone had thought all of it through from start to finish, but the concept proved fodder for a dozen or more dystopian novels and, in the Netflix age, more than one long and drawn-out series.

Planned to be eight miles apart, the terrain had something to say about that, and often the distances between posts ended up being more rather than less. The concrete cast structures, fifteen feet underground with seven-inch thick walls were bitumen tanked, covered with compacted soil, and pierced by air shafts at one end and an access shaft at the other. A significant number of posts remained to this day, forgotten and often the subject of forays by intrepid internet warriors.

Of course, lists of these posts and their locations were easily accessible via the World Wide Web. But that did not mean to say the posts themselves were easy to visit. If one cared to look online, reports, whether official or otherwise, gave an indication of the state of repair of every one. In Mid-Wales, the Tregaron ROC post, located on the east side of a factory, had been demolished. The only signs of its existence an area of un-mown grass indicating the boundaries of the compound, now housing a junction box and telegraph pole. Its nearest neighbour to the east, nearly fifteen miles away, sat in a field seventy-odd yards north of the village town hall at Abergwesyn. A casual observer noting the structures from a distance might imagine that this isolated spot in a valley floor might be the crumbling remains of a building, or even a family burial site. But they would be wrong. At the bottom of the access shaft in the concrete bunker sat a well-preserved room with table, shelf, and cupboard still in position.

In between these two, at the apex of a triangle with ten-mile sides, another had been built a mile from the Diffwys Outdoor Centre, and a couple of miles from one of the country's most remote telephone boxes on the moor road between Abergwesyn and Tregaron. The post, named Cwm Berwyn, appeared on the Corps website as having been filled in and inaccessible.

The post sat on a mound, 200 metres from the lake at the edge of a plantation. The compound was now overgrown with gorse. The hatch had been removed and steel bars used to seal it. Stones had been used to infill the access shaft up to within six inches of the bars, rendering ingress impossible.

Filled in and inaccessible.

The words had the ring of officialdom about them. Anyone wanting to visit the site would see how the surface concrete features had been removed, along with the louvred air vents, leaving only a hatch-less hole and its seal. These visitors, satisfied, but disappointed, would have no reason to walk west for fifty metres to another mound, less overgrown, just inside a forestry plantation, where the true post was located. And why would they? No grey concrete access shaft showed above ground, and the two metal ventilation pipes that might indicate the position of the post were obscured by young conifers.

Planted very deliberately.

Roger Hunt found the site several years before and hit on a plan to preserve it long before Moyles had entered his life. His old dad had been in the ROC, manning the station in Newick, Sussex. It would have killed him if he knew that selfie-taking vandals might want to graffiti the walls which, at Cwm Berwyn, on unchaining the hatch with bolt-cutters, Hunt had found remarkably well preserved. He'd found old bedding, fire blankets, two mattresses, GPO connection boxes, and a duties chart leaning against a wall above a table, and even fall-out charts in the chemical loo.

And so, every year Hunt came back, sometimes two or three times, and built, in concrete, a surround to the second, mock-access shaft some seventy yards away. He'd never been disturbed as he put bars over his pretend access way and filled the shallow hole with stones to a two-foot depth. He did the same at the other end, burying broken pipes and a bit of half demolished concrete rectangle to indicate air shafts.

At the real post, he'd removed the access shaft's above ground housing and levelled it, placing a plastic tray over its surface and carefully covering it all with a fallen tree trunk to allow vegetation to take hold in the soil within the plastic tray. A lever system meant he could lift the tray and access the shaft, now invisible from the surface, with ease.

Where the real ventilation shaft was, he placed a mound of decaying branches to cover the whole thing.

On the Tuesday after Christmas, while the December wind and rain howled across the desolate moor, Roger Hunt sat deep in the post, warm from heat supplied by solar generators with hidden cables running up into the tree canopy to the panels themselves. He had a dozen back-up car batteries. He'd stocked the post well. He could stay where he was for weeks. Months even. And, if and when he ventured up, the likelihood of meeting another person in this uninhabited spot was virtually zero.

He'd grow a beard.

Speak with an accent.

He had his ebike hidden in the forest and could be in Tregaron in half an hour, Lampeter not long after that. They were both towns that had their share of eccentrics. People who'd chosen lives, if not totally off the grid, then teetering on the edge. He could fit in when supplies were needed.

But for now, he was content to hibernate, let the weather and the police do their worst. He had a radio. He had a phone and half a dozen prepaid SIM cards. Not that he was intending to contact anyone. Not even Megan Roach.

And, while he sat, like a wounded animal, he brooded. He hadn't expected the police to find the church so quickly. And if Napier lived, that would be a pity. Unfinished business thanks to bloody DCI Warlow and that other DI, the good-looking one. Damn the two of them. Damn the whole lot of them.

His life, the one he'd known, no longer existed.

He no longer existed.

Not as Roger Hunt.

Quite what he'd become remained unresolved in his

head. Someone, or something apart from the herd, he could sense that. An animal in its den in the forest.

He thought of the police officers hunting him now.

They would never find him here. But they might when he set out to finish what he'd begun.

Because that remained the goal.

As he scraped a final spoonful of baked beans into his mouth from the can, the radio played music from the world above. No longer Christmas tunes, thank God. But it failed to ease his troubled soul. He'd wanted Napier to suffer. Wanted him to lie in the shallow grave thinking that no one would ever come for him.

The conflagration, the petrol, had been a failsafe. But he'd watched the police tip the shelter. His bonfire had not taken hold. Pity.

Hunt thought little of plans for the future. He thought only of those that had destroyed his old life. Those that had to pay. Hughes was still alive according to the radio. As was Napier.

They *would* pay. He had time.

As for the two officers who had thwarted him. By doing so, they had declared themselves, and their people, his enemy.

So be it.

Visit my website and join up to the Rhys Dylan VIP Reader's Club and get a FREE novella, *The Wolf Hunts Alone*, by visiting: **https://rhysdylan.com**

The Wolf Hunts Alone.

One man and his dog… will track you down.

DCI Evan Warlow is at a crossroads in his life. Living alone, contending with the bad hand fate has dealt him, he finds solace in simple things like walking his neighbour's dog.

But even that is not as safe as it was. Dogs are going missing from a country park. And not only one, now three have disappeared. When he takes it upon himself to root out the cause of the lost animals, Warlow faces ridicule and a thuggish enemy.

But are these simply dog thefts? Or is there a more sinister malevolence at work? One with its sights on bigger, two legged prey.

Only one thing is for certain; Warlow will not rest until he finds out.

———

By joining the club, you will also be the first to hear about new releases via the few but fun emails I'll send you. This includes a no spam promise from me, and you can unsubscribe at any time.

ACKNOWLEDGMENTS

As with all writing endeavours, the existence of this novel depends upon me, the author, and a small army of 'others' who turn an idea into a reality. My wife, Eleri, who gives me the space to indulge my imagination and picks out my stupid mistakes. Others who help with making the book what it is like Sian Phillips, Tim Barber and of course, proofers and ARC readers. Thank you all for your help. Special mention goes to Ela the dog who drags me away from the writing cave and the computer for walks, rain or shine. Actually, she's a bit of a princess so the rain is a no-no. Good dog!

But my biggest thanks goes to you, lovely reader, for being there and actually reading this. It's great to have you along and I do appreciate you spending your time in joining me on this roller-coaster ride with Evan and the rest of the team.

CAN YOU HELP?

With that in mind, and if you enjoyed it, I do have a favour to ask. Could you spare a moment to **leave a review or a rating**? A few words will do, but it's really the only way to help others like you discover the books. Probably the best way to help authors you like. Just visit the book's page on Amazon and leave a few words, or a rating, if you have the time. I've made it easy with country specific links which will take you to the page. Tidy!

AUTHOR'S NOTE

No One Near: It has always struck me that going on holiday means experiencing new places and meeting new people, even if it's the wait staff you see every day at the hotel. But, that would be some people's idea of a nightmare. People who crave peace and tranquility—a rare commodity. These days, rental properties will often advertise the attraction of not being joined on to, or even close to, another property. Seclusion. Well, this tale is all about being careful what you wish for. It also gave me the opportunity to write about some close to home places which I know very well. As I often say, places you should definitely try and visit. There *is* a town called Llandeilo with hotel and bakeries, a Talley Abbey, too. The ROC bunkers *are* real, though you might struggle to find the one at Cwm Berwyn. The book also introduces a real black hat: One Roger Hunt. As suggested in the last chapter, he will, unfortunately, most definitely be back.

Those of you who've read *The Wolf Hunts Alone* will know how much Warlow loves his dogs. And who knows what and who he is going to come up against next! So once again, thank you for sparing your precious time on this new endeavour. I hope I'll get the chance to show you more of this part of the world and that it'll give you the urge to visit.

Not everyone here is a murderer. Not everyone... Cue tense music!

By they way, there is map and a glossary on the website to help you with all those pesky Welsh words. All the best, and see you all soon, Rhys.

READY FOR MORE?

DCI Evan Warlow and the team are back in...

The Light Remains

When a revered sports legend falls victim to a brutal home invasion, a nation is shaken to its core. Outrage swells and the press and powers that be demand answers. Warlow, fresh from a well-earned vacation, is thrown into the cauldron to lead the investigation. But the victim, despite his iconic status, has secrets of his own. Amidst the chaos of jealousy and rivalry that swirls around the case, a darker underbelly emerges. The pursuit of truth transforms into a gripping hunt, but whose truth is the team hunting?

As is often the case, something else lurks in the labyrinth of deception. Something vile and twisted that could strike again at any moment... unless it's found.

Tick-Tock — January 2024

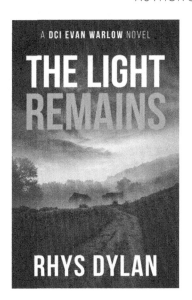

Made in United States
North Haven, CT
02 February 2024

48240880R00189